The Best Barbara Robinson Treasury Ever

THREE HILARIOUS NOVELS

HarperCollins*Publishers*

Contents

For Jack, of course

BARBARA ROBINSON

★

The Best Christmas Pageant Ever

Pictures by Judith Gwyn Brown

HarperCollins*Publishers*

1

The Herdmans were absolutely the worst kids in the history of the world. They lied and stole and smoked cigars (even the girls) and talked dirty and hit little kids and cussed their teachers and took the name of the Lord in vain and set fire to Fred Shoemaker's old broken-down toolhouse.

The toolhouse burned right down to the ground, and I think that surprised the Herdmans. They set fire to things all the time, but that was the first time they managed to burn down a whole building.

I guess it was an accident. I don't suppose they woke up that morning and said to one another,

"Let's go burn down Fred Shoemaker's toolhouse" . . . but maybe they did. After all, it was a Saturday, and not much going on.

It was a terrific fire—two engines and two police cars and all the volunteer firemen and five dozen doughnuts sent up from the Tasti-Lunch Diner. The doughnuts were supposed to be for the firemen, but by the time they got the fire out the doughnuts were all gone. The Herdmans got them—what they couldn't eat they stuffed in their pockets and down the front of their shirts. You could actually *see* the doughnuts all around Ollie Herdman's middle.

I couldn't understand why the Herdmans were hanging around the scene of their crime. Everybody knew the whole thing was their fault, and you'd think they'd have the brains to get out of sight.

One fireman even collared Claude Herdman and said, "Did you kids start this fire, smoking cigars in that toolhouse?"

But Claude just said, "We weren't smoking cigars."

And they weren't. They were playing with Leroy Herdman's "Young Einstein" chemistry set, which he stole from the hardware store, and that was how they started the fire.

Leroy said so. "We mixed all the little powders together," he said, "and poured lighter fluid around on them and set fire to the lighter fluid. We wanted to see if the chemistry set was any good."

Any other kid—even a mean kid—would have been a little bit worried if he stole $4.95 worth of something and then burned down a building with it. But Leroy was just mad because the chemistry set got burned up along with everything else before he had a chance to make one or two bombs.

The fire chief got us all together—there were fifteen or twenty kids standing around watching the fire—and gave us a little talk about playing with matches and gasoline and dangerous things like that.

"I don't say that's what happened here," he told us. "I don't *know* what happened here, but that could have been it, and you see the result. So let this be a good lesson to you, boys and girls."

Of course it was a great lesson to the Herdmans—they learned that wherever there's a fire there will be free doughnuts sooner or later.

I guess things would have been different if they'd burned down, say, the Second Presbyterian

Church instead of the toolhouse, but the toolhouse was about to fall down anyway. All the neighbors had pestered Mr. Shoemaker to do something about it because it looked so awful and was sure to bring rats. So everybody said the fire was a blessing in disguise, and even Mr. Shoemaker said it was a relief. My father said it was the only good thing the Herdmans ever did, and if they'd *known* it was a good thing, they wouldn't have done it at all. They would have set fire to something else . . . or somebody.

They were just so all-around awful you could hardly believe they were real: Ralph, Imogene, Leroy, Claude, Ollie, and Gladys—six skinny, stringy-haired kids all alike except for being different sizes and having different black-and-blue places where they had clonked each other.

They lived over a garage at the bottom of Sproul Hill. Nobody used the garage anymore, but the Herdmans used to bang the door up and down just as fast as they could and try to squash one another—that was their idea of a game. Where other people had grass in their front yard, the Herdmans had rocks. And where other people had hydrangea bushes, the Herdmans had poison ivy.

4

There was also a sign in the yard that said "Beware Of The Cat."

New kids always laughed about that till they got a look at the cat. It was the meanest looking animal I ever saw. It had one short leg and a broken tail and one missing eye, and the mailman wouldn't deliver anything to the Herdmans because of it.

"I don't think it's a regular cat at all," the mailman told my father. "I think those kids went up in the hills and caught themselves a bobcat."

"Oh, I don't think you can tame a wild bobcat," my father said.

"I'm sure you can't," said the mailman. "They'd never try to *tame* it; they'd just try to make it wilder than it was to begin with."

If that was their plan, it worked—the cat would attack anything it could see out of its one eye.

One day Claude Herdman emptied the whole first grade in three minutes flat when he took the cat to Show-and-Tell. He didn't feed it for two days so it was already mad, and then he carried it to school in a box, and when he opened the box the cat shot out—right straight up in the air, people said.

It came down on the top blackboard ledge and

clawed four big long scratches all the way down the blackboard. Then it just tore around all over the place, scratching little kids and shedding fur and scattering books and papers everywhere.

The teacher, Miss Brandel, yelled for everybody to run out in the hall, and she pulled a coat over her head and grabbed a broom and tried to corner the cat. But of course she couldn't see, with the coat over her head, so she just ran up and down the aisles, hollering "Here, kitty!" and smacking the broom down whenever the cat hissed back. She knocked over the Happy Family dollhouse and a globe of the world, and broke the aquarium full of twenty gallons of water and about sixty-five goldfish.

All the time she kept yelling for Claude to come and catch his cat, but Claude had gone out in the hall with the rest of the class.

Later, when Miss Brandel was slapping Band-Aids on everyone who could show her any blood, she asked Claude why in the world he didn't come and get his cat under control.

"You told us to go out in the hall," Claude said, just as if he were the ordinary kind of first-grader who did whatever teachers said to do.

The cat settled down a little bit once it got something to eat—most of the goldfish and Ramona Billian's two pet mice that she brought to Show-and-Tell. Ramona cried and carried on so—"I can't even bury them!" she said—that they sent her home.

The room was a wreck—broken glass and papers and books and puddles of water and dead goldfish everywhere. Miss Brandel was sort of a wreck too, and most of the first graders were hysterical, so somebody took them outdoors and let them have recess for the rest of the day.

Claude took the cat home and after that there was a rule that you couldn't bring anything alive to Show-and-Tell.

The Herdmans moved from grade to grade through the Woodrow Wilson School like those South American fish that strip your bones clean in three minutes flat . . . which was just about what they did to one teacher after another.

But they never, never got kept back in a grade.

When it came time for Claude Herdman to pass to the second grade he didn't know his ABC's or his numbers or his colors or his shapes or his "Three Bears" or how to get along with anybody. But Miss Brandel passed him anyway.

For one thing, she knew she'd have Ollie Herdman the next year. That was the thing about the Herdmans—there was always another one coming along, and no teacher was crazy enough to let herself in for two of them at once.

I was always in the same grade with Imogene Herdman, and what I did was stay out of her way. It wasn't easy to stay out of her way. You couldn't do it if you were very pretty or very ugly, or very smart or very dumb, or had anything unusual about you, like red hair or double-jointed thumbs.

But if you were sort of a medium kid like me, and kept your mouth shut when the teacher said, "Who can name all fifty states?" you had a pretty good chance to stay clear of Imogene.

As far as anyone could tell, Imogene was just like the rest of the Herdmans. She never learned anything either, except dirty words and secrets about everybody.

Twice a year we had to go to the health room to get weighed and measured, and Imogene always managed to find out exactly what everybody weighed. Sometimes she would hang around waiting for the nurse, Miss Hemphill, to give her a Band-Aid; sometimes she would sneak behind the curtain where they kept a folding cot and just stay there the whole time, with one eye on the scales.

"Why are you still here, Imogene?" Miss Hemphill asked one day. "You can go back to your room."

"I think you better look and see if I've got what Ollie has."

"What does Ollie have?"

Imogene shrugged. "We don't know. Red spots all over."

Miss Hemphill looked at her. "What did the doctor say?"

"We didn't have a doctor." Imogene began scrunching her back up and down against the medicine cabinet.

"Well, does Ollie have a fever? Is he in bed?"

"No, he's in the first grade."

"Right now?" Miss Hemphill stared. "Why, he shouldn't be in school with red spots! It could be measles or chicken pox . . . any number of things . . . contagious things. What are you doing?"

"Scratching my back," Imogene said. "Boy, do I itch!"

"The rest of you boys and girls go back to your classroom," Miss Hemphill said, "and, Imogene, you stay right here."

So we all went back to our room, and Miss

Hemphill went to the first grade to look at Ollie, and Imogene stayed in the health room and copied down everybody's weight from Miss Hemphill's records.

Your weight was supposed to be a big secret, like what you got on your report card.

"It's nobody's business what you get on your report card," all the teachers said. And Miss Hemphill said the same thing—"It's nobody's business what you weigh."

Not even the fat kids could find out what they weighed, but Imogene always knew.

"Don't let Albert Pelfrey on the swing!" she would yell at recess. "He'll bust it. Albert Pelfrey weighs a hundred and forty-three pounds. Last time he weighed a hundred and thirty-seven." So right away everybody knew two things about Albert—we knew exactly how fat he was, and we also knew that he was getting fatter all the time.

"You have to go to fat-camp this summer," Imogene hollered at him. "Miss Hemphill wrote it down on your paper."

Fat-camp is a place where they feed you lettuce and grapefruit and cottage cheese and eggs for a month, and you either give up and cheat or give up and get skinny.

"I am not!" Albert said. "I'm going to Disneyland with my Uncle Frank."

"That's what you think!" Imogene told him.

Albert had to believe her—she was always right about things like that—so all year he had fatcamp to look forward to instead of Disneyland.

Sometimes Imogene would blackmail the fat kids if they had anything she wanted . . . like Wanda Pierce's charm bracelet.

Wanda Pierce weighed about a ton—she even had fat eyes—and her hobby was this charm bracelet. It had twenty-two charms and every single one did something: the little wheels turned, or the little bitty piano keys went "plink," or the little tiny drawers opened and closed.

Besides being a fat kid, Wanda was also a rich kid, so every time you turned around she had a new charm.

"Look at my new charm," she would say. "It cost $6.95 without the tax. It's a bird, and when you push this little knob, its wings flutter. It cost $6.95."

They were great charms, but everybody got sick of hearing about them, so it was almost a relief when Imogene blackmailed her out of it.

"I know how much you weigh, Wanda,"

Imogene told her. "I wrote it down on this piece of paper. See?"

It must have been an awful amount, because even Wanda looked horrified. So Imogene got her charm bracelet, and she got Lucille Golden's imitation alligator pocketbook with "Souvenir of Florida" written on it. For a while she got ten cents a week from Floyd Brush, till Floyd caught double pneumonia and lost fifteen pounds and didn't care anymore.

My friend Alice Wendleken was so nasty-clean that she had detergent hands by the time she was four years old. Just the same, Alice picked up a case of head lice when she was at summer camp, and somehow Imogene found out about that. She would sneak up on Alice at recess and holler "Cooties!" and smack Alice's head. She nearly knocked Alice cross-eyed before one of the teachers saw her and took both of them in to the principal.

"Now, what's this all about?" the principal wanted to know, but Alice wouldn't say.

"*I had* to hit her," Imogene told him. "She's got cooties, and I saw one crawling in her hair, and I don't want them on me."

"You did not see one!" Alice said. "I don't have them anymore!"

"What do you mean, you don't have them anymore?" the principal said. "Did you have them *lately*?" It really shook him up—he didn't want a whole school full of kids with cooties. So he sent Alice to the health room and the nurse went all through her head with a fine-tooth comb and a magnifying glass, and finally said it was all right.

But it was too late—everybody called Alice "Cooties" the whole rest of the year.

If Imogene didn't know a secret about a person, she would make one up. She would catch you in the girls' room or out in the hall and whisper, "I know what you did!" and then you'd go crazy trying to figure out what it was you did that Imogene knew about.

It was no good trying to get secrets on the Herdmans. Everybody already knew about the awful things they did. You couldn't even tease them about their parents, or holler "Your father's in jail!" because they didn't care. Actually, they didn't know what their father was or where he was or anything about him, because when Gladys was two years old he climbed on a railroad train and disappeared. Nobody blamed him.

Now and then you'd see Mrs. Herdman, walking the cat on a length of chain around the block.

But she worked double shifts at the shoe factory, and wasn't home much.

My mother's friend, Miss Philips, was a social-service worker and she tried to get some welfare money for the Herdmans, so Mrs. Herdman could just work one shift and spend more time with her children. But Mrs. Herdman wouldn't do it; she liked the work, she said.

"It's not the work," Miss Philips told my mother, "and it's not the money. It's just that she'd rather be at the shoe factory than shut up at home with that crowd of kids." She sighed. "I can't say I blame her."

So the Herdmans pretty much looked after themselves. Ralph looked after Imogene, and Imogene looked after Leroy, and Leroy looked after Claude and so on down the line. The Herdmans were like most big families—the big ones taught the little ones everything they knew . . . and the proof of that was that the meanest Herdman of all was Gladys, the youngest.

We figured they were headed straight for hell, by way of the state penitentiary . . . until they got themselves mixed up with the church, and my mother, and our Christmas pageant.

2

Mother didn't expect to have anything to do with the Christmas pageant except to make me and my little brother Charlie be in it (we didn't want to) and to make my father go and see it (he didn't want to).

Every year he said the same thing—"I've seen the Christmas pageant."

"You haven't seen this year's Christmas pageant," Mother would tell him. "Charlie is a shepherd this year."

"Charlie was a shepherd last year. No . . . you go on and go. I'm just going to put on my bathrobe and sit by the fire and relax. There's never anything different about the Christmas pageant."

"There's something different this year," Mother said.

"What?"

"Charlie is wearing your bathrobe."

So that year my father went . . . to see his bathrobe, he said.

Actually, he went every year but it was always a struggle, and Mother said that was her contribution to the Christmas pageant—getting my father to go to it.

But then she got stuck with the whole thing when Mrs. George Armstrong fell and broke her leg.

We knew about this as soon as it happened, because Mrs. Armstrong only lived a block and a half away. We heard the siren and saw the ambulance and watched the policemen carry her out of the house on a stretcher.

"Call Mr. Armstrong at his work!" she yelled at the policemen. "Shut off the stove under my potatoes! Inform the Ladies' Aid that I won't be at the meeting!"

One of the neighbor women called out, "Helen, are you in much pain?" and Mrs. Armstrong yelled back, "Yes, terrible! Don't let those children tear up my privet hedge!"

Even in pain, Mrs. Armstrong could still give orders. She was so good at giving orders that she was just naturally the head of anything she belonged to, and at church she did everything but preach. Most of all, she ran the Christmas pageant every year. And here she was, two weeks before Thanksgiving, flat on her back.

"I don't know what they'll do now about the pageant," Mother said.

But the pageant wasn't the only problem. Mrs. Armstrong was also chairman of the Ladies' Aid Bazaar, and coordinator of the Women's Society Potluck Supper, and there was a lot of telephoning back and forth to see who would take over those jobs.

Mother had a list of names, and while she was calling people about the Ladies' Aid Bazaar, Mrs. Homer McCarthy was trying to call Mother about the pot-luck supper. But Mrs. McCarthy got somebody else to do that, and Mother got somebody else to do the bazaar. So the only thing left was the Christmas pageant.

And Mother got stuck with that.

"I could run the pot-luck supper with one hand tied behind my back," Mother told us. "All you have to do is make sure everybody doesn't bring meat loaf. But the Christmas pageant!"

Our Christmas pageant isn't what you'd call four-star entertainment. Mrs. Armstrong breaking her leg was the only unexpected thing that ever happened to it. The script is standard (the inn, the stable, the shepherds, the star), and so are the costumes, and so is the casting.

Primary kids are angels; intermediate kids are shepherds; big boys are Wise Men; Elmer Hopkins, the minister's son, has been Joseph for as long as I can remember; and my friend Alice Wendleken is Mary because she's so smart, so neat and clean, and, most of all, so holy-looking.

All the rest of us are the angel choir—lined up according to height because nobody can sing parts. As a matter of fact, nobody can *sing*. We're strictly a no-talent outfit except for a girl named Alberta Bottles, who whistles. Last year Alberta whistled "What Child Is This?" for a change of pace, but nobody liked it, especially Mrs. Bottles, because Alberta put too much into it and ran out of air and passed out cold on the manger in the middle of the third verse.

Aside from that, though, it's always just the Christmas story, year after year, with people shuffling around in bathrobes and bedsheets and sharp wings.

"Well," my father said, once Mother got put in charge of it, "here's your big chance. Why don't you cancel the pageant and show movies?"

"Movies of what?" Mother said.

"I don't know. Fred Stamper has five big reels of Yellowstone National Park."

"What does Yellowstone National Park have to do with Christmas?" Mother asked.

"I know a good movie," Charlie said. "We had it at school. It shows a heart operation, and two kids got sick."

"Never mind," Mother said. "I guess you all think you're pretty funny, but the Christmas pageant is a tradition, and I don't plan to do anything different."

Of course nobody even thought about the Herdmans in connection with the Christmas pageant. Most of us spent all week in school being pounded and poked and pushed around by Herdmans, and we looked forward to Sunday as a real day of rest.

Once a month the whole Sunday school would go to church for the first fifteen minutes of the service and do something special—sing a song, or act out a parable, or recite Bible verses. Usually the little kids sang "Jesus Loves Me," which was all they were up to.

But when my brother Charlie was in with the little kids, his teacher thought up something different to do. She had everybody write down on a piece of paper what they liked best about Sunday school, or draw a picture of what they liked best. And when we all got in the church she stood up in front of the congregation and said, "Today some of our youngest boys and girls are going to tell you what Sunday school means to them. Betsy, what do you have on your paper?"

Betsy Cathcart stood up and said, "What I like best about Sunday school is the good feeling I get when I go there."

I don't think she wrote that down at all, but it sounded terrific, of course.

One kid said he liked hearing all the Bible stories. Another kid said, "I like learning songs about Jesus."

Eight or nine little kids stood up and said what they liked, and it was always something good about Jesus or God or cheerful friends or the nice teacher.

Finally the teacher said, "I think we have time for one more. Charlie, what can you tell us about Sunday school?"

My little brother Charlie stood up and he

didn't even have to look at his piece of paper. "What I like best about Sunday school," he said, "is that there aren't any Herdmans here."

Well. The teacher should have stuck with "Jesus Loves Me," because everybody forgot all the nice churchy things the other kids said, and just remembered what Charlie said about the Herdmans.

When we went to pick him up after church his teacher told us, "I'm sure there are many things that Charlie likes about Sunday school. Maybe he will tell you what some of them are." She smiled at all of us, but you could tell she was really mad.

On the way home I asked Charlie, "What are some of the other things you like that she was talking about?"

He shrugged. "I like all the other stuff but she said to write down what we liked best, and what I like best is no Herdmans."

"Not a very Christian sentiment," my father said.

"Maybe not, but it's a very practical one," Mother told him—last year Charlie had spent the whole second grade being black-and-blue because he had to sit next to Leroy Herdman.

In the end it was Charlie's fault that the Herdmans showed up in church.

For three days in a row Leroy Herdman stole the dessert from Charlie's lunch box and finally Charlie just gave up trying to do anything about it. "Oh, go on and take it," he said. "I don't care. I get all the dessert I want in Sunday school."

Leroy wanted to know more about that. "What kind of dessert?" he said.

"Chocolate cake," Charlie told him, "and candy bars and cookies and Kool-Aid. We get refreshments all the time, all we want."

"You're a liar," Leroy said.

Leroy was right. We got jelly beans at Easter and punch and cookies on Children's Day, and that was it.

"We get ice cream, too," Charlie went on, "and doughnuts and popcorn balls."

"Who gives it to you?" Leroy wanted to know.

"The minister," Charlie said. He didn't know who else to say.

Of course that was the wrong thing to tell Herdmans if you wanted them to stay away. And sure enough, the very next Sunday there they were, slouching into Sunday school, eyes peeled for the refreshments.

"Where do you get the cake?" Ralph asked the Sunday-school superintendent, and Mr. Grady said, "Well, son, I don't know about any cake, but they're collecting the food packages out in the kitchen." What he meant was the canned stuff we brought in every year as a Thanksgiving present for the Orphans Home.

It was just our bad luck that the Herdmans picked that Sunday to come, because when they saw all the cans of spaghetti and beans and grape drink and peanut butter, they figured there might be some truth to what Charlie said about refreshments.

So they stayed. They didn't sing any hymns or say any prayers, but they did make a little money, because I saw Imogene snake a handful of coins out of the collection basket when it went past her.

At the end of the morning Mr. Grady came to every class and made an announcement.

"We'll be starting rehearsals soon for our Christmas pageant," he said, "and next week after the service we'll all gather in the back of the church to decide who will play the main roles. But of course we want every boy and girl in our Sunday school to take part in the pageant, so be sure your parents know that you'll be staying a little later next Sunday."

Mr. Grady made this same speech every year,

so he didn't get any wild applause. Besides, as I said, we all knew what part we were going to play anyway.

Alice Wendleken must have been a little bit worried, though, because she turned around to me with this sticky smile on her face and said, "I hope you're going to be in the angel choir again. You're so good in the angel choir."

What she meant was, I hope you won't get to be Mary just because your mother's running the pageant. She didn't have to worry. I didn't want to be Mary. I didn't want to be in the angel choir either, but everybody had to be something.

All of a sudden Imogene Herdman dug me in the ribs with her elbow. She has the sharpest elbows of anybody I ever knew. "What's the pageant?" she said.

"It's a play," I said, and for the first time that day (except when she saw the collection basket) Imogene looked interested. All the Herdmans are big moviegoers, though they never pay their own way. One or two of them start a fight at the box office of the theater while the others slip in. They get their popcorn the same way, and then they spread out all over the place so the manager can never find them all before the picture's over.

"What's the play about?" Imogene asked.

"It's about Jesus," I said.

"Everything here is," she muttered, so I figured Imogene didn't care much about the Christmas pageant.

But I was wrong.

3

Mrs. Armstrong, who was still trying to run things from her hospital bed, said that the same people always got the main parts. "But it's important to give everybody a chance," she told Mother over the telephone. "Let me tell you what I do."

Mother sighed, and turned off the heat under the pork chops. "All right, Helen," she said.

Mrs. Armstrong called Mother at least every other day, and she always called at suppertime. "Don't let me interrupt your supper," she always said, and then went right ahead and did it anyway, while my father paced up and down the hall, saying things under his breath about Mrs. Armstrong.

"Here's what I do," Mrs. Armstrong said. "I get them all together and tell them about the rehearsals, and that they must be on time and pay close attention. Then I tell them that the main parts are Mary and Joseph and the Wise Men and the Angel of the Lord. And then I always remind them that there are no small parts, only small actors."

"Do they understand what that means?" Mother asked.

"Oh, yes," Mrs. Armstrong said.

Later Mother asked me if I knew what that meant, about small parts and small actors.

I didn't really know—none of us did. It was just something Mrs. Armstrong always said. "I guess it means that the short kids have to be in the front row of the angel choir, or else nobody can see them."

"I thought so," Mother said. "It doesn't mean that at all. It really means that every single person in the pageant is just as important as every other person—that the littlest baby angel is just as important as Mary."

"Go and tell that to Alice Wendleken," I said, and Mother told me not to be so fresh. She didn't get very mad, though, because she knew I was right. You could have a Christmas pageant without *any* baby angels, but you couldn't have one without a Mary.

Mrs. Armstrong knew it too. "I always start with Mary," she told Mother over the telephone. "I tell them that we must choose our Mary carefully, because Mary was the mother of Jesus."

"I know that," Mother said, wanting to get off the telephone and cook the pork chops.

"Yes. I tell them that our Mary should be a cheerful, happy little girl who is unselfish and kind to others. Then I tell them about Joseph, that he was God's choice to be Jesus' father, and our Joseph ought to be a little boy . . ." She went on and on and got as far as the second Wise Man when Mother said, "Helen, I'll have to go now. There's somebody at the door."

Actually there was somebody at the door. It was my father, standing out on the porch in his coat and hat, leaning on the doorbell.

When Mother let him in he took off his hat and bowed to her. "Lady, can you give me some supper? I haven't had a square meal in three days."

"Oh, for goodness sake," Mother said, "Come on in. What will the neighbors think, to see you standing out there ringing your own doorbell? And why didn't you ring the doorbell ten minutes ago?"

Mrs. Armstrong called Mother two more times that week—to tell her that people could hem up costumes, but couldn't cut them—and to tell her not to let the angel choir wear lipstick. And by Sunday, Mother was already sick of the whole thing.

After church we all filed into the back seven pews, along with two or three Sunday-school teachers who were supposed to keep everybody quiet. It was a terrible time to try to keep everybody quiet—all the little kids were tired and all the big kids were hungry, and all the mothers wanted to go home and cook dinner, and all the fathers wanted to go home and watch the football game on TV.

"Now, this isn't going to take very long," Mother told us. My father had said it better not take very long, because he wanted to watch the football game too. He also wanted to eat, he said— he hadn't had a decent meal all week.

"First I'm going to tell you about the rehearsals," Mother said. "We'll have our rehearsals on Wednesdays at 6:30. We're only going to have five rehearsals so you must all try to be present at every one."

"What if we get sick?" asked a little kid in the front pew.

"You won't get sick," Mother told him, which was exactly what she told Charlie that morning when Charlie said he didn't want to be a shepherd and would be sick to his stomach if she made him be one.

"Now you little children in the cradle room and the primary class will be our angels," Mother said. "You'll like that, won't you?"

They all said yes. What else could they say?

"The older boys and girls will be shepherds and guests at the inn and members of the choir." Mother was really zipping along, and I thought how mad Mrs. Armstrong would be about all the things she was leaving out.

"And we need Mary and Joseph, the three Wise Men, and the Angel of the Lord. They aren't hard parts, but they're very important parts, so those people must absolutely come to every rehearsal."

"What if *they* get sick?" It was the same little kid, and it made you wonder what kind of little kid he was, to be so interested in sickness.

"They won't get sick either," Mother said, looking a little cross. "Now, we all know what kind of person Mary was. She was quiet and gentle and kind, and the little girl who plays Mary should try to be that kind of person. I know that many of you would like to be Mary in our pageant, but of course we can only have one Mary. So I'll ask for volunteers, and then we'll all decide together which girl should get the part." That was pretty safe to say, since the only person who ever raised her hand was Alice Wendleken.

But Alice just sat there, chewing on a piece of her hair and looking down at the floor . . . and the only person who raised her hand this time was Imogene Herdman.

"Did you have a question, Imogene?" Mother asked. I guess that was the only reason she could think of for Imogene to have her hand up.

"No," Imogene said. "I want to be Mary." She looked back over her shoulder. "And Ralph wants to be Joseph."

"Yeh," Ralph said.

Mother just stared at them. It was like a detective movie, when the nice little old gray-haired lady sticks a gun in the bank window and says "Give me all your money" and you can't believe it. Mother couldn't believe this.

"Well," she said after a minute, "we want to be

sure that everyone has a chance. Does anyone else want to volunteer for Joseph?"

No one did. No one ever did, especially not Elmer Hopkins. But he couldn't do anything about it, because he was the minister's son. One year he didn't volunteer to be Joseph and neither did anyone else, and afterward I heard Reverend Hopkins talking to Elmer out in the hall.

"You're going to be Joseph," Reverend Hopkins said. "That's it."

"I don't want to be Joseph," Elmer told him. "I'm too big, and I feel dumb up there, and all those little kids give me a pain in the neck."

"I can understand that," Reverend Hopkins said. "I can even sympathize, but till somebody else volunteers for Joseph, you're stuck with it."

"Nobody's ever going to do that!" Elmer said. "I even offered Grady Baker fifty cents to be Joseph and he wouldn't do it. I'm going to have to be Joseph for the rest of my life!"

"Cheer up," Reverend Hopkins told him. "Maybe somebody will turn up."

I'll bet he didn't think the somebody would be Ralph Herdman.

"All right," Mother said, "Ralph will be our Joseph. Now, does anyone else want to volunteer for Mary?" Mother looked all around, trying to catch somebody's eye—*anybody's* eye. "Janet? . . . Roberta? . . . Alice, don't you want to volunteer this year?"

"No," Alice said, so low you could hardly hear her. "I don't want to."

Nobody volunteered to be Wise Men either, except Leroy, Claude, and Ollie Herdman.

So there was my mother, stuck with a Christmas pageant full of Herdmans in the main roles.

There was one Herdman left over, and one main role left over, and you didn't have to be very smart to figure out that Gladys was going to be the Angel of the Lord.

"What do I have to do?" Gladys wanted to know.

"The Angel of the Lord was the one who brought the good news to the shepherds," Mother said.

Right away all the shepherds began to wiggle around in their seats, figuring that any good news Gladys brought them would come with a smack in the teeth.

Charlie's friend Hobie Carmichael raised his hand and said, "I can't be a shepherd. We're going to Philadelphia."

"Why didn't you say so before?" Mother asked.

"I forgot."

Another kid said, "My mother doesn't want me to be a shepherd."

"Why not?" Mother said.

"I don't know. She just said don't be a shepherd."

One kid was honest. "Gladys Herdman hits too hard," he said.

"Why, Gladys isn't going to hit anybody!" Mother said. "What an idea! The Angel just visits the shepherds in the fields and tells them Jesus is born."

"And hits 'em," said the kid.

Of course he was right. You could just picture Gladys whamming shepherds left and right, but Mother said that was perfectly ridiculous.

"I don't want to hear another word about it," she said. "No shepherds may quit—or get sick," she added, before the kid in the front pew could ask.

While everybody was leaving, Mother grabbed Alice Wendleken by the arm and said, "Alice, why in the world didn't you raise your hand to be Mary?"

"I don't know," Alice said, looking mad.

But I knew—I'd heard Imogene Herdman telling Alice what would happen to her if she dared to volunteer: all the ordinary, everyday Herdman-things like clonking you on the head, and drawing pictures all over your homework papers, and putting worms in your coat pocket.

"I don't care," Alice told her. "I don't care what you do. I'm always Mary in the pageant."

"And next spring," Imogene went on, squinching up her eyes, "when the pussy willows come out, I'll stick a pussy willow so far down your ear that nobody can reach it—and it'll sprout there, and it'll grow and grow, and you'll spend the rest of your life with a pussy-willow bush growing out your ear."

You had to admire her—that was the worst thing any of them ever thought up to do. Of course some people might not think that could happen, but it could. Ollie Herdman did it once. He got this terrible earache in school, and when the nurse looked down his ear with her little lighted tube she yelled so loud you could hear her all the way down the hall. "He's got something growing down there!" she hollered.

They had to take Ollie to the hospital and put him under and dig this sprouted pussy willow out of his ear.

So that was why Alice kept her mouth shut about being Mary.

"You know she wouldn't do all those things she said," I told Alice as we walked home.

"Yes, she would," Alice said. "Herdmans will do anything. But your mother should have told them no. Somebody should put Imogene out of the pageant, and all the rest of them too. They'll do something terrible and ruin the whole thing."

I thought she was probably right, and so did lots of other people, and for two or three days all anybody could talk about was the Herdmans being Mary and Joseph and all.

Mrs. Homer McCarthy called Mother to say that she had been thinking and thinking about it, and if the Herdmans wanted to participate in our Christmas celebration, why didn't we let them hand out programs at the door?

"We don't have programs for the Christmas pageant," Mother said.

"Well, maybe we ought to get some printed and put the Herdmans in charge of that."

Alice's mother told the Ladies' Aid that it was sacrilegious to let Imogene Herdman be Mary. Somebody we never heard of called up Mother on the telephone and said her name was Hazelbeck and she lived on Sproul Hill, and was it true that Imogene Herdman was going to be Mary the mother of Jesus in a church play?

"Yes," Mother said. "Imogene is going to be Mary in our Christmas pageant."

"And the rest of them too?" the lady asked.

"Yes, Ralph is going to be Joseph and the others are the Wise Men and the Angel of the Lord."

"You must be crazy," this Mrs. Hazelbeck told Mother. "I live next door to that outfit with their yelling and screaming and their insane cat and their garage door going up and down, up and down all day long, and let me tell you, you're in for a rowdy time!"

Some people said it wasn't fair for a whole family who didn't even go to our church to barge in and take over the pageant. My father said somebody better lock up the Women's Society's silver service. My mother just said she would rather be in the hospital with Mrs. Armstrong.

But then the flower committee took a potted geranium to Mrs. Armstrong and told her what was going on and she nearly fell out of bed, traction bars and all. "I feel personally responsible," she said. "Whatever happens, I accept the blame. If I'd been up and around and doing my duty, this never would have happened."

And that made my mother so mad she couldn't see straight.

"If she'd been up and around it wouldn't have happened!" Mother said. "That woman! She must be surprised that the sun is still coming up every morning without her to supervise the sunrise. Well, let me tell you—"

"Don't tell me," my father said. "I'm on your side."

"I just mean that Helen Armstrong is not the only woman alive who can run a Christmas pageant. Up till now I'd made up my mind just to do the best I could under the circumstances, but *now*—" She stabbed a meat fork into the pot roast. "I'm going to make this the very best Christmas pageant anybody ever saw, and I'm going to do it with Herdmans, too. After all, they raised their hands and nobody else did. And that's that."

And it was too. For one thing, nobody else wanted to take over the pageant, with or without Herdmans; and for another thing, Reverend Hopkins got fed up with all the complaints and told everybody where to get off.

Of course, he didn't say "Go jump in the lake, Mrs. Wendleken" or anything like that. He just reminded everyone that when Jesus said "Suffer the little children to come unto me" Jesus meant all the little children, including Herdmans.

So that shut everybody up, even Alice's mother, and the next Wednesday we started rehearsals.

4

The first pageant rehearsal was usually about as much fun as a three-hour ride on the school bus, and just as noisy and crowded. This rehearsal, though, was different. Everybody shut up and settled down right away, for fear of missing something awful that the Herdmans might do.

They got there ten minutes late, sliding into the room like a bunch of outlaws about to shoot up a saloon. When Leroy passed Charlie he knuckled him behind the ear, and one little primary girl yelled as Gladys went by. But Mother had said she was going to ignore everything except blood, and since the primary kid wasn't bleeding, and neither was Charlie, nothing happened.

Mother said, "And here's the Herdman family. We're glad to see you all," which was probably the biggest lie ever said right out loud in the church.

Imogene smiled—the Herdman smile, we called it, sly and sneaky—and there they sat, the closest thing to criminals that we knew about, and they were going to represent the best and most beautiful. No wonder everybody was so worked up.

Mother started to separate everyone into angels and shepherds and guests at the inn, but right away she ran into trouble.

"Who were the shepherds?" Leroy Herdman wanted to know. "Where did they come from?"

Ollie Herdman didn't even know what a shepherd was . . . or, anyway, that's what he said.

"What was the inn?" Claude asked. "What's an inn?"

"It's like a motel," somebody told him, "where people go to spend the night."

"What people?" Claude said. "Jesus?"

"Oh, honestly!" Alice Wendleken grumbled. "Jesus wasn't even born yet! Mary and Joseph went there."

"Why?" Ralph asked.

44

"What happened first?" Imogene hollered at my mother. "Begin at the beginning!"

That really scared me because the beginning would be the Book of Genesis, where it says "In the beginning . . ." and if we were going to have to start with the Book of Genesis we'd never get through.

The thing was, the Herdmans didn't know anything about the Christmas story. They knew that Christmas was Jesus' birthday, but everything else was news to them—the shepherds, the Wise Men, the star, the stable, the crowded inn.

It was hard to believe. At least, it was hard for me to believe—Alice Wendleken said she didn't have any trouble believing it. "How would they find out about the Christmas story?" she said. "They don't even know what a Bible is. Look what Gladys did to that Bible last week."

While Imogene was snitching money from the collection plate in my class, Gladys and Ollie drew mustaches and tails on all the disciples in the primary-grade Illustrated Bible.

"They never went to church in their whole life till your little brother told them we got refreshments," Alice said, "and all you ever hear about Christmas in school is how to make ornaments out of aluminum foil. So how would they know about the Christmas story?"

She was right. Of course they might have read about it, but they never read anything except "Amazing Comics." And they might have heard about it on TV, except that Ralph paid sixty-five cents for their TV at a garage sale, and you couldn't see anything on it unless somebody held onto the antenna. Even then, you couldn't see much.

The only other way for them to hear about the Christmas story was from their parents, and I guess Mr. Herdman never got around to it before he climbed on the railroad train. And it was pretty clear that Mrs. Herdman had given up ever trying to tell them anything.

So they just didn't know. And Mother said she had better begin by reading the Christmas story from the Bible. This was a pain in the neck to most of us because we knew the whole thing backward and forward and never had to be told anything except who we were supposed to be, and where we were supposed to stand.

". . . Joseph and Mary, his espoused wife, being great with child . . ."

"Pregnant!" yelled Ralph Herdman.

Well. That stirred things up. All the big kids

began to giggle and all the little kids wanted to know what was so funny, and Mother had to hammer on the floor with a blackboard pointer. "That's enough, Ralph," she said, and went on with the story.

"I don't think it's very nice to say Mary was pregnant," Alice whispered to me.

"But she was," I pointed out. In a way, though, I agreed with her. It sounded too ordinary. Anybody could be pregnant. "Great with child" sounded better for Mary.

"I'm not supposed to talk about people being pregnant." Alice folded her hands in her lap and pinched her lips together. "I'd better tell my mother."

"Tell her what?"

"That your mother is talking about things like that in church. My mother might not want me to be here."

I was pretty sure she would do it. She wanted to be Mary, and she was mad at Mother. I knew, too, that she would make it sound worse than it was and Mrs. Wendleken would get madder than she already was. Mrs. Wendleken didn't even want cats to have kittens or birds to lay eggs, and she wouldn't let Alice play with anybody who had two rabbits.

But there wasn't much I could do about it, except pinch Alice, which I did. She yelped, and Mother separated us and made me sit beside Imogene Herdman and sent Alice to sit in the middle of the baby angels.

I wasn't crazy to sit next to Imogene—after all, I'd spent my whole life staying away from Imogene—but she didn't even notice me . . . not much, anyway.

"Shut up," was all she said. "I want to hear her."

I couldn't believe it. Among other things, the Herdmans were famous for never sitting still and never paying attention to anyone—teachers, parents (their own or anybody else's), the truant officer, the police—yet here they were, eyes glued on my mother and taking in every word.

"What's that?" they would yell whenever they didn't understand the language, and when Mother read about there being no room at the inn, Imogene's jaw dropped and she sat up in her seat.

"My God!" she said. "Not even for Jesus?"

I saw Alice purse her lips together so I knew that was something else Mrs. Wendleken would hear about—swearing in the church.

"Well, now, after all," Mother explained, "nobody knew the baby was going to turn out to be Jesus."

"You said Mary knew," Ralph said. "Why didn't she tell them?"

"*I* would have told them!" Imogene put in. "Boy, would I have told them! What was the matter with Joseph that he didn't tell them? Her pregnant and everything," she grumbled.

"What was that they laid the baby in?" Leroy said. "That manger . . . is that like a bed? Why would they have a bed in the barn?"

"That's just the point," Mother said. "They *didn't* have a bed in the barn, so Mary and Joseph had to use whatever there was. What would you do if you had a new baby and no bed to put the baby in?"

"We put Gladys in a bureau drawer," Imogene volunteered.

"Well, there you are," Mother said, blinking a little. "You didn't have a bed for Gladys so you had to use something else."

"Oh, we had a bed," Ralph said, "only Ollie was still in it and he wouldn't get out. He didn't like Gladys." He elbowed Ollie. "Remember how you didn't like Gladys?"

I thought that was pretty smart of Ollie, not to like Gladys right off the bat.

"*Anyway,*" Mother said, "Mary and Joseph

used the manger. A manger is a large wooden feeding trough for animals."

"What were the wadded-up clothes?" Claude wanted to know.

"The what?" Mother said.

"You read about it—'she wrapped him in wadded-up clothes.'"

"*Swaddling* clothes." Mother sighed. "Long ago, people used to wrap their babies very tightly in big pieces of material, so they couldn't move around. It made the babies feel cozy and comfortable."

I thought it probably just made the babies mad. Till then, I didn't know what swaddling clothes were either, and they sounded terrible, so I wasn't too surprised when Imogene got all excited about that.

"You mean they tied him up and put him in a feedbox?" she said. "Where was the Child Welfare?"

The Child Welfare was always checking up on the Herdmans. I'll bet if the Child Welfare had ever found Gladys all tied up in a bureau drawer they would have done something about it.

"And, lo, the Angel of the Lord came upon them," Mother went on, "and the glory of the

Lord shone round about them, and—"

"Shazam!" Gladys yelled, flinging her arms out and smacking the kid next to her.

"What?" Mother said. Mother never read "Amazing Comics."

"Out of the black night with horrible vengeance, the Mighty Marvo—"

"I don't know what you're talking about, Gladys," Mother said. "This is the Angel of the Lord who comes to the shepherds in the fields, and—"

"Out of nowhere, right?" Gladys said. "In the black night, right?"

"Well . . ." Mother looked unhappy. "In a way."

So Gladys sat back down, looking very satisfied, as if this was at least one part of the Christmas story that made sense to her.

"Now when Jesus was born in Bethlehem of Judaea," Mother went on reading, "behold there came Wise Men from the East to Jerusalem, saying—"

"That's you, Leroy," Ralph said, "and Claude and Ollie. So pay attention."

"What does it mean, Wise Men?" Ollie wanted to know. "Were they like schoolteachers?"

"No, dumbbell," Claude said. "It means like

President of the United States."

Mother looked surprised, and a little pleased—like she did when Charlie finally learned the times-tables up to five. "Why, that's very close, Claude," she said. "Actually, they were kings."

"Well, it's about time," Imogene muttered. "Maybe they'll tell the innkeeper where to get off, and get the baby out of the barn."

"They saw the young child with Mary, his mother, and fell down and worshipped him, and presented unto him gifts: gold, and frankincense, and myrrh."

"What's that stuff?" Leroy wanted to know.

"Precious oils," Mother said, "and fragrant resins."

"Oil!" Imogene hollered. "What kind of a cheap king hands out oil for a present? You get better presents from the firemen!"

Sometimes the Herdmans got Christmas presents at the Firemen's Party, but the Santa Claus always had to feel all around the packages to be sure they weren't getting bows and arrows or dart guns or anything like that. Imogene usually got sewing cards or jigsaw puzzles and she never liked them, but I guess she figured they were better than oil.

Then we came to King Herod, and the Herdmans never heard of him either, so Mother had to explain that it was Herod who sent the Wise Men to find the baby Jesus.

"Was it him that sent the crummy presents?" Ollie wanted to know, and Mother said it was worse than that—he planned to have the baby Jesus put to death.

"My God!" Imogene said. "He just got born and already they're out to kill him!"

The Herdmans wanted to know all about Herod—what he looked like, and how rich he was, and whether he fought wars with people.

"He must have been the main king," Claude said, "if he could make the other three do what he wanted them to."

"If I was a king," Leroy said, "I wouldn't let some other king push me around."

"You couldn't help it if he was the main king."

"I'd go be king somewhere else."

They were really interested in Herod, and I figured they liked him. He was so mean he could have been their ancestor—Herod Herdman. But I was wrong.

"Who's going to be Herod in this play?" Leroy said.

"We don't show Herod in our pageant," Mother said. And they all got mad. They wanted somebody to be Herod so they could beat up on him.

I couldn't understand the Herdmans. You would have thought the Christmas story came right out of the F.B.I. files, they got so involved in it—wanted a bloody end to Herod, worried about Mary having her baby in a barn, and called the Wise Men a bunch of dirty spies.

And they left the first rehearsal arguing about whether Joseph should have set fire to the inn, or just chased the innkeeper into the next county.

5

When we got home my father wanted to hear all about it.

"Well," Mother said, "just suppose you had never heard the Christmas story, and didn't know anything about it, and then somebody told it to you. What would you think?"

My father looked at her for a minute or two and then he said, "Well, I guess I would think it was pretty disgraceful that they couldn't find any room for a pregnant woman except in the stable."

I was amazed. It didn't seem natural for my father to be on the same side as the Herdmans. But then, it didn't seem natural for the Herdmans to be on the *right* side of a thing. It would have made more sense for them to be on Herod's side.

"Exactly," Mother said. "It was perfectly disgraceful. And I never thought about it much. You hear all about the nice warm stable with all the animals breathing, and the sweet-smelling hay—but that doesn't change the fact that they put Mary in a barn. Now, let me tell you . . ." She told my father all about the rehearsal and when she was through she said, "It's clear to me that, deep down, those children have *some* good instincts after all."

My father said he couldn't exactly agree. "According to you," he said, "their chief instinct was to burn Herod alive."

"No, their chief instinct was to get Mary and the baby out of the barn. But even so, it was *Herod* they wanted to do away with, and not Mary or Joseph. They picked out the right villain—that must mean something."

"Maybe so." My father looked up from his newspaper. "Is that what finally happened to Herod? What *did* happen to Herod, anyway?"

None of us knew. I had never thought much about Herod. He was just a name, somebody in the Bible, Herodtheking.

But the Herdmans went and looked him up.

The very next day Imogene grabbed me at recess. "How do you get a book out of the library?" she said.

"You have to have a card."

"How do you get a card?"

"You have to sign your name."

She looked at me for a minute, with her eyes all squinched up. "Do you have to sign your own name?"

I thought Imogene probably wanted to get one of the dirty books out of the basement, which is where they keep them, but I knew nobody would let her do that. There is this big chain across the stairs to the basement and Miss Graebner, the librarian, can hear it rattle no matter where she is in the library, so you don't stand a chance of getting down there.

"Sure you have to sign your own name," I said. "They have to know who has the books." I didn't see what difference it made—whether she signed the card with her own name, or signed the card Queen Elizabeth—Miss Graebner still wasn't going to let Imogene Herdman take any books out of the public library.

I guess she couldn't stop them from using the library, though, because that was where they found out about Herod.

They went in that afternoon, all six of them, and told Miss Graebner that they wanted library cards. Usually when anybody told Miss Graebner that they wanted a library card, she got this big happy smile on her face and said, "Good! We want all our boys and girls to have library cards."

She didn't say that to the Herdmans, though. She just asked them *why* they wanted library cards.

"We want to read about Jesus," Imogene said.

"Not Jesus," Ralph said, "that king who was out to get Jesus . . . Herod."

Later on Miss Graebner told my mother that she had been a librarian for thirty-eight years and loved every minute of it because every day brought something new and different. "But now," she said, "I might as well retire. When Imogene Herdman came in and said she wanted to read about Jesus, I knew I'd heard everything there was to hear."

At the next rehearsal Mother started, again, to separate everyone into angels and shepherds and guests at the inn but she didn't get very far. The Herdmans wanted to rewrite the whole pageant and hang Herod for a finish. They couldn't stand it

that he died in bed of old age.

"It wasn't just Jesus he was after," Ralph told us. "He killed all kinds of people."

"He even killed his own wife," Leroy said.

"And nothing happened to him," Imogene grumbled.

"Well, he died, didn't he?" somebody said. "Maybe he died a horrible death. What did he die of?"

Ralph shrugged. "It didn't say. Flu, I guess."

They were so mad about it that I thought they might quit the pageant. But they didn't—not then or ever—and all the people who kept hoping that the Herdmans would get bored and leave were out of luck. They showed up at rehearsals, right on time, and did just what they were supposed to do.

But they were still Herdmans, and there was at least one person who didn't forget that for a minute.

One day I saw Alice Wendleken writing something down on a little pad of paper, and trying to hide it with her other hand.

"It's none of your business," she said.

It *wasn't* any of my business, but it wasn't any of Alice's, either. What she wrote was "Gladys Herdman drinks communion wine."

"It isn't wine," I said. "It's grape juice."

"I don't care what it is, she drinks it. I've seen her three times with her mouth all purple. They steal crayons from the Sunday-school cupboards, too, and if you shake the Happy Birthday bank in the kindergarten room it doesn't make a sound. They stole all the pennies out of that."

I was amazed at Alice. I would never think to go and shake the Happy Birthday bank.

"And every time you go in the girls' room," she went on, "the whole air is blue, and Imogene Herdman is sitting there in the Mary costume, smoking cigars!"

Alice wrote all these things down, and how many times each thing happened. I don't know why, unless it made her feel good to see, in black and white, just how awful they were.

Since none of the Herdmans had ever gone to church or Sunday school or read the Bible or anything, they didn't know how things were supposed to be. Imogene, for instance, didn't know that Mary was supposed to be acted out in one certain way—sort of quiet and dreamy and out of this world.

The way Imogene did it, Mary was a lot like Mrs. Santoro at the Pizza Parlor. Mrs. Santoro is a

big fat lady with a little skinny husband and nine children and she yells and hollers and hugs her kids and slaps them around. That's how Imogene's Mary was—loud and bossy.

"Get away from the baby!" she yelled at Ralph, who was Joseph. And she made the Wise Men keep their distance.

"The Wise Men want to honor the Christ Child," Mother explained, for the tenth time. "They don't mean to harm him, for heaven's sake!"

But the Wise Men didn't know how things were supposed to be either, and nobody blamed Imogene for shoving them out of the way. You got the feeling that *these* Wise Men were going to hustle back to Herod as fast as they could and squeal on the baby, out of pure meanness.

They thought about it, too.

"What if we *didn't* go home another way?" Leroy demanded. Leroy was Melchior. "What if we went back to the king and told on the baby— where he was and all?"

"He would murder Jesus," Ralph said. "Old Herod would murder him."

"He would not!" That was Imogene, with fire in her eye, and since the Herdmans fought one another just as fast as they fought everybody else,

Mother had to step in and settle everyone down.

I thought about it later though and I decided that if Herod, a king, set out to murder Jesus, a carpenter's baby son, he would surely find some way to do it. So when Leroy said, "What if we went back and told on the baby?" it gave you something to think about.

No Jesus . . . ever.

I don't know whether anybody else got this flash. Alice Wendleken, for one, didn't.

"I don't think it's very nice to talk about the baby Jesus being murdered," she said, stitching her lips together and looking sour. That was one more thing to write down on her pad of paper, and one more thing to tell her mother about the Herdmans—besides the fact that they swore and smoked and stole and all. I think she kept hoping that they would do one great big sinful thing and her mother would say, "Well, that's that!" and get on the telephone and have them thrown out.

"Be sure and tell your mother that I can step right in and be Mary if I have to," she told me as we stood in the back row of the angel choir. "And if *I'm* Mary we can get the Perkins baby for Jesus. But Mrs. Perkins won't let Imogene Herdman get her hands on him." The Perkins baby would have made a terrific Jesus, and Alice knew it.

The way things stood, we didn't have any baby at all—and this really bothered my mother because you couldn't very well have the best Christmas pageant in history with the chief character missing.

We had lots of babies offered in the beginning—all the way from Eugene Sloper who was so new he was still red, up to Junior Caudill who was almost four (his mother said he could scrunch up). But when all the mothers found out about the Herdmans they withdrew their babies.

Mother had called everybody she knew, trying to scratch up a baby, but the closest she came was Bernice Watrous, who kept foster babies all the time.

"I've got a darling little boy right now," Bernice told Mother. "He's three months old, and so good I hardly know he's in the house. He'd be wonderful. Of course he's Chinese. Does that matter?"

"No," Mother said. "It doesn't matter at all."

But Bernice's baby got adopted two weeks before Christmas, and Bernice said she didn't like to ask to borrow him back right away.

So that was that.

"Listen," Imogene said. "I'll get us a baby."

"How would you do that?" Mother asked.

"I'll steal one," Imogene said. "There's always two or three babies in carriages outside the A&P supermarket."

"Oh, Imogene, don't be ridiculous," Mother said, "You can't just walk off with somebody's baby, you know!" I doubt if Imogene *did* know that—she walked off with everything else.

"We just won't worry anymore about a baby," Mother said. "We'll use a baby doll. That'll be better anyway."

Imogene looked pleased. "A doll can't bite you," she pointed out. Which just went to prove that Herdmans started out mean, right from the cradle.

6

Our last rehearsal happened to be the night before the pot-luck supper, and when we got there the kitchen was full of ladies in aprons, counting out dishes and silverware and making applesauce cake for the dessert.

"I'm sorry about this," one of the ladies told Mother, "but with so much to do at this time of year, the committee decided to come in this evening and set up the tables and all. I just hope we won't bother you."

"Oh, you won't," Mother said. "We won't be in the kitchen. You won't even know we're here."

Mother was wrong—everybody in that end of town knew we were there before the evening was over.

"Now, this is going to be a dress rehearsal," Mother told us all, and right away three or four baby angels began hollering that they forgot their wings. Half the angel choir had forgotten their robes, and Hobie Carmichael said he didn't have any kind of a costume.

"Wear your father's bathrobe," Charlie told him. "That's what I do."

"He doesn't have a bathrobe."

"What does he hang around the house in?"

"His underwear," Hobie said.

I looked at Alice Wendleken to see if she was going to write that down on her pad of paper, but Alice was standing all by herself in a corner, patting her hair. Her hair was all washed and curled, and her robe was clean and pressed. She had even put vaseline on her eyelids, so they would shine in the candlelight and everyone would say "Who is that lovely girl in the angel choir? Why isn't she Mary?" I guess Alice was afraid to move, for fear she might spoil herself.

"Don't worry about your wings," Mother said. "The main point of a dress rehearsal isn't the costumes. The main point is to go right straight through without stopping. And that's what we're going to do, just as if we were doing it for the whole congregation. I'm going to sit in the back of the church and be the audience."

But it didn't work that way. The baby angels came in at the wrong place and had to go back out again, and a whole gang of shepherds didn't come in at all, for fear of Gladys. Imogene couldn't find the baby Jesus doll, and wrapped up a great big memorial flower urn in the blanket, and then dropped it on Ralph's foot. And half the angel choir sang "Away in a Manger" while the other half sang "O, Little Town of Bethlehem."

So we had to start over a lot.

"I've got the baby here," Imogene barked at the Wise Men. "Don't touch him! I named him Jesus."

"No, no, no." Mother came flying up the aisle. "Now, Imogene, you know you're not supposed to say anything. Nobody says anything in our pageant, except the Angel of the Lord and the choir singing carols. Mary and Joseph and the Wise Men make a lovely picture for us to look at while we think about Christmas and what it means."

I guess Mother had to say things like that, even though everybody knew it was a big lie. The Herdmans didn't look like *anything* out of the Bible— more like trick-or-treat. Imogene even had on great big gold earrings, and she wouldn't take them off.

"Now, Imogene," Mother said. "You know Mary didn't wear earrings."

"I have to wear these," Imogene said.

"Why is that?"

"I got my ears pierced, and if I don't keep something in 'em, they'll grow together."

"Well, they won't grow together in an hour and a half," Mother said.

"No . . . but I better leave 'em in." Imogene pulled on her earrings, which made you shudder—it was like looking at the pictures in *National Geographic* of natives with their ears stretched all the way to their shoulders.

"What did the doctor say about leaving something in them?" Mother said.

"What doctor?"

"Well, who pierced your ears?"

"Gladys," Imogene said.

That really made you shudder—the thought of Gladys Herdman piercing ears. I thought she probably used an ice pick, and for the next six months I kept watching Imogene, to see her ears turn black and fall off.

"All right," Mother said, "but we'll try to find

something smaller and more appropriate for you to wear in the pageant. Now we'll start again and go right straight through, and—"

"I think I ought to tell them what his name is," Imogene said.

"No. Besides, you remember it wasn't Mary who named the baby."

"I told you!" Ralph whacked Imogene on the back. "*I* named him."

"Joseph didn't name the baby either," Mother said. "God sent an angel to tell Mary what his name should be."

Imogene sniffed. "I would have named him Bill."

Alice Wendleken sucked in her breath, and I could hear her scratching down on her pad of paper that Imogene Herdman would have called the baby Bill instead of Jesus.

"What angel was that?" Ralph wanted to know. "Was that Gladys?"

"No," Mother said. "Gladys is the angel who comes to the shepherds with the news."

"Yeh," Gladys said. "Unto you a child is born!" she yelled at the shepherds.

"Unto *me!*" Imogene yelled back at her. "Not them, me! I'm the one that had the baby!"

"No, no, no." Mother sat down on a front pew. "That just means that Jesus belongs to everybody. Unto *all* of us a child is born. Now," she sighed. "Let's start again, and—"

"Why didn't they let Mary name her own baby?" Imogene demanded. "What did that angel do, just walk up and say, 'Name him Jesus'?"

"Yes," Mother said, because she was in a hurry to get finished.

But Alice Wendleken had to open her big mouth. "I know what the angel said," Alice piped up. "She said, 'His name shall be called Wonderful, Counselor, Mighty God, Everlasting Father, the Prince of Peace.'"

I could have hit her.

"My God!" Imogene said. "He'd never get out of the first grade if he had to write all that!"

There was a big crash at the back of the church, as if somebody dropped all the collection plates. But it wasn't the collection plates—it was Mrs. Hopkins, the minister's wife, dropping a whole tray of silverware.

"I'm sorry," she said. "I was just passing by, and I thought I'd take a peek . . ."

"Would you like to sit down and watch the rehearsal?" Mother asked.

"No-o-o." Mrs. Hopkins couldn't seem to take her eyes off Imogene. "I'd better go check on the applesauce cake."

"You didn't have to say that," I told Alice. "All that about Wonderful, Everlasting Father, and all."

"Why not?" Alice said, patting her hair. "I thought Imogene wanted to know."

By that time everyone was hot and tired, and most of the baby angels had to go to the bathroom, so Mother said we would take a five-minute recess. "And then we'll start over," she said, looking sort of hopeless, "and go right straight through without stopping, won't we?"

Well, we never did go right straight through. The five-minute recess was a big mistake, because it stretched to fifteen minutes, and Imogene spent the whole time smoking cigars in one of the johns in the ladies' room. Then Mrs. Homer McCarthy went to the ladies' room and opened the door and smelled something funny and saw some smoke— and she ran right to the church office and called the fire department.

We were singing "Angels We Have Heard on High" when what we heard was the fire engine, pulling up on the lawn of the church, with the siren blaring and the red lights flashing. The firemen hurried in and made us all go outside, and they dragged a big hose in the front door and went looking for a fire to put out.

The street was full of baby angels crying, and shepherds climbing all over the fire truck, and firemen, and all the ladies on the pot-luck committee, and neighbors who came to see what was going on, and Reverend Hopkins who ran over from the parsonage in his pajamas and his woolly bathrobe.

Nobody knew what had happened, including the Herdmans, but I guess they figured that whatever it was, they had done it, so they left.

"Why in the world did you call the fire department?" Mother asked Mrs. McCarthy, when she finally heard the whole story.

"Because the ladies' room was full of thick smoke!"

"It couldn't have been," Mother said. "You just got excited. Didn't you know it was cigar smoke?"

Mrs. McCarthy stared at her. "No, I didn't. I don't expect to find cigar smoke in the ladies' room of the church!" She whirled around and marched back to the kitchen.

But by that time the kitchen was fuller of smoke than the ladies' room, because, while everybody was milling around in the street, all the

applesauce cake burned up.

Of course the ladies on the pot-luck committee were mad about that. Mrs. McCarthy was mad, and Alice said her mother would be good and mad when she heard about it. Most of the baby angels' mothers were mad because they couldn't find out what had happened—and somebody said Mrs. Hopkins was mad because Reverend Hopkins was running around the streets in his pajamas.

It turned out to be the one great big sinful thing Alice kept hoping for.

Mrs. Wendleken read Alice's notes, got on the telephone that very night and called up everybody she could think of in the Ladies' Aid and the Women's Society. And she called most of the flower committee, and all the Sunday-school teachers, and Reverend Hopkins.

And Reverend Hopkins came to see Mother. "I can't make head or tail of it," he said. "Some people say they set fire to the ladies' room. Some people say they set fire to the kitchen. One lady told me that Imogene threw a flower pot at Ralph. Mrs. Wendleken says all they do is talk about sex and underwear."

"That was Hobie Carmichael," Mother said, "talking about underwear. And they didn't set fire

76

to anything. The only fire was in the kitchen, where the pot-luck committee let their applesauce cake burn up."

"Well . . ." Reverend Hopkins looked unhappy. "The whole church is in an uproar. Do you think we should call off the pageant?"

"Certainly not!" Mother said. By that time she was mad, too. "Why, it's going to be the best Christmas pageant we've ever had!"

Of all the lies she'd told so far, that was the biggest, but you had to admire her. It was like General Custer saying, "Bring on the Indians!"

"Maybe so," Reverend Hopkins said. "I'm just afraid that no one will come to see it."

But he was wrong.

Everybody came . . . to see what the Herdmans would do.

7

On the night of the pageant
we didn't have any supper because Mother forgot
to fix it. My father said that was all right. Between
Mrs. Armstrong's telephone calls and the pageant
rehearsals, he didn't expect supper anymore.

"When it's all over," he said, "we'll go someplace and have hamburgers." But Mother said
when it was all over she might want to go someplace and hide.

"We've never once gone through the whole
thing," she said. "I don't know what's going to happen. It may be the first Christmas pageant in history where Joseph and the Wise Men get in a fight,

and Mary runs away with the baby."

She might be right, I thought, and I wondered what all of us in the angel choir ought to do in case that happened. It would be dumb for us just to stand there singing about the Holy Infant if Mary had run off with him.

But nothing seemed very different at first.

There was the usual big mess all over the place—baby angels getting poked in the eye by other baby angels' wings and grumpy shepherds stumbling over their bathrobes. The spotlight swooped back and forth and up and down till it made you sick at your stomach to look at it and, as usual, whoever was playing the piano pitched "Away in a Manger" so high we could hardly hear it, let alone sing it. My father says "Away in a Manger" always starts out sounding like a closetful of mice.

But everything settled down, and at 7:30 the pageant began.

While we sang "Away in a Manger," the ushers lit candles all around the church, and the spotlight came on to be the star. So you really had to know the words to "Away in a Manger" because you couldn't see anything—not even Alice Wendleken's vaseline eyelids.

After that we sang two verses of "O, Little Town of Bethlehem," and then we were supposed to hum some more "O, Little Town of Bethlehem" while Mary and Joseph came in from a side door. Only they didn't come right away. So we hummed and hummed and hummed, which is boring and also very hard, and before long doesn't sound like any song at all—more like an old refrigerator.

"I knew something like this would happen," Alice Wendleken whispered to me. "They didn't come at all! We won't have any Mary and Joseph—and now what are we supposed to do?"

I guess we would have gone on humming till we all turned blue, but we didn't have to. Ralph and Imogene were there all right, only for once they didn't come through the door pushing each other out of the way. They just stood there for a minute as if they weren't sure they were in the right place—because of the candles, I guess, and the church being full of people. They looked like the people you see on the six o'clock news— refugees, sent to wait in some strange ugly place, with all their boxes and sacks around them.

It suddenly occurred to me that this was just the way it must have been for the real Holy

Family, stuck away in a barn by people who didn't much care what happened to them. They couldn't have been very neat and tidy either, but more like *this* Mary and Joseph (Imogene's veil was cockeyed as usual, and Ralph's hair stuck out all around his ears). Imogene had the baby doll but she wasn't carrying it the way she was supposed to, cradled in her arms. She had it slung up over her shoulder, and before she put it in the manger she thumped it twice on the back.

I heard Alice gasp and she poked me. "I don't think it's very nice to burp the baby Jesus," she whispered, "as if he had colic." Then she poked me again. "Do you suppose he could have had colic?"

I said, "I don't know why not," and I didn't. He *could* have had colic, or been fussy, or hungry like any other baby. After all, that was the whole point of Jesus—that he didn't come down on a cloud like something out of "Amazing Comics," but that he was born and lived . . . a real person.

Right away we had to sing "While Shepherds Watched Their Flocks by Night"—and we had to sing very loud, because there were more shepherds than there were anything else, and they made so much noise, banging their crooks around like a lot of hockey sticks.

Next came Gladys, from behind the angel choir, pushing people out of the way and stepping on everyone's feet. Since Gladys was the only one in the pageant who had anything to say she made the most of it: "Hey! Unto you a child is born!" she hollered, as if it was, for sure, the best news in the world. And all the shepherds trembled, sore afraid —of Gladys, mainly, but it looked good anyway.

Then came three carols about angels. It took that long to get the angels in because they were all primary kids and they got nervous and cried and forgot where they were supposed to go and bent their wings in the door and things like that.

We got a little rest then, while the boys sang "We Three Kings of Orient Are," and everybody in the audience shifted around to watch the Wise Men march up the aisle.

"What have they got?" Alice whispered.

I didn't know, but whatever it was, it was heavy—Leroy almost dropped it. He didn't have his frankincense jar either, and Claude and Ollie didn't have anything although they were supposed to bring the gold and the myrrh.

"I knew this would happen," Alice said for the second time. "I bet it's something awful."

"Like what?"

"Like . . . a burnt offering. You know the Herdmans."

Well, they did burn things, but they hadn't burned this yet. It was a ham—and right away I knew where it came from. My father was on the church charitable works committee—they give away food baskets at Christmas, and this was the Herdman's food-basket ham. It still had the ribbon around it, saying Merry Christmas.

"I'll bet they stole that!" Alice said.

"They did not. It came from their food basket, and if they want to give away their own ham I guess they can do it." But even if the Herdmans didn't *like* ham (that was Alice's next idea) they had never before in their lives given anything away except lumps on the head. So you had to be impressed.

Leroy dropped the ham in front of the manger. It looked funny to see a ham there instead of the fancy bath-salts jars we always used for the myrrh and the frankincense. And then they went and sat down in the only space that was left.

While we sang "What Child Is This?" the Wise

84

Men were supposed to confer among themselves and then leave by a different door, so everyone would understand that they were going home another way. But the Herdmans forgot, or didn't want to, or something, because they didn't confer and they didn't leave either. They just sat there, and there wasn't anything anyone could do about it.

"They're ruining the whole thing!" Alice whispered, but they weren't at all. As a matter of fact, it made perfect sense for the Wise Men to sit down and rest, and I said so.

"They're supposed to have come a long way. You wouldn't expect them just to show up, hand over the ham, and leave!"

As for ruining the whole thing, it seemed to me that the Herdmans had improved the pageant a lot, just by doing what came naturally—like burping the baby, for instance, or thinking a ham would make a better present than a lot of perfumed oil.

Usually, by the time we got to "Silent Night," which was always the last carol, I was fed up with the whole thing and couldn't wait for it to be over. But I didn't feel that way this time. I almost wished for the pageant to go on, with the Herdmans in charge, to see what else they would do that was different.

Maybe the Wise Men would tell Mary about their problem with Herod, and she would tell them to go back and lie their heads off. Or Joseph might go with them and get rid of Herod once and for all. Or Joseph and Mary might ask the Wise Men to take the Christ Child with them, figuring that no one would think to look there.

I was so busy planning new ways to save the baby Jesus that I missed the beginning of "Silent Night," but it was all right because everyone sang "Silent

Night," including the audience. We sang all the verses too, and when we got to "Son of God, Love's pure light" I happened to look at Imogene and I almost dropped my hymn book on a baby angel.

Everyone had been waiting all this time for the Herdmans to do something absolutely unexpected. And sure enough, that was what happened.

Imogene Herdman was crying.

In the candlelight her face was all shiny with tears and she didn't even bother to wipe them away. She just sat there—awful old Imogene—in her crookedy veil, crying and crying and crying.

Well. It *was* the best Christmas pageant we ever had.

Everybody said so, but nobody seemed to know why. When it was over people stood around the lobby of the church talking about what was different this year. There was something special, everyone said—they couldn't put their finger on what.

Mrs. Wendleken said, "Well, Mary the mother of Jesus had a black eye; that was something special. But only what you might expect," she added.

She meant that it was the most natural thing in the world for a Herdman to have a black eye. But actually nobody hit Imogene and she didn't hit anyone else. Her eye wasn't really black either, just all puffy and swollen. She had walked into the corner of the choir-robe cabinet, in a kind of daze—as if she had just caught onto the idea of God, and the wonder of Christmas.

And this was the funny thing about it all. For years, I'd thought about the wonder of Christmas, and the mystery of Jesus' birth, and never really understood it. But now, because of the Herdmans, it didn't seem so mysterious after all.

When Imogene had asked me what the pageant was about, I told her it was about Jesus, but that was just part of it. It was about a new baby, and his mother and father who were in a lot of trouble—no money, no place to go, no doctor, nobody they knew. And then, arriving from the East (like my uncle from New Jersey) some rich friends.

But Imogene, I guess, didn't see it that way. Christmas just came over her all at once, like a case of chills and fever. And so she was crying, and walking into the furniture.

Afterward there were candy canes and little tiny Testaments for everyone, and a poinsettia plant for my mother from the whole Sunday school. We put the costumes away and folded up the collapsible manger, and just before we left, my father snuffed out the last of the tall white candles.

"I guess that's everything," he said as we stood at the back of the church. "All over now. It was quite a pageant." Then he looked at my mother. "What's that you've got?"

"It's the ham," she said. "They wouldn't take it back. They wouldn't take any candy either, or any of the little Bibles. But Imogene did ask me for a set of the Bible-story pictures, and she took out the Mary picture and said it was exactly right, whatever that means."

I think it meant that no matter how she herself was, Imogene liked the idea of the Mary in the picture—all pink and white and pure-looking, as if she never washed the dishes or cooked supper or did anything at all except have Jesus on Christmas Eve.

But as far as I'm concerned, Mary is always going to look a lot like Imogene Herdman—sort of nervous and bewildered, but ready to clobber anyone who laid a hand on her baby. And the Wise Men are always going to be Leroy and his brothers, bearing ham.

When we came out of the church that night it

was cold and clear, with crunchy snow underfoot and bright, bright stars overhead. And I thought about the Angel of the Lord—Gladys, with her skinny legs and her dirty sneakers sticking out from under her robe, yelling at all of us, everywhere:

"Hey! Unto you a child is born!"

OTHER BOOKS BY BARBARA ROBINSON

The Best Christmas Pageant Ever

My Brother Louis Measures Worms
And Other Louis Stories

BARBARA ROBINSON

THE ~~WORST~~ Best SCHOOL YEAR EVER

HarperCollins*Publishers*

This book is for my daughters,
Carolyn and Margie,
who brighten all the corners
of my life. . . .
—B.R.

THE HERDMANS . . .
BACK AGAIN!

When we studied the Old West, everybody had to do a special report on A Cowboy's Life or Famous Indian Chiefs or Notorious Outlaw Families like the James brothers. Boomer Malone picked the James brothers, but then he couldn't find them in the children's encyclopedia.

"That's all right, Boomer," Miss Kemp said. "It doesn't have to be the James brothers. Pick another outlaw family."

So Boomer did. He picked the Herdmans.

Of course, the Herdmans weren't in the Old West, and they weren't in the children's encyclopedia either. They were right there in the Woodrow Wilson School, all six of them spread

1

out, one to a class, because the only teacher who could put up with two of them at once would have to be a Miss King Kong. My father said he bet that was in the teachers' contracts along with sick leave and medical benefits: only one Herdman at a time.

Boomer's paper was the best one, three whole pages of one crime after another. He should have gotten A plus, but Miss Kemp made him do the whole paper over.

"I'm ashamed of you, Boomer," she said, "calling your own schoolmates an outlaw family."

The Herdmans didn't care. They knew they were outlaws. So did Miss Kemp, but I guess she had to pretend they were like everybody else.

They weren't, and if they *had* been around in the Old West, they would have burned it all down or blown it all up and we wouldn't have to study about it.

Plus, of course, we wouldn't have to live with Herdmans every day, in school and out. . . .

1

Unless you're somebody like Huckleberry Finn, the first day of school isn't too bad. Most kids, by then, are bored with summer and itchy from mosquito bites and poison ivy and nothing to do. Your sneakers are all worn out and you can't get new ones till school starts and your mother is sick and tired of yelling at you to pick things up and you're sick and tired of picking the same things up.

Plus, the first day of school is only half a day for kids.

My little brother, Charlie, once asked my mother what the teachers do for the rest of the day.

"They get things ready—books and papers and lessons."

3

"That's not what Leroy Herdman says," Charlie told her. "Leroy says as soon as the kids are gone, they lock all the doors and order in pizza and beer."

"Well, they don't," Mother said, "and how would Leroy know anyway?"

"He forgot something," Charlie said, "and he went back to get it and he couldn't get in."

"They saw him coming and locked the doors," Mother said. "Wouldn't you?"

Well, yes. Anyone would, because the Herdmans—Ralph, Imogene, Leroy, Claude, Ollie, and Gladys—were the worst kids in the history of the world. They weren't honest or cheerful or industrious or cooperative or clean. They told lies and smoked cigars and set fire to things and hit little kids and cursed and stayed away from school whenever they wanted to and wouldn't learn anything when they were there.

They were always there, though, on the first day, so you always knew right away that this was going to be another exciting Herdman year in the Woodrow Wilson Elementary School.

At least there was only one of them in each grade, and since they never got kept back, you always had the same one to put up with. I had

Imogene, and what I did was stay out of her way, but it wasn't easy.

This time she grabbed me in the hall and shoved an oatmeal box in my face. "Hey," she said, "you want to buy a science project?"

I figured that Imogene's idea of a science project would probably explode or catch fire or smell really bad or be alive and bite me—and, in fact, I could hear something squealing and scratching around in the oatmeal box.

"Miss Kemp already wrote this year's assignment on the board," I said, "and it isn't a science project."

"Fine time to tell me," Imogene grunted. "What is it? The assignment." She shook her oatmeal box. "Is it mice?"

So I was half right—Imogene's science project was alive, but it probably wouldn't bite me unless it was great big mice, and I didn't want to find out.

"No," I said, "it's about people."

"Mice would be better," Imogene said.

Later that morning Miss Kemp explained her assignment, and I thought Imogene might be right, because the assignment sounded weird.

"For this year's project," she said, "we're going to study each other. That's the assignment on the

5

blackboard, Compliments for Classmates."

All over the room hands were going up and kids were saying "Huh?" and "What does it mean?" and "How many pages?" But Miss Kemp ignored all this.

"It means exactly what it says," she said. "You're to think of a special compliment for each person in this class, and please don't groan"—a lot of people did anyway—"because this is the assignment for the *year*. You have all year to think about it, and next June, before the last day of school, you'll draw names from a hat and think of more compliments for just that one person."

Somebody asked if it could be a famous person instead, and somebody else asked if it could be a dead famous person, like George Washington.

Miss Kemp said no. "This is a classroom project, so it has to be people in this class. We know all about George Washington's good points, but . . ." She looked around and picked on Boomer. "We don't know all Boomer's good points. More important, *Boomer* probably doesn't know all his good points."

"How many compliments?" Junior Jacobs wanted to know.

"Up to you," Miss Kemp said.

Alice Wendleken raised her hand. "Would beautiful hair and shiny hair count as one compliment?"

This sounded to me as if Alice planned to compliment herself, which would save someone else the trouble, but Miss Kemp said, "I'm not talking about beautiful hair and nice teeth, Alice. I mean characteristics, personal qualities, something special."

This could be hard, I thought. Take Albert Pelfrey. When you think of Albert Pelfrey, you think *fat*. Even Albert thinks *fat*. It's hard to think anything else, so I would really have to study Albert to find some special personal quality that wasn't just about being fat. And besides Albert there were twenty-eight other people, including Imogene Herdman.

"What's a compliment?" Imogene asked me.

"It's something nice you tell someone, like if someone is especially helpful or especially friendly."

Alice looked Imogene up and down. "Or especially clean," she said.

"Okay." Imogene frowned. "But mice would still be better."

Mice would probably be *easier* for Imogene

because the Herdmans always had animals around. As far as I know they weren't mean to the animals, but the animals they weren't mean to were mean all by themselves, like their cat, which was crazy and had to be kept on a chain because it bit people.

Now and then you would see Mrs. Herdman walking the cat around the block on its chain, but she worked two shifts at the shoe factory and didn't have much time left over to hang around the house and walk the cat.

There wasn't any Mr. Herdman. Everybody agreed that after Gladys was born, he just climbed on a freight train and left town, but some people said he did it right away and some people said he waited a year or two.

"Gladys probably bit him," my friend Alice Wendleken said.

"Not if she was a baby?" I asked. "Babies don't have any teeth."

"She probably had hard, hard gums." Alice knew what she was talking about, because Gladys bit her all the time. Mrs. Wendleken always poured iodine all over the bites, so Alice had to go around for days with big brown splotches on her arms and legs. Alice was always afraid she would die anyway (of Gladys-bite) and have to be buried looking splotched up and ugly instead of beautiful in her blue-and-white dress with the ruffles.

It wasn't all that special to get bitten by Gladys. She bit everybody, including my little brother, Charlie. Charlie came home yelling and screaming that Gladys bit him, and Gladys came too, which shows you how fearless they were. Any other kid who bit a kid and broke the skin and drew blood would go hide somewhere, but not Gladys.

"Gladys Herdman!" It's always your whole name when my mother is mad. "Do you know what I think about a little girl who bites people? I think she ought to have to wear a sign around her neck that says 'Beware of Gladys.'"

I guess Mother thought that would really put Gladys in her place, but Gladys just said "Okay" and went home and made the sign and wore it for a week. Nobody paid much attention—we didn't need a sign to make us beware of Gladys.

Besides everything else they did, the Herdmans would steal anything they could carry, and it was surprising what all they could carry—not just candy and gum and gerbils and goldfish. They even stole Mrs. Johanneson's concrete birdbath, for the goldfish, I guess. And last spring they stole my friend Louella McCluskey's baby brother, Howard, from in front of the grocery store.

Of course Howard wasn't supposed to be in front of the grocery store. Louella was supposed to be baby-sitting him, which she did every Tuesday afternoon while her mother went to the beauty parlor. Louella got paid fifty cents to do this, and on that particular Tuesday we were in the grocery store spending her fifty cents.

When we came out—no Howard. The stroller was still there, though, and that's why we didn't think of the Herdmans right away. Usually if you missed something, you would just naturally figure the Herdmans had it. But when they stole a thing, they always stole all of the thing. It wasn't like them to take the baby and leave the stroller.

Louella turned the stroller over and looked underneath it as if she thought Howard might have fallen through, which was pretty dumb. Then we walked up and down the street, hollering for Howard, which was also dumb. How could Howard answer? He couldn't even talk. He couldn't walk either, or crawl very much. He couldn't get out of the stroller in the first place.

"Well, somebody must have taken him,"

Louella said. "Some stranger has just walked off with my baby brother."

"You better tell a policeman," I said.

"No, I don't want to. They would get my mother out of the beauty parlor and I don't want her to know."

"She'll know when you come home without Howard," I said.

"I won't go home. Not till I find him. Now let's just think. Who would take Howard?"

I couldn't imagine who would take Howard. Even my mother said Howard was the homeliest baby she'd ever laid eyes on, but she did say that he would probably be just fine once he grew some hair. That was his main trouble—having no hair. Here he was, bald as an egg, and Mrs. McCluskey kept rubbing his head with Vaseline to make the hair grow. So when you looked at Howard, all you saw was this shiny white head. Not too good.

"Probably someone who just loves babies," Louella said, but that could be anybody. It would be easier to think of someone who hates babies, but if you hated them you certainly wouldn't steal one.

Then Louella had another idea. "Let's just walk down the street," she said, "pushing the

11

stroller. Maybe someone has seen Howard and when they see us with an empty stroller they'll figure we're looking for him and tell us where he is."

I was pretty disgusted. "Louella," I said, "you know that won't happen."

But it did. The first person we met was my little brother, Charlie, and the first thing he said was "If you're looking for Howard, the Herdmans have got him."

Louella looked relieved, but not very, and I didn't blame her. If you had to choose between a total stranger having your baby brother and the Herdmans having him, you would pick the total stranger every time.

"What have they done with him?" Louella asked.

"They're charging kids a quarter to look at him."

"Why would anybody pay a quarter to look at Howard?" I said. "We can look at Howard anytime."

"They don't tell you it's Howard. They've got a sign up that says, 'See the Amazing Tattooed Baby! 25 cents.'"

"They tattooed him!" Louella yelped. "My mother will kill me!"

Actually, they didn't tattoo him. What they did was wipe off the Vaseline and draw pictures all over his head with waterproof marker.

Charlie was dumb enough to fall for their sign. He paid his quarter to see an amazing tattooed baby, and of course he was mad as could be when it turned out to be Howard McCluskey with pictures drawn all over his head.

So he tagged along behind us, insisting that Louella get his money back, but we both knew that Louella would have all she could do just to get Howard back.

"If it was anything but the baby," she said, "I wouldn't even *try* to get it back—not from the Herdmans."

"They already collected six-fifty," Charlie said. "You ought to make them pay you some of that for the use of Howard."

"I'll probably have to pay them," Louella grumbled.

She was right. When we got to the Herdmans', there were three or four kids lined up outside the fence, and Louella marched up and said to Imogene Herdman, "You give me back my baby brother!"

But Imogene pretended not to hear her and

13

just went on collecting money. "You want to see the tattooed baby?" She jiggled the money box at Louella. "It'll cost you a quarter."

"It's no tattooed baby," Louella said, "it's my little brother."

Imogene squinched her eyes together. "How do you know?"

"I just know."

"You do not. It could be anybody's baby. It could be some baby you never heard of. It'll cost you a quarter to find out."

Sure enough, it was Howard and he was a sight. The whole top of his head was red and green and blue and purple with pictures of dogs and cats and trees and tic-tac-toe games.

"I don't know what you're so mad about," Leroy Herdman said. "He looks a lot better than he did."

In a way Leroy was right. Howard looked a lot more *interesting*, but nobody expected Mrs. McCluskey to think so.

We took Howard out back of my house and tried to wash off his head, which is how we found out the pictures were all waterproof.

"Now what'll I do?" Louella asked.

"Tell your mother the Herdmans did it," Charlie said.

"She'll just want to know why I let them do it, and how they got hold of him in the first place. Maybe we should use some soap."

We tried all kinds of things on Howard, but the only thing that worked at all was scouring powder, and that didn't work too well. It made his head gritty and it didn't take off all the purple.

"If you don't stand too close to him," Louella said, "and then squint your eyes . . . does the purple look to you like veins?"

It didn't to me. "But after all," I told Louella, "I *know* what it is. Your mother doesn't know what it is, so maybe it will look like veins to her."

It didn't. Mrs. McCluskey was so mad that she got a sick headache and spots before her eyes and had to lie down for two days. The first thing she did after she got up was go to work on Howard's head to try and get the purple off, and she discovered two or three patches of soft fuzz.

So then she wasn't mad at the Herdmans anymore. She said that something about all the drawing or the Magic Marker ink must have started his hair to grow. But she was still mad at Louella, which didn't seem fair. After all, it *could* have been the scouring powder.

I said that to my mother, and I knew right away that it was a mistake, because she said,

"What scouring powder?" and then, "Beth Bradley, come back here! What scouring powder?"

So then I got punished for putting scouring powder on Howard's head, and Louella got punished for leaving him in front of the grocery store, and Charlie got punished by not having any Choco-Whoopee bars from the ice cream man till next week.

"That's what your quarter was for," Mother told him. "Next time you'll think twice before you throw away your quarter on something silly."

Of course, Howard got some hair, but he was just a baby and he didn't care whether he had any hair or not. The Herdmans, who caused all the trouble in the first place, got $6.50.

If anybody but the Herdmans had stolen a baby and scribbled all over his head and then charged people money to look at him, they would have been shut up in the house for the rest of their natural lives. But since it *was* the Herdmans, most people just said how lucky Mrs. McCluskey was to get Howard back all in one piece, and that was that.

The truth is that no one wanted to fool around with them, so you knew that unless they tried to hold up the First National Bank or burn down the public library, you weren't going to see the last of them—especially if you had to go to the Woodrow Wilson School, and be in the same class with Imogene, and figure out something good to say about her before the end of the year.

2

A lot of people, like Alice Wendleken's mother, thought the Herdmans ought to be in jail, kids or not, but I knew that wouldn't happen.

Our jail is just two cells in the basement of the town hall, and the Herdmans aren't allowed in the town hall anymore since Gladys and Ollie put all the frogs in the drinking fountain there. They were little tiny frogs, and Miss Farley, the town clerk, drank two or three of them off the top of the bubbler by mistake. She didn't have her glasses on, she said, and didn't see them till somebody hollered, "Evelyn, stop! You're drinking frogs!"

Miss Farley was hysterical! She said she could feel them jerking and jumping all up and down

18

her windpipe. But even so she chased Gladys and Ollie all around the block, and she said if she ever caught any Herdmans inside the town hall again, she would put on roller skates and run them out of town so fast their heels would smoke.

Of course they didn't care. "What'd she eat our frogs for anyway?" Gladys said. "It's not our fault she ate our frogs. She'll get warts in her stomach, where she can't scratch them."

"Warts don't itch," Alice Wendleken told her.

"These will," Gladys said. "We caught the frogs in a patch of poison ivy."

The town hall wasn't the only place in town where the Herdmans weren't allowed in to get a drink of water or go to the bathroom or call their mother or anything. They also weren't allowed in the drugstore or the movie theater or the A&P or the Tasti-Lunch Diner.

They used to be allowed in the post office, but that didn't last. Somebody got hold of all their school pictures and put them up right next to the "WANTED" posters, and it seemed so natural for them to be there that nobody noticed till Ollie Herdman went up and asked the postmaster, Mr. Blair, how much money he could get for his brother Claude.

"I don't know what you mean," Mr. Blair said.

"Some of those people are worth five hundred dollars," Ollie said. "How much can I get for Claude?"

So Mr. Blair went to see what he was talking about and sure enough, there were the Herdmans right up with the bank robbers and the mad bombers and all.

Mr. Blair had a fit. "How did these pictures get up here?" he said. "Did you put these pictures up here?"

Ollie said no, it was a big surprise to him.

"Well, it's a big surprise to me too," Mr. Blair said, "but I can tell you that the F.B.I. is not going to pay you anything for Claude, or any of the rest of you either. How did you happen to pick on Claude?"

"Because he's the one I've got," Ollie said.

Mr. Blair said later that he didn't like the sound of that. "I figured he probably had Claude tied to a tree somewhere." So he mentioned it to the policeman on the corner, and the policeman said he'd better go investigate because with Herdmans you never could tell.

He didn't have to go far. There was a big crowd of people and a lot of commotion halfway down the block, and sure enough, Ollie had shut Claude up in the men's room of the Sunoco station.

When the policeman got there, Claude was banging on the door and hollering for someone to let him out, and there was a whole big family from South Dakota wanting to get in. The mother said they had driven almost a hundred and fifty miles looking for a Sunoco station because they were the cleanest, but what good was clean if you couldn't get in?

"I gave the key to one of those Herdmans," the manager said, "and he went off with it. I should have my head examined."

"But you don't need a key to get *out*," the policeman said. "Why doesn't Claude just open the door?"

"I can't," Claude yelled. "The door's stuck."

Ollie claimed later that he didn't have anything to do with that; that he hadn't even planned to shut Claude up in the men's room or anywhere else, but when the door jammed shut he went off to get help, and that was when he saw the pictures at the post office.

"You were going to get help at the post office?" the manager asked.

"I was going to get my sister Imogene."

"And she was at the post office?"

"No," Ollie said, "she wasn't there."

That was typical Herdman—there was a lie in it somewhere, but you couldn't put your finger on where.

Of course all that was later. In the meantime Mr. Blair and the Sunoco station manager had to get the fire department to break in the door and get Claude out. By that time the South Dakota people had left, and a lot of other people who wanted gas got tired of waiting and went somewhere else, and in all the excitement somebody walked off with two cans of motor oil and a wrench. Herdmans, probably, but nobody could prove it, just like nobody could prove that Ollie really meant to hand Claude over to the F.B.I. for money.

So then the Herdmans weren't allowed in the post office *or* the Sunoco station, and they got thrown out of the new Laundromat the very day it opened.

They planned to wash their cat in one of the machines, but they didn't know it would cost money, so they just dropped him in and went off to locate some quarters.

Of course the cat didn't like it in the washing

machine, and it made so much noise hissing and spitting and scratching that the manager, Mr. Cleveland, went to see what was wrong.

"I thought it was a short circuit," he said, "or a loose connection—something electrical. That's the kind of noise it was."

People said it *looked* electrical, all right. When he opened the lid, the cat shot out with its tail and its ears and all its hair standing straight up. It skittered around all over the tops of the machines and clawed through everybody's laundry baskets, and knocked over boxes of soap and bottles of bleach and a big basket of flowers that said "Good Luck to the Laundromat."

Finally someone opened the door, and the last they saw of the cat it was roaring down the street, all tangled up in a tablecloth.

Of course the Laundromat was a mess and all the customers were mad and couldn't find their clothes and wanted their money back for the stuff the cat had spilled. Pretty soon people began to sneeze from all the cat hair and soap powder in the air, and one lady broke out in big red blotches all over because she was allergic to cats. Mr. Cleveland sent everyone outdoors till things settled down.

But things didn't settle down. Santoro's Pizza

Parlor was across the street, and when Mr. Santoro saw all these people coming out of the Laundromat sneezing and coughing and choking, he yelled, "What's the matter? Is it a fire?"

Somebody yelled back, "No—cat hair." But Mr. Santoro thought they said "bad air." He figured there was something wrong with the new plumbing connections, maybe a gas leak, and he ran to the top of the street to warn people away in case of an explosion.

Some of the people he warned away were Herdmans—Imogene and Ralph and Leroy, on their way back with fifty cents for the washing machine.

"You children get away from here!" he said. "The Laundromat may explode!"

I guess they were pretty surprised. They probably figured the cat did it, but they didn't know how. They also probably figured that if the cat was smart enough to blow up a Laundromat, it was smart enough to get away. So they just left.

Mr. Santoro called the fire department too and they came right away. But of course there wasn't any fire and there wasn't any gas leak, and by that time there wasn't any cat and there weren't any Herdmans either, just a lot of angry customers and a reporter from the newspaper who went around interviewing everybody.

Most of the people didn't even know what had happened because it happened so fast, so the newspaper story was pretty mysterious. "LAUNDROMAT OPENING MARRED BY UNUSUAL DISTURBANCE," it said. "FIREMEN RESPOND TO ANONYMOUS ALARM. CUSTOMERS DESCRIBE WILD ANIMAL." My father said at least they got that part right.

Mr. Cleveland had to clean up the mess and replace everybody's stuff and pay for the blotched-up lady to get an allergy shot, so he was pretty mad. Mr. Santoro was mad because they called him "anonymous," and of course the firemen were mad because they knew the Herdmans did it, whatever it was.

In the meantime the Herdmans were home, waiting for the cat to show up. The cat, crazier than usual because it was all wrapped up in a tablecloth, was tearing all over town, yowling and spitting and scratching at anything that got in its way.

It ran in the barber shop and streaked up one side of the chair where Mr. Perry was shaving someone.

"All of a sudden," Mr. Perry said, "there was a cat. So I lathered the cat by mistake. Missed my customer and lathered the cat."

Then the cat ran through the lobby of the movie theater and picked up some popcorn there, and by that time you couldn't tell what it was or what it had *ever* been.

It finally clawed its way up a tree in front of the library, and the librarian, Miss Graebner, called the fire department to come and get it down.

"I think it's a cat," she said, "and it looks like it's been through a war."

"No," the fire chief said, "it's been through a washing machine, and as far as I'm concerned it can stay in that tree till the middle of next year." Of course, Miss Graebner was mad about that.

The only people who weren't mad were the Herdmans, because when the cat finally came home, it was all clean and fluffy from the shaving lather, and that's what they wanted in the first place.

3

Naturally my mother wasn't too crazy about the Herdmans since they were always mopping up the floor with Charlie, but she had too much to do, she said, to spend time complaining about them—she would leave that to Alice Wendleken's mother, who was so good at it.

Mrs. Wendleken complained about them all the time, to everybody. It was her second favorite subject, besides how smart Alice was, and how pretty, and how talented, and how it would all go to waste if Gladys Herdman bit her to death.

Every time you turned around, Mrs. Wendleken was volunteering Alice to be the star of something—the main fairy or the head elf or the

Clean Up Our Streets poster girl—and when the Chamber of Commerce bought a respirator for the hospital they put a picture of it in the paper and, sure enough, there was Alice hooked up to the respirator.

Mrs. Wendleken said she didn't have anything to do with that. The photographer just looked around and said, "I wonder if that pretty little girl would be willing to pose with the respirator." But nobody believed her.

Alice didn't get any applause for this either, but she carried the picture around anyway, and showed it to anyone who would hold still. She showed it to Imogene Herdman at recess, and Imogene took one look and hollered, "Get away from me! Don't touch me! Whatever you've got, I don't want it!"—which brought the school nurse in a hurry in case Alice had smallpox or something.

It emptied the playground in a hurry too. Everybody figured that if it was something Imogene Herdman was scared to catch, it would wipe out the rest of us because ordinary germs didn't even slow the Herdmans down. They never got mumps or pinkeye or colds or stomachaches or anything. A snake once bit Leroy Herdman and

Leroy's leg swelled up a little bit, but that was all.

The snake died. Leroy brought it to school and tied it all up and down the light cord in the teachers' supply closet, and about five minutes later the kindergarten teacher, Miss Newman, came in and pulled the cord.

She had all the day's helpers with her—six kindergarten kids carrying pots of red finger paint—and when Miss Newman screamed, they all dropped their pots and finger paint flew all over the place.

Then somebody upset two big boxes of chalk and they all tramped around in that, and when the janitor heard the racket and opened the door, he just took one look and went straight to get the principal. He said there had been some terrible accident and the supply closet was full of bloody people, apparently all cut up and screaming in pain.

By the time the principal got there, Miss Newman had pulled herself together and was herding the little kids down the hall to the washroom, and then the recess bell rang.

So the hall was full of kids, and teachers calling to Miss Newman, "What happened? What happened?" and the principal telling everyone to "Move along, move right along. Nothing here to see." Of course there was plenty to see—the whole thing looked like a big disaster we had just read about in history called The Children's Massacre.

In all the commotion Leroy Herdman just walked into the supply closet, untied his snake and put it in his pocket, and walked out again.

When we got back from recess, the principal and Miss Newman and the janitor and the boys' basketball coach were all crawling around the floor of the supply closet, and Miss Newman was saying, "I tell you there was a snake crawling up the light cord!"

Of course they never did find it, because nobody looked in Leroy's pocket.

I couldn't understand why the snake died and Leroy didn't, but when I asked my father, he said that Leroy probably stretched his story. "A snake bit him," my father said, "and then he found a different snake that was already dead. That's what I think."

My mother said she bet it wasn't a snake at all, that Leroy just tied a whole lot of poor worms together. But I decided that Leroy was telling the truth for the first time in his life, that the snake was perfectly healthy, bit Leroy, and immediately died. So maybe Mrs. Wendleken wasn't far wrong to pour iodine all over Alice, and maybe Alice should shut up about this treatment and just be glad she wasn't dead, like the snake.

Two or three days later Leroy stuck the snake in the third-grade pencil sharpener, tail first, and that teacher went all to pieces too. It was bad enough, she said, to find a snake in the pencil sharpener, but then she almost sharpened it by mistake.

The snake was pretty worn out by then, so they threw it away, but nobody in the third grade would go near the pencil sharpener for the rest of the week.

My mother's friend Miss Philips worked for the welfare department, and one of her jobs was to check up on the Herdmans, so Mother told her about the snakebite in case Leroy should get some kind of shot for it. But Miss Philips just said she didn't know of any shot that would benefit Leroy, and anyway, all her sympathies were with the snake.

"I went once to that garage where those kids live," she said, "but I never got inside and I barely got out of the yard alive. It was full of rocks and poison ivy and torn-up bicycles and pieces of cars and great big holes they'd dug. I fell in one of the holes and the cat jumped on me out of a window. Good thing I had a hat on or I'd be bald. Now I just drive past the place once a month, and if they haven't managed to blow it up or burn it down, I figure they're all right."

"But a snakebite," Mother said. "Don't you think that's unusual?"

"I certainly do," Miss Philips said. "It's the first time something bit one of them instead of the other way around."

The whole thing got into the newspaper: "REPTILE FOUND IN WOODROW WILSON SCHOOL," the article said. "TEACHERS AND STUDENTS ALARMED." That probably meant Miss Newman and all the kindergarten kids. "PARENTS SEEK ACTION" probably meant Mrs. Wendleken, seeking to get the Herdmans expelled or arrested or something. "SCHOOL OFFICIAL INSPECTS PREMISES" *was* Mr. Crabtree, the principal, who stuck his head in the third-grade room and said that if one more snake showed up anywhere he would personally kill it, skin it, cook it, and feed it to whoever was responsible.

I don't know whether that would have scared Leroy or not, but it didn't matter anyway because he wasn't there. Imogene said he stayed home to

32

bury the snake, and she had this messy scribbled-up note that said, "Leroy is absent at a funeral."

"I'm sorry to hear that, Imogene," the teacher said. "Was it a member of your family? Why aren't you at the funeral?"

"It was a friend of Leroy's," Imogene said. "I didn't like him."

Mrs. Wendleken was mad because the newspaper article didn't say it was Leroy Herdman's snake that caused all this trouble, and she was mad at the principal because he wouldn't say so either.

"I can't *prove* who the snake belonged to," Mr. Crabtree said, "and even if I could, why would I? It wasn't a boa constrictor, you know, and it was dead to begin with."

But I guess Mrs. Wendleken was really out to nail Leroy, and she wouldn't give up. "Of course it was Leroy's snake! Everybody knows it was Leroy's snake. Why else would he bury it? Why would Leroy Herdman bury someone else's snake?"

"I don't know." Mr. Crabtree was fed up with the snake and Leroy Herdman and Mrs. Wendleken too. "But if he *did* bury a snake for somebody else, it's the first cooperative thing he's

33

ever done in his life, and I just think we ought to drop the whole subject, don't you?"

That would probably have been the end of it, except that Mrs. Wendleken described this conversation to my mother, who described it to Miss Philips. Then Miss Philips went to school and told Mr. Crabtree that she had a plan to civilize the Herdmans or, at least, one of them.

"It's about the snake . . ." she began, but Mr. Crabtree wouldn't let her say any more.

"I'll do it," he said. "I don't even care what it is you want, just so I don't have to hear any more about that snake."

So Leroy got named Good School Citizen of the Month—"for an act of kindness," the award read.

Of course this was one big surprise to everybody, especially Leroy, and it nearly killed Alice Wendleken, who had piled up more good deeds and good grades and extra-credit projects and perfect-attendance records than anybody else in the whole history of the Woodrow Wilson School, and expected to be the Good School Citizen of the Month for the rest of her life.

Nobody could figure out what kind thing Leroy had done, but Miss Philips told my mother.

"He buried a snake?" Mother said. "That's it?"

"That's it," Miss Phillips said.

"Well, I guess if you were the snake you might call it an act of kindness, but I don't understand . . ."

"I just thought he might decide to live up to the honor," Miss Philips explained. "He might be a changed person."

Mother said she wouldn't count on it. "He probably doesn't even know what it was he did."

"He didn't even do it," Charlie told her. "Imogene just said he did. Nobody buried the snake. The janitor threw it in the trash masher. I saw him."

"Well, don't tell anyone," Mother said. "Mrs. Wendleken would never shut up about it."

Mother was right about Leroy. He *didn't* know what he did or how he got to be a Good School Citizen, and when Charlie wouldn't tell him, he buried Charlie up to his neck in the trash masher barrel, which would have been tough on Charlie if the janitor didn't happen to see him before he mashed up the trash.

So Leroy wasn't a changed person, unless you want to count that he only buried Charlie up to his neck instead of all the way.

4

The janitor, Mr. Sprague, said that was that—no more trash masher. He told the principal that we could have a trash masher or we could have the Herdmans, but we couldn't have both under one roof.

"I can't stand around and guard the thing all day," he said. "There's six of them and only one of me, and every time I leave the basement to go sweep a floor, they shove something else into it."

They'd already mashed up the fourth-grade ant farm and the plastic dinosaur exhibit, and then Leroy went ahead and mashed up the Good School Citizen Award too, once he found out he couldn't eat it or spend it or sell it to anybody.

Alice reported this to her mother, and Mrs. Wendleken was so disgusted about the whole thing that she resigned from the PTA, which my father said was good news for the PTA.

Of course, Mrs. Wendleken didn't come right out and say, "I quit because I'm mad at everybody." She just said it wasn't fair for her to run the PTA Talent Show because Alice was in it. She said Mother could do that because Mother *didn't* have any talented children in it.

"Does that mean we aren't talented, or just that we aren't in it?" Charlie asked me, and I said, "Both."

Actually *nobody* had any talented children in it, and they really had to scratch around to get kids to do anything, so it was no night of a thousand stars, which was what all the posters said— "Night of a Thousand Stars! An Evening of Family Entertainment! PTA Talent Show!"

When my father saw the list of acts, he said he hoped there would be more talent in the refreshments than there was going to be in the show.

"There aren't any refreshments," Mother told him. "This is just an evening of family entertainment."

He shook his head. "Not unless you have refreshments, it won't be."

I guess Mother took another look at the list, because that night she called around for people to make cookies and brownies and cupcakes and punch, and the next day the posters said, "Night of a Thousand Stars! An Evening of Family Entertainment! PTA Talent Show!"—with "Delicious Refreshments!" crowded in at the bottom.

This was a big mistake, because "refreshments" is one long word that all the Herdmans understand, and right away you knew that they'd figure some way to get at them.

"They can't," Alice said. "They'd have to be in the show, and they can't do anything talented."

"They can steal," Charlie said.

Alice looked at him the way my mother looks at the bottom of the hamster cage. "That's not a talent," she said.

Maybe not, but the Herdmans did it better than anybody else. Still, it was hard to see how they would do it for an audience or what they would call it on the program or what they would steal, because there wasn't much left that they hadn't already stolen.

Last year they were all absent on October 4

and we had Arbor Day because for the last three years the Herdmans stole the tree, and the principal said at least this year we'd finally get it planted, even if it died over the winter.

"Maybe they've got some talent we don't know about," I said. And sure enough, three days later Gladys Herdman took a pair of kindergarten safety scissors and cut Eugene Preston's hair in the shape of a dog. It could have been a cat, though, or a horse or a pig. Something with four legs and a tail, anyway, or else something with five legs and no tail.

You had to look right down at the top of his head to see it, but this was what you mostly saw of Eugene anyway because he was the shortest kid in the second grade or the first grade or even kindergarten. So naturally he got picked on a lot, and if you had to choose which kid in the Woodrow Wilson School would get his hair cut in the shape of a dog for no reason, you would choose Eugene.

Of course he was already a nervous wreck from being the shortest kid around, and you knew it wasn't going to calm him down to have people holler, "Here, Fido!" or "Here, Spot!" at him. And if his hair was anything like the rest of him, he would probably be this way for years. So things didn't look good for Eugene.

"A dog?" my father said when he heard about it. "I can't believe it looks like a dog. Who says it looks like a dog?"

"The art teacher," Charlie said. "I heard her tell the principal. She said if it just wasn't on Eugene's head she would display it as an example of living sculpture."

"Why don't you tell that to Eugene?" Mother said. "It might make him feel better to know that he's a living sculpture."

I didn't think so. For one thing, nobody knew what a living sculpture was. I helped Eugene look it up in the encyclopedia, but we looked under *living* instead of *sculpture* and never got past *living sacrifice*, which was all about torture, and *that* sure didn't make Eugene feel better.

"Come on, Eugene," I said. "Don't be crazy. No one's going to make you be a sacrifice."

"Hah!" he said. "How about Gladys Herdman?"

He was really worried, and between being worried and short and having his hair all chopped up, Eugene began to twitch and wiggle and bite his fingernails and bang himself on the head.

40

"I can't help it," he said. "It makes me feel better."

Actually, there wasn't a kid in the Woodrow Wilson School who didn't wiggle or twitch or tie knots in his hair or *something*. Boomer Malone once ate a whole pencil without even knowing it till he got to the eraser and broke off a tooth. Some kids banged their heads, too, when they didn't have anything else to do, and of course the Herdmans banged *other* kids on the head, but nobody did it as hard as Eugene.

This was fascinating to Gladys Herdman. She quit hitting him and hollering at him and just followed him around everywhere—waiting for him to knock himself out, we all thought.

"Why do you do that all the time?" she asked him, but Eugene was scared to tell her the truth. He figured if he said, "It makes me feel better," she would pound him black and blue and claim it was a good deed.

My mother thought Eugene ought to enter the talent show. "It would take his mind off his troubles," she said, "and there must be *something* he could do."

I couldn't imagine what, except maybe stand up on the stage and be short, and I never heard of a show where part of the entertainment was somebody being short. So I was pretty surprised, along with everybody else, to learn that Eugene had a hidden talent that he would perform at the talent show.

"And then on TV, probably," Gladys Herdman said. Gladys was the one who discovered this talent but she wouldn't tell anybody what it was and she wouldn't let Eugene tell anybody either, not even his mother—so Mrs. Preston didn't know whether to get him a costume or a guitar or elevator shoes or what.

My mother didn't know what to put on the stage for him to use. "Maybe he needs a microphone," she said. "Maybe he needs some special music. I'd really like to know, because I want Eugene to be a success." It would be wonderful, she told us, if Eugene could win first prize in the talent show.

What she really meant was, it would be wonderful if *anybody* besides Alice Wendleken would win first prize for a change, but I knew that wouldn't happen unless Alice broke both her arms and couldn't play the piano.

I guess Charlie thought it was worth a try, though, because he asked Eugene what he needed for his talent act.

"He needs walnuts," Charlie reported, "but he says he'll bring his own. He doesn't want to. He's scared to be in the talent show, but he's more scared of Gladys."

"What's he going to do with walnuts?" Mother asked.

"I don't know. Unless . . . maybe he's going to juggle them." Charlie brightened up. "That would be good! Even if he drops some, that would be good!"

It seemed to me that if Eugene could juggle *anything* we would all know about it, but maybe not. My friend Betty Lou Sampson is double-jointed and can fold herself into a pretzel, but she won't do it in front of people, because of being shy. It could be the same way with Eugene, I thought.

I also thought he might back out, but on the night of the talent show there he was, so for once we had something different to look forward to.

There isn't usually anything different or surprising about the talent show. One year a girl named Bernice Potts signed up to do an animal act and the animal turned out to be a goldfish, which was different. But then the act turned out to be Bernice talking to the fish and the fish talking back and Bernice telling the audience what the fish said. Charlie loved this, but he was in the first grade then and believed anything anybody told him.

Mrs. Wendleken said this act didn't belong in the talent show because it didn't have anything to do with human talent. "Even if the fish *could* talk," she said, "that would just mean the fish was talented, not Bernice."

Mrs. Wendleken didn't think Eugene should be juggling walnuts either, according to Alice. "*If* he can do it," Alice sniffed, "which he probably can't."

Eugene didn't even try. He came out on the stage carrying a big bowl of walnuts while Mother was introducing him. "Our next talented performer," she said, "is from the second grade. It's Eugene Preston, and Eugene is going to—"

Mother never got a chance to finish, because Eugene began smashing walnuts on his forehead one after another, just as fast as he could, and walnut shells flew everywhere.

People sitting in the back of the auditorium couldn't figure out what he was doing, and people sitting in the front of the auditorium knew what he was doing but couldn't believe he was doing it. The principal, who was sitting in the back row, thought kids were throwing things at Eugene, so he started up the aisle and ran smack into Mrs. Preston, who was yelling for someone to stop Eugene before he killed himself with walnuts.

Nobody heard her. There was too much noise. Kids were jumping up and down and clapping and hollering, "Go, Eugene! Go, Eugene!" and then, "Go, Hammerhead! Go, Hammerhead!" Boomer Malone began counting walnuts: ". . . twenty-two, twenty-three, twenty-four . . ." And pretty soon everybody was chanting, ". . . thirty-six, thirty-seven, thirty-eight . . ." Boomer said Mrs. Preston fainted when Eugene got to forty-five walnuts, but she didn't really faint. She just collapsed onto a seat, moaning something about "scrambled brains."

Eugene used all his walnuts and then he set his bowl down on the stage and walked off. He looked taller to me, but that's probably because I was looking up at him for a change.

Eugene didn't win first prize, but neither did Alice. Her piano solo was called "Flying Fingers," and it would have been pretty flashy except that there were so many walnut shells stuck in the piano keys that she kept having to stop and start over. Eugene was the popular favorite, but I guess the judges didn't want to reward a scramble-your-brains act, in case that *did* eventually happen to him, so they gave the first prize to the kindergarten rhythm band, which was probably the best thing to do. It made all the kindergarten mothers happy and it didn't make anyone else very mad.

Of course, kids were all over Eugene, telling him that he should have won, that he was the best, and wanting to feel his head.

"Did you always crack nuts that way?" someone asked, and Eugene said no, that it was Gladys Herdman's idea.

"Why?" Charlie said. "What was in it for Gladys?"

If you didn't know any better you might think that Gladys felt guilty because of Eugene's dog haircut, but no one at the Woodrow Wilson School would think that. So when we went to get the delicious refreshments, no one was very surprised to find they were all gone.

Mrs. McCluskey was in charge of the food, and when Mother asked her what happened she said, "I'd just put the last plate of cupcakes on the table when Gladys Herdman ran in here yelling that Eugene Preston had gone crazy in the auditorium and was trying to kill himself. Now normally I wouldn't pay any attention to *anything* a Herdman told me, but I could hear a lot of noise and stamping around and people yelling, 'Eugene! Eugene!' so naturally I went to see." She shrugged. "I still don't know what happened to Eugene, but I know what happened to the refreshments."

Everybody knew what happened to the refreshments but as usual you couldn't prove anything because the evidence was gone and Gladys was gone.

Mrs. Wendleken didn't agree. She said the evidence was Eugene. "It's obvious that Gladys Herdman got that poor little boy to knock himself silly and cause a big commotion, and then she went to the cafeteria and walked off with every last cookie!"

Maybe so, but Eugene *didn't* knock himself silly and you couldn't feel very sorry for him because he was a big celebrity with his name in the newspaper—"Unusual Performance by Plucky Eugene Preston Earns Standing Ovation at Woodrow Wilson Talent Show." The article also mentioned the kindergarten rhythm band, but not by name ("Too many of them," the reporter said) and not by musical number ("Could have been almost anything").

Besides, Eugene wasn't even Eugene anymore except to his mother and the teachers. And sometimes even the teachers forgot and called him Hammerhead, just like everyone else.

5

Every now and then I would remember about the assignment for the year—Compliments for Classmates—and turn to that page in my notebook. So far I had thought up compliments for six people, including Alice. For Alice, I put down "Important."

"I'm not sure I'd call that a compliment," my mother said.

"Alice would," I told her. Actually, Alice would probably consider it just a natural fact, like "The earth is round," "The sky is blue," "Alice Wendleken is important."

Alice began being important right away in the first grade because she was the only first-grade kid who had ever been inside the teachers' room. So whenever something had to be delivered there, Alice got to deliver it.

"I have a note to go to the teachers' room," our teacher would say, "way up on the third floor, so Alice, I'll ask you to be my messenger since you know exactly where it is."

Then Alice would stand up and straighten her dress and pat her hair and carry the note in both hands out in front of her as if it was news from God. Most of all, she would never tell what was in the room.

Whenever the teachers didn't have anything else to do, they went and hid in the teachers' room, but nobody else ever got in there. You couldn't *see* in, either, because the door was wood and frosted glass almost to the top.

Boomer Malone once got Charlie to climb on his shoulders and look in, but all Charlie could see was a sign that said "Thank God It's Friday," and another sign that said "Thank God It's June."

This got spread around school, and kids went home and told about the swear words in the teachers' room, so after that they put up a curtain and nobody could see anything.

"There isn't anything to see," my mother said.

"Just some chairs and tables and a sofa and a big coffeepot and a little refrigerator."

"No TV?" Charlie said.

"No TV."

"What do they do in there?"

Mother sighed. "I suppose they relax," she said, "and talk to each other, and have lunch."

"That's not what Imogene Herdman says," Charlie muttered.

"Well," Mother said, "if you believe what Imogene Herdman says, you'll believe anything."

"They go in there to smoke cigarettes and drink Cokes" was what Imogene had said. "And if somebody has a cake, they put it in a Sears, Roebuck sack and pretend it's something they bought, and then they go in there and eat it where nobody can see them. And they don't let anybody in who doesn't know the password."

Charlie brightened right up. "What's the password?"

"They pick a new one every day," Imogene said, "and then they put it in the morning announcements, like in what's for lunch. Once it was *macaroni and cheese*."

I figured Imogene was making this up as she went along, so you had to be impressed with her

51

imagination. I even got out my notebook and started to write that down: Imogene Herdman— "Has imagination." But then I realized it wasn't imagination, it was just a big lie. I also realized that finding a compliment for Imogene Herdman was probably the hardest thing I'd have to do all year and I'd better start thinking about it.

Of course, Charlie kept waiting for "macaroni and cheese" to show up in the morning announcements. He was going to walk past the teachers' room and say "macaroni and cheese" and see what happened. But the next time it was on the lunch menu, Charlie was stuck in the nurse's room with a nosebleed and didn't get to try it.

Imogene told him it didn't make any difference because the password that day was *softball*.

"Did you try it?" Charlie asked. "Did you get in?"

"I don't want in." Imogene gave him this dark, squinty-eyed look. "If a kid gets in that room, they never let him out. Remember Pauline Ellison?"

Charlie shook his head.

"Neither does anyone else. She got in the teachers' room. Remember Kenneth Weaver? Did you see Kenneth Weaver lately?"

"No, because he's got the mumps."

"That's what you think. Kenneth doesn't have the mumps. Kenneth got caught in the teachers' room."

I guess this was too much, even for Charlie. "I don't believe you," he said.

Imogene grinned her girl-Godzilla grin. "Neither did Kenneth," she said. "I told him he better not go near the teachers' room but"—she shrugged—"he did it anyway."

For once nobody believed Imogene. Nobody *told* her so, but Alice Wendleken said that from now on Imogene couldn't shove people around anymore because she was a proven liar, and no matter what she said everybody would laugh at her and maybe knock her down. Nobody believed *that* either, but it sounded great.

"Just wait till Kenneth comes back!" everybody said. But Kenneth didn't come back.

Charlie hunted me up at recess with this news. "He's never coming back," he said. "The teacher gathered up his books and moved Bernadette Slocum into his seat and said, 'Well, we'll certainly miss Kenneth, won't we?' It's just like Imogene said!"

"Oh, come on, Charlie," I said. "You know they haven't got him shut up in the teachers' room."

Still . . . you had to wonder. First Imogene said Kenneth was gone, and then he *was* gone. What if Imogene was right?

I wasn't the only one who thought about this, and I wasn't the only one who found reasons to stay away from the teachers' room, and even to stay away from the whole third floor. Kids suddenly couldn't climb stairs for one reason or another or kids got dizzy if they went above the second floor. Alice had what she called a twisted toe and limped around holding on to chairs and tables, all on one floor, naturally.

But Louella McCluskey told the real truth, for everyone. "I don't *think* Imogene Herdman is right," she said, "and I don't *think* kids disappear into the teachers' room, but maybe she is and maybe they do, and I'm not going to take any chances."

Then two teachers and a district supervisor and Mrs. Wendleken all got locked in the teachers' room by accident. They were in there for an hour and a half, banging on the door and yelling and even throwing things out the window. They took down the curtain and climbed up on chairs and waved their arms around at the top of the door, but nobody saw them and nobody heard them because nobody ever went near the teachers' room.

They were all pretty mad, especially the district supervisor, and Mrs. Wendleken was hysterical by the time somebody let them out. By that time, too, they were all worn out and hoarse from yelling and dizzy from waving their arms around in the air.

Who finally let them out was Imogene.

She said that she stood around trying to decide what to do, and that made Mrs. Wendleken hysterical all over again. "What to do!" she said. "Open the door and let us out is what to do!"

"But it's the teachers' room," Imogene said, looking shocked, as if she had this rule burned into her brain. "We're not allowed in the teachers' room."

"You're allowed to let people *out* of the teachers' room!" Mrs. Wendleken hollered.

Then the district supervisor got mad at Mrs. Wendleken. "This child has saved the day," she said. "We ought to thank her. And let me tell you, there are plenty of schools in this district where the students spend every waking minute trying to break into the teachers' room, or sneak into the teachers' room. You wouldn't believe the wild tales I've heard. Now here's a student who seems to understand that teachers need a little privacy. I hope you have more boys and girls like . . . is it Imogene?"

"We have five more exactly like her," one of the teachers said.

The district supervisor said that was wonderful and nobody argued with her—too tired, I guess, from jumping up and down yelling for help.

This whole thing got in the newspaper. "SCHOOL PERSONNEL LOCKED IN THIRD FLOOR ROOM," it said. "RELEASED BY ALERT STUDENT." It didn't name the alert student but it named everybody else who was there.

"Except Kenneth Weaver," Charlie said. "It doesn't say anything about Kenneth Weaver."

"That proves it, Charlie," I said. "He never was in there."

"Why in the world would Kenneth Weaver be in the teachers' room?" Mother said. "That whole family moved to Toledo."

"Did they take Kenneth?" Charlie asked.

"Certainly they took Kenneth! Who would

move away and leave their children?"

"Mr. Herdman," I said, but Mother said that was different.

Alice Wendleken cut out the newspaper article and gave it to Imogene. "I thought you'd want to keep it," she said, "since it's about you. Of course nobody knows it's about you because they didn't print your name. I wonder why they didn't print your name."

"They didn't print Kenneth's name either," Imogene said. "So what?"

"So Kenneth wasn't there!" Alice said.

Imogene stuck her nose right up against Alice's nose, which naturally made Alice nervous and also cross-eyed. "Why do you think I opened the door to that room?" she said. "You think I opened the door to let all those teachers out? Who cares if they never get out? I let Kenneth out."

"My mother was in there," Alice said, "and she didn't see Kenneth."

"Did you ask her?"

"No, because I know Kenneth Weaver is in Toledo."

"He is now," Imogene said.

This was typical Herdman—too shifty to figure

out, and Alice didn't even try.

Aside from congratulating Imogene, the district supervisor said that the worst part of being shut up in there for an hour and a half was the furniture. "Lumpy old sofa," she said, "broken-down chairs, terrible lighting. It doesn't surprise me that the door was broken. Everything in that room is broken."

So the teachers got a new sofa and chairs, and the furniture store donated a new rug, and they painted the walls and fixed the door and bought new curtains and a big green plant.

They left the door open too for a couple of days so everybody could see the new stuff, which just went to prove, Alice said, "that there's nobody hidden there and never was."

Imogene shrugged. "Suit yourself."

Charlie was feeling brave too. "Where would they be?" he said. "There's no place for them."

"Sure there is." Imogene pointed. "How about that? The plant that ate Chicago."

"The plant?" Mother said that evening. "Well, I would have chosen some normal kind of plant like a fern, but I guess they wanted something scientific for the teachers' room. That plant is a Venus's-flytrap. It eats flies . . . swallows them right up."

Charlie looked at me, his eyes wide, and I knew what he was thinking—that maybe you could say the password by accident, disappear into the teachers' room, and never be seen again because of death by plant.

"It eats *flies*, Charlie," I said. "Nothing but flies."

"Well, after all, it's just a plant," Mother said. "It doesn't know flies from hamburger. I guess it eats anything it can get hold of."

Once Charlie spread that word around, you would normally have had kids lining up to feed stuff to the plant—pizza, potato chips, M&M cookies—and they would probably have had to keep the door locked and put up a big sign that said "Private, Keep Out, Teachers Only." But none of this happened because nobody would go near the teachers' room, not even to watch a plant eat lunch.

When the district supervisor came back to see the new furniture, she mentioned this and said that the teachers could thank "that thoughtful girl. What was her name? Imogene" for all this peace and privacy.

I guess she was right, in a way, but I didn't see any teachers rushing to thank Imogene. And never mind how much I needed to find a compliment for her, I certainly couldn't write down "Imogene Herdman is thoughtful," no matter what the district supervisor said.

6

Once a year we had to take an IQ test and a psychology test and an aptitude test, which showed what you might grow up to be if the Herdmans let you get out of the Woodrow Wilson School alive. But the only test the Herdmans ever bothered to take was the eye test.

This surprised everybody, because it meant that at least they knew the letters of the alphabet. You had to cover up one eye with a little piece of paper and read the letters on a chart, and then cover up the other eye and read them again. If you couldn't do it, it meant that you had to have glasses.

Sometimes it just meant that you were scared, like Lester Yeagle.

"If you don't do it right," Gladys Herdman told Lester, "it means your eyes are in backward, and they have to take them out and put them in the other way."

This made Lester so nervous that he couldn't tell *L* from *M* or *X* from *K* and when the doctor said, "Well, let's just switch eyes," he went all to pieces and had to go lie down in the nurse's room till his mother could come and get him.

Besides having three other kids and a baby, Mrs. Yeagle was a schoolbus driver, so she couldn't waste much time just letting Lester be hysterical. But Lester was too hysterical to tell her what happened—all he said was "Herdman."

"Which one?" Mrs. Yeagle said. "Which one did it?" and Lester said Gladys did it.

"Did what?" the nurse wanted to know. "Gladys wasn't even there."

"I don't know what," Mrs. Yeagle said, "and I can't wait around to find out because I had to leave the baby with the Avon lady and it's almost time to drive the bus. Come on, Lester, honey . . . maybe you can find out," she told the nurse.

Of course Gladys said she didn't do anything, and the eye doctor said *he* certainly didn't do anything. "But I got a look at that kid's braces," he said, "and I'll bet that's his problem."

I didn't think so. Having braces was no problem—*not* having braces was a problem. Gloria Coburn's little sister got braces and Gloria didn't, and Gloria cried and carried on for weeks. "I'll grow up ugly with an overbite," she said, and she didn't even know for sure what one was. She just wanted braces like everyone else.

That night the nurse called Mrs. Yeagle to say that apparently Gladys didn't do anything to Lester. "We think the trouble may be his braces," she suggested.

"What braces?" Mrs. Yeagle said. "Lester doesn't have braces." But then she went and looked in his mouth and she nearly died.

"What have you got in there?" she yelled. "What is all that? It looks like paper clips!"

Sure enough, Lester had paper clips bent around his teeth and he got hysterical all over again because his mother pried them off.

The nurse said she never heard of paper clips, "but you know they all want to have braces or bands or something. And they don't know how much braces cost."

"Well, these cost thirty-five cents," Mrs. Yeagle said. "According to Lester, Gladys Herdman put them on him and that's what she charged him. And let me tell you, that kid better never try to get on my bus! Or any other Herdmans either!"

Getting thrown off the bus was almost the worst thing that could happen to you. You had to go to school anyway, no matter what, so if you got thrown off the bus it meant that your father had to hang around and take you, or your mother had to stop whatever she was doing and take you, so you got yelled at right and left. You even got yelled at when it happened to someone else— "Don't *you* get thrown off the bus!" your mother would say.

Mrs. Herdman probably never said this, but she didn't have to worry about it anyway. The Herdmans never got thrown off a bus because nobody ever let them on one. Sometimes, though, they would hang around what would have been their bus stop if they had one, smoking cigars and starting fights and telling little kids that the bus was full of bugs.

"Big bugs," Gladys told Maxine Cooper's little brother, Donald. "Didn't you ever hear them? They chomp through anything to get food. You better give me your lunch, Donald. I'll take it to school for you."

Of course that was the end of Donald's lunch, but at least, Maxine said, it was just a day-old bologna sandwich and some carrot sticks so they probably wouldn't do that again.

"They're just jealous," Alice told her, "because they have to walk while everybody else gets to ride and be warm and comfortable."

"Come on, Alice," I said. "If you think the schoolbus is warm and comfortable, you must be out of your mind."

But Imogene Herdman was standing right behind us, so Alice ignored me and said again how wonderful it was to ride the schoolbus, and how she would hate to be the Herdmans who *couldn't* ride the schoolbus because they were so awful.

After that they began to show up every morning at Maxine's bus stop, looking sneaky and dangerous, like some outlaw gang about to hold up the stagecoach.

"But they don't do anything," Maxine said, looking worried. "They just stand around. It's scary."

It scared Donald, all right, and after three or four days he wouldn't even come out the door, so Maxine stood on her front porch and yelled, "My mother says for you to go home!"

"We can't go home!" Imogene yelled back. "We have to go to school."

Then they all nodded at each other, Maxine said, just as if they were this big normal family of ordinary kids who got up and brushed their teeth and combed their hair and marched out ready to learn something.

Maxine felt pretty safe on her own porch, so she said, "Then why don't you just get on the bus and go!"

"Get on *your* bus?" Imogene said. "Get on Bus Six?" And Gladys hollered that she wouldn't get on Bus 6 if it was the last bus in the world, and Leroy said, "Me neither."

"And then when the bus came," Maxine told us, "they all ran behind the McCarthys' front hedge and just stood there, staring at us."

"What did Mrs. Yeagle do?" I asked.

"She yelled at them, 'Don't you kids even think about getting on my bus!' and Ollie said, 'I'll never get on Bus Six!' He said it twice. Listen . . ." Maxine leaned forward and lowered her voice. "I think the Herdmans are scared of the bus."

This was the craziest thing I'd ever heard. "It's just a bus," I said.

"I *know* that," Maxine said, "but it's my bus and I have to ride on it, and I don't want to ride on a doomed bus!"

This sounded crazy too, but nobody laughed, because if the Herdmans *were* scared of Bus 6, it was the *only* thing in the world they were scared of, so you had to figure they must know something no one else knew.

Whatever it was, they weren't telling, but every day there they were at the bus stop, whispering and shaking their heads.

Charlie thought they were stealing pieces of the bus, one little piece at a time, and someday the whole bus would just fall apart and scatter kids all over the street.

Eugene Preston brought in a copy of *Amazing Comics*, about a robot bus that suddenly began to go backward and sideways and turn itself over and lock all its doors, so the people were trapped inside, yelling and screaming. In the comic book the Mighty Marvo showed up and rescued everybody, but Eugene said he wouldn't want to count on the Mighty Marvo if he was up against the Herdmans.

"I just know something's going to happen," Maxine said. "I keep hearing this strange noise on the bus."

I don't know how she would hear anything except kids hollering, but Eloise Albright said she heard a strange noise too. Some kids said they smelled something on the bus, but who doesn't?—egg sandwiches, poison ivy medicine, Alice Wendleken's Little Princess perfume.

Lester finally asked his mother if there was anything wrong with their bus, but she just said, "Yes, it's full of kids."

Then Bus 6 was assigned to take the third grade to a dairy farm to study cows, and Ollie Herdman refused to go. "Not me," Ollie said. "Not on *that* bus!"

Of course this was good news for the cows, and the teacher was pretty happy, but the rest of the third grade was scared to death. Boomer Malone's little sister Gwenda said the suspense was awful—waiting for the bus to blow up or turn over—and between that and having to milk a cow, the whole third grade was wiped out for the rest of the day.

By this time Maxine was a nervous wreck, along with Donald and Lester and everybody else on Bus 6. More and more kids were feeling sick to their stomachs and then feeling fine as soon as the bus left, and they all said the same thing—

that they were scared to ride the bus because the Herdmans wouldn't get on it.

"What kind of reason is that?" my mother wanted to know. "Of course they won't get on the bus. Thelma Yeagle won't *let* them on the bus. Nobody *wants* them on the bus!"

"Something bad is going to happen," Charlie told her, "and the Herdmans know what it is. That's why they won't get on. They know Bus Six is doomed."

"Doomed!" Mother stared at him. "You watch too much television. Is that what everybody thinks?"

We said yes.

"Then why doesn't somebody just put the Herdmans on the bus and make them ride it?" Mother said.

Since it wasn't my bus, I thought that was a good idea and so did Charlie and so did Mr. Crabtree, I guess, because that's what he did.

"We have to ride your bus, Lester," Gladys said. She grinned this big grin so Lester could see her teeth all shiny with paper clips. "The principal said."

"I thought you were scared to ride this bus," Maxine told Imogene. "You said it was doomed."

"I didn't say that," Imogene told her. "*You* said

that." She climbed on the bus and walked up and down the aisle, picking out a seat next to some victim. "It looks all right to me."

Mrs. Yeagle was pretty mad at first, but she told my mother it wasn't all bad to have the Herdmans on the bus. "They told everybody to shut up," she said, "and everybody did."

Not for long, though. Claude and Leroy stole a bunch of baby turtles from the pet store and took them on the bus and put them down some kids' shirts. Leroy said later that he was amazed at what happened. He thought the turtles were dead and he was going to take them back to the pet store and complain.

The turtles weren't dead. They probably saw who had them and decided to stay in their shells till they were big enough to bite back. But it was nice and warm inside the shirts, so they began to stick their heads out and crawl around.

Of course nobody knew they had turtles down their backs. Nobody knew *what* they had down their backs, but Donald Cooper thought it was the big bugs, hungry and tired of peanut butter sandwiches. "I've got the big bugs on me!" he yelled, and right away all the other kids began to yell and scream and jump up and down and thrash around so Mrs. Yeagle had to stop the bus and get everybody settled down.

It was another week before all the turtles came out from under the seats and behind the seat backs, so it was a good thing that they were little to begin with and didn't grow very fast.

Once the Herdmans had collected all the turtles, they got off the bus and never came back. "Don't want to ride this dumb bus," Ralph muttered, and I guess that was the real truth. They just wanted to get *on* the bus, take over the territory, wham a few kids, pick out the best lunch (Gwenda Malone's, usually, because Gwenda always had two desserts and no healthy food), and then get *off* the bus and stay off, which they did.

For once, though, they weren't the only ones who got what they wanted. Lester's baby teeth fell out like popcorn—"All those paper clips," Mrs. Yeagle said—and his second teeth came in all crooked and sideways, so he had more braces and bigger braces and fancier braces than anybody else in the Woodrow Wilson School, and maybe the whole world.

7

When Louella McCluskey's mother went to work part-time at the telephone company, she let Louella baby-sit her little brother, Howard, again during spring vacation.

"Just don't you let the Herdmans get him this time," she said. "He's got hair now so they can't draw all over his head but I don't know what else they might do."

Howard had hair all right, but it was no big improvement because it started way above his ears and grew straight up, like grass.

"If it was up to me," Louella said, "I'd shave his head and let him start all over."

"Just mention that to Leroy," I said.

Louella turned pale. "My mother would kill me, and I'd never get to watch television or go to the movies for the rest of my life."

Louella kept Howard out of sight for the whole time, but when school started again, the regular baby-sitter quit, so Mrs. McCluskey got special permission for Louella to bring Howard to school—"Just for a few days," she said. "Just till I find someone else."

"Now what'll I do?" Louella said. "I can't learn compound fractions and watch out for Howard all the time, and he'll be right there in the same room with Imogene Herdman!"

She was really worried and you couldn't blame her, so I wasn't too surprised when she showed up with Howard on a leash.

Miss Kemp was pretty surprised, though. "Is that necessary, Louella?" she asked. "After all, your little brother is our guest here in the sixth grade. Is that how we want to treat a guest, class?"

Some kids said no, but a lot of kids said yes because they figured Howard was going to be a pain in the neck. So then Miss Kemp spent ten minutes talking about manners and hospitality, but I guess *she* figured Howard might be a pain in the

73

neck too because she didn't make Louella untie him.

She did make her get a longer leash, though, because Howard got knocked on his bottom every time he tried to go somewhere.

"He better learn not to do that," Imogene Herdman said. "Claude had to learn not to do that."

Miss Kemp looked at her. "Not to do what?"

"Not to go past the end of his leash."

"Why was Claude on a leash?"

"Because we didn't have a dog," Imogene said.

Miss Kemp frowned and sort of shook her head—the way you do when you've got water in your ears and everything sounds strange and far-away—but she didn't ask to hear any more and you couldn't blame her.

Louella poked me. "If they wanted a dog," she said, "they could just go to the Animal Rescue. That's where we got our dog."

That might be okay for Louella, but I didn't think the Animal Rescue people would give the Herdmans a rescued goldfish, let alone a whole dog, and the Herdmans probably knew it.

Maybe they even went there and said, "We want a dog," and the Animal Rescue said, "Not on your life." So then, I guess, they just looked around and said, "Okay, Claude, you be the dog," and then Claude was the dog till he got tired of it or they got tired of it.

You had to wonder what he *did* when he was the dog—bite people, maybe, except they had Gladys to do that.

Boomer Malone thought he might bark and guard the house.

"From what?" I asked.

Boomer shrugged. "I don't know . . . robbers?"

"Boomer, who are the main robbers around here?"

"Oh, yeah." He nodded. "They are."

Kids who *didn't* have dogs thought he might come when somebody called him, or sit up and beg, or roll over, or fetch papers. Kids who *did* have dogs said their dogs barked to get in and barked to get out, and chased cars, and swiped food off the table, and tore up the neighbors' trash, and all those things sounded more like Claude. You could see, though, how he would get tired of it.

"He probably got tired of being on a leash," Alice said. "Not like *some* people I know." She meant Howard. Alice had already told Louella what she thought about Howard. "I tried to teach your little brother to read," she'd said, "so he would be ready for kindergarten like I was. But I don't think they'll even let him *in* kindergarten. He's pretty dumb."

"He's too little to be dumb," Louella grumbled. "If you want to teach him something, you could teach him to go to the bathroom."

Well, I knew that wouldn't happen because Alice won't even say the word *bathroom*. It's a good thing you can just raise your hand to be excused, because if Alice had to say where she was going she would never go, and I don't know what would happen to her.

Dumb or not, Howard was okay for such a little kid stuck in the sixth grade. He had lots of paper and crayons, and little boxes of cereal to eat, and different people brought him different things to play with and look at. Alice showed up with great big pieces of cardboard that said A and B and C, but Howard didn't like those much. He scribbled all over them, which, Alice said, just proved how dumb he was, that he didn't even recognize the alphabet. "He'll never get into kindergarten," she said again. To hear Alice, you would think getting into kindergarten was better than getting into heaven, and a whole lot harder.

"They'll never let him in with *that!*" she said the first time she saw Howard's blanket, and for once you had to think she might be right. Howard's blanket was gross. Louella said it used to be blue and it used to have bunnies on it, but now it just looked like my father's car-washing rag.

"He has to have it," Louella said. "If he didn't have his blanket, Miss Kemp would probably have to throw him out. If he doesn't have his blanket, he cries and yells and jumps up and down, and if he still doesn't have his blanket, he holds his breath and turns purple."

Right away Boomer Malone scooped up the blanket and sat on it, which would have caused a big argument except that everyone *wanted* to see Howard turn purple. It was recess and there was already a bunch of kids gathered around Howard at one end of the playground, and naturally more kids came to see what was going on, and by the time Howard quit hollering and began to hold his breath, half the Woodrow Wilson School was there, trying to see over and around people.

"What's he doing?" I heard someone say. "Is he purple yet?"

He wasn't, and I didn't think he would *live* to be purple, with his eyes popping and all his little head veins standing out.

"Louella," I said, "do something . . . he's going to explode!"

"No, he won't," she said. "He never does. You can't explode from holding your breath. It's a scientific fact. He won't even pass out. You'll see."

I didn't want to see—what if Louella was wrong?—but it didn't matter anyway because all of a sudden Imogene Herdman charged up, shoving kids out of the way right and left, and began to pound on Louella.

"You said he would turn purple!" she said. "Look at him, he's not purple. I can't stand around here all day waiting for him to turn purple. Here, kid." She threw Howard his blanket and Howard let out this big loud shuddery sob. Then he went on sobbing and hiccuping and hugging his blanket while Imogene stalked off and the whole big crowd of kids grumbled at Louella as if it was her fault.

"I should just take his blanket away right now," Louella said, "and let everybody look at him and that would be that. But as far as I know he never had to hold his breath two times so close together and I don't know what that would do to him."

I thought it would probably kill him, so I was glad she didn't do it, but I knew plenty of kids *would* do it if they got the chance.

My mother said it better not be me or Charlie if we knew what was good for us. "That poor child has been scribbled on and scrubbed with scouring powder. He's been bald and shiny-headed and now what hair he's got looks as if someone planted it. Isn't that enough for one little boy?"

Either Imogene agreed with my mother or else she had plans to exhibit Howard at some later date ("See the Amazing Purple Baby! 25 cents") and didn't want him used up. From then on she kept one eye on Howard and the other eye on his blanket, and when Wesley Potter tried to snatch Howard's blanket, he never knew what hit him.

Imogene smacked Wesley flat and then stood him up and *held* him up by the ears and said, "You leave that blanket alone and you leave that kid alone or I'll wrap your whole head in chewing gum so tight they'll have to peel it off along with all your hair and your eyebrows and your lip skin and everything!"

That took care of Wesley and everybody else who heard it, but it made Louella nervous.

"Why is she being nice to Howard?" Louella said. "Why did she get his blanket back? That's twice she's gotten Howard's blanket back. Why?"

I didn't know why but I knew she wouldn't have to do it again because nobody wants to go through life wrapped in gum *or* skinned bald, and that would be your choice.

"Maybe she likes him," I said.

"Why would she like him?" Louella said. "I don't even like him and he's my own brother."

"But that's normal," I said. "I'm not crazy about Charlie either. If Howard was somebody else's brother you'd like him. *I* like him. There's nothing not to like unless he *is* your brother and you have to bring him to school and watch out for him and keep him on a leash and all."

"Keep him on a leash . . ." Louella repeated. "Remember what Imogene said? They kept Claude on a leash because they didn't have a dog?"

"So?"

"Well, they still don't have a dog, and here's Howard already on a leash . . . O-o-h!" Louella squealed. "Imogene is going to make him be their dog and my mother will kill me!"

"Come on, Louella," I said. "You can't make a

person be a dog. They could *pretend* Howard is their dog, but . . ."

"Just look at Howard," Louella said. "He'll pretend anything Imogene wants him to."

This was true. Howard was hugging his blanket and feeling his one favorite corner (which was even rattier than the whole rest of the blanket) and looking at Imogene the way you would look at the tooth fairy, handing out ten dollars a tooth.

"She'll feed him dog biscuits and teach him to bite!" Louella moaned.

"Maybe he'll bite Gladys," I said, "and there's nothing wrong with dog biscuits. Everybody eats dog biscuits at least once to see what they taste like."

I personally didn't care for them, but when Charlie was little he was crazy about this one brand called Puppy Pleasers. I once asked him how they tasted and he knew exactly.

"If you take a chocolate bar to the beach," he said, "and put it in the sand and let it melt and then pick up the melted chocolate bar and the sand and stick it all in the freezer, and when it's frozen bust it up into little pieces, is how Puppy Pleasers taste."

At the time I thought Charlie would either die

of grit or slowly turn to sand from the feet up and I didn't know what we would do with him—stand him up in the backyard, maybe, and plant flowers around him.

I didn't know what the Herdmans would do with their dog, Howard, either. Whenever Charlie and I asked for a dog, my mother always said, "What are you going to do with him?" and we never knew what to say. We thought the dog would do it all and we would just hang around and watch.

Mother said that's exactly what she *thought* we thought. "When you find a dog that's smart enough to take care of itself and let itself in and out of the house and answer the phone, let me know," she said.

Louella said we would have to watch Imogene, "Or else she'll try to run off with Howard and take him home and name him some dog name, like Rover or Spot."

Luckily, she never got the chance. Mrs. McCluskey got her wires crossed at the telephone company and shut down the whole system for half an hour. She never knew a thing like that could happen, she said, and it made her so nervous that she just quit her job, right on the spot.

And after that Louella didn't have to bring Howard to school anymore.

This was a big relief to Louella and you could tell it made Miss Kemp happy too, but she gave a little speech anyway, about how we would miss Howard and how he would be a big part of our sixth-grade experience and how we would always remember him.

"Sounds like he died," Imogene muttered. She was mad, I thought, because of wasting all her good deeds—getting Howard's blanket back and making kids leave him alone—and then not getting anything for it, like a substitute dog, if that was what she wanted.

"There is one thing," Miss Kemp went on. "It seems Howard went off without his blanket. Has anyone seen Howard's blanket?"

No one had. Or else no one would *admit* they had, not with Imogene sitting there blowing this huge bubble of gum out and in and out and in, ready to park it on anyone who looked guilty. It's too bad you can't study bubble gum and get graded for it, because Imogene would get straight A's. Her bubbles were so big and so thin you could see her whole face through the bubble, like looking at somebody through their own skin.

"What if we can't find it?" I asked Louella.

"We better find it," she said, "or else Howard will go crazy because all he does is sob and cry and hold his breath and hiccup."

He had also turned purple, she said, and he had almost passed out, so you had to figure that if somebody didn't turn up with Howard's blanket soon he would never make it to next week, let alone kindergarten.

We looked for the blanket off and on the rest of that day, although Alice said it would be better if we didn't find it. "It's old and horrible and full of germs," she said, and she told Louella, "You should be glad it's lost. Howard will thank you someday."

This is what your mother says when she makes you wear ugly shoes. She says, "This will give your toes room to grow and you'll thank me someday." Hearing Alice say things like this makes you want to squirt her with canned cheese. Even Miss Kemp does, I think, because she said, "Alice, I can assure you that by the time Howard gets to 'someday,' he won't even *remember* this blanket."

Somebody muttered, "Don't be too sure"— Imogene.

There was good news the next day—Howard

had lived through the night without going crazy *or* purple—and even better news when Imogene showed up with his blanket. She said she found it at the bus stop underneath a bush.

Nobody believed this. The Herdmans stole everything that wasn't nailed down, just out of habit. Why not Howard's blanket? "But so what?" Louella said, as long as Imogene brought it back.

The next day the art teacher, Miss Harrison, stopped Louella in the hall and gave her a bunch of stubby crayons for Howard. "I just heard about your little brother's blanket," she said. "Louella, you aren't going to find it because I threw it away. The last time we had art I used it to wipe the pastels off the chalkboard and then I just threw it away. I'm really sorry, but I didn't know it was Howard's blanket. It looked like my car-washing rag."

Louella shook her head. "We found Howard's blanket."

Miss Harrison shook *her* head. "You're just saying that to make me feel better. No, as soon as I heard it was missing, I knew what I'd done and where it was—gone, in the trash."

"She's wrong," Louella said.

"Maybe you're wrong," I said.

Louella thought for a minute. "Well, Howard wouldn't be wrong and *he* thinks it's his blanket. You can't get it away from him."

We did get it away from him but we had to wait till he was asleep. Then we had to unfasten his fingers and quickly give him this old worn-out bathrobe of Louella's.

"See?" said Louella. "It's the same blanket."

It certainly looked like the same blanket—old, faded, sort of dirty gray, with one corner that was especially old and faded and dirty gray. There was something else too—a capital *H*, scribbled and wobbly and almost faded out.

"It even has his initial on it," I said. "*H*, for Howard."

"Huh-uh," Louella said. "There's no initial on Howard's blanket."

I started to show her the *H*, and then I saw the *other* initial. It was an *I*.

I.H. There was only one *I.H.* in the whole Woodrow Wilson School—Imogene Herdman. "Louella," I said, "Imogene didn't find this blanket underneath a bush or anywhere else. This was her *own* blanket."

Louella refused to believe this and you couldn't blame her. It was hard enough just to imagine that Imogene ever *was* a baby, let alone a baby with her own blanket to drag around and hang on to.

"Besides," Louella said, "if it was hers, she wouldn't give it away. The Herdmans never gave anything away in their whole life."

"But what about the initials?" I said.

"They aren't really initials," Louella said. "I think they're just what's left of the bunny pattern."

I guess Louella believed this, but I knew better. They were Imogene's initials, all right, and this was Imogene's blanket. Maybe somebody took it away from her when *she* was a baby, and maybe *she* yelled and held her breath and turned purple, so she would know exactly how Howard felt. She would be sympathetic.

I could hardly wait to write this down on the Compliments for Classmates page in my notebook, but it looked too weird: "Imogene Herdman—sympathetic."

Nobody would believe this and I would have to explain it and Imogene would probably wrap *my* head in chewing gum if I told everyone that she once had a blanket with a favorite chewed corner and everything.

8

Two or three times a year all the Herdmans would be absent at the same time and it was like a vacation. You knew you wouldn't get killed at recess, you wouldn't have to hand over your lunch, and you wouldn't have to hide your money if you had any.

We even had easy lessons when they were absent. Boomer Malone said the teachers did that on purpose to give us all time to heal and get our strength back, but my mother said it was probably the teachers who had to get their strength back.

Nobody knew why they were absent. Nobody cared. They didn't have to bring a note from home either like everyone else, to say what was the matter.

"Why bother?" the school nurse told my mother. "They would write it themselves, no one could read it, and it would be a lie. Besides, if they ever did have something contagious, they wouldn't stay home. They'd come here and breathe on everybody."

You never knew *when* they would be absent either, but nobody thought this made any difference till they were all absent on a fire-drill day and our school won the Fire Department Speed and Safety Award.

"I can't believe this improvement," the fire chief said. "Last time it took you thirty-four minutes to vacate the building. What happened?"

"You know what happened," Mr. Crabtree said. "We lost half the kindergarten. Ollie Herdman led them out a basement door and took them all downtown."

"I mean, what happened this time?"

"Nothing happened this time," Mr. Crabtree said, "because Ollie isn't here. Neither is Ralph or Imogene or Leroy or Claude or Gladys."

"Where are they?"

"They're absent," Mr. Crabtree said.

The chief sighed. "I thought maybe they moved away. Oh, well . . ." He sighed again and said in that case he'd better get back to the firehouse and be ready for anything.

Everyone was pretty excited about the Speed and Safety Award, because we had never won anything before and probably never would again till the last Herdman was gone from Woodrow Wilson School.

So far, though, we could only be excited about the honor of it because we wouldn't get the actual award till Fire Prevention Day. There was a Fire Prevention Day every year, but all we ever got were Smokey the Bear stickers, so this was a big step up. There would be a special assembly with the fire chief and the mayor there, and the newspaper would send someone to take pictures and interview kids about fire prevention.

Of course fire prevention was the last thing the Herdmans knew anything about—except to be against it, I guess—so you had to hope the reporter wouldn't pick one of them to interview. You had to hope they wouldn't show up for this big event wearing beer advertisement T-shirts. You had to hope they wouldn't *show up*.

"Maybe they won't," Charlie said. "Maybe

they don't even know we won the award."

It's true that the Herdmans didn't know much if you count things like who invented the telephone, but they always knew what was going on around them, which in this case was plenty. There were signs and posters about fires and firemen everywhere; all the blackboards said "Woodrow Wilson Elementary School, Speed and Safety Winner!" Kids were making bookmarks and placemats, and writing poems and stories about our big accomplishment. We didn't even have hot dogs and hamburgers at lunch—we had Fire Dogs and Smokey Burgers.

How could the Herdmans miss all this? They didn't.

Somebody in the second grade brought in this great big stuffed bear and they stood it up in the hall with a sign around its neck—"Smokey says Congratulations to the Woodrow Wilson School!"—and the very next day there was the bear with its paws full of matches and cigarette lighters, firecrackers in its lap, and a half-smoked cigar sticking out of its mouth . . . Smokey, the Fire-Bug Bear.

"Oh, that is so disgusting!" Alice said. "What if someone reports it to the fire department? We might not even get the award. As usual, they're going to mess everything up and ruin the whole assembly, hitting people and tripping people and folding little kids up in the seats!"

I guess Mr. Crabtree came in the back door that day and didn't know what had happened to the bear, because the first announcement was all about the outstanding fire-prevention display by the second grade. "I want every student to stop by the second-grade room and see our very own Smokey the Bear," he said, "and let's be sure to thank those second graders for this . . ." Then there were some whispers and a *thwip* sound as somebody put a hand over the microphone, but you could still hear voices and a few words: ". . . matches . . . horrible wet cigar . . . get rid of that bear . . ."

Then the secretary, Mrs. Parker, got on and shuffled some papers and cleared her throat and said that Mr. Crabtree had been called away suddenly and she would finish the announcements: Picture money was due by Friday; a Fred Flintstone lunch box had been left on Bus 4; there would be a meeting of the Fire Safety Team in the lunchroom after school.

Right away Alice wrote this down on a piece of

paper, as if she had so many important engagements that she *had* to write them all down.

Imogene poked me. "What's the Fire Safety Team?"

"It's for the assembly," I said. "It's some kids who are going to demonstrate what to do in case of fire."

Imogene shrugged. "Throw water on it and get out of the way." Then she squinched up her eyes. "What kids? Who's on this team?"

I was going to say "I don't know" or "Who cares"—something so loose that Imogene wouldn't want to waste her time—but as usual Alice had to blow her own horn.

"I am," she said. "There's ten of us plus two alternates in case somebody gets sick at the last minute."

It's not unusual for people to get sick at the last minute if they're mixed up with Herdmans, so that got Imogene's attention, but it wasn't enough to hold her attention till Alice said, "We're going to have T-shirts that say 'Fire Safety Team, Woodrow Wilson School,' so we'll all look alike in the picture."

I didn't even bother to say "Shut up, Alice"— it was too late. You could tell that Imogene was

93

already seeing herself in the Fire Safety T-shirt *and* in the picture, and there was only one thing that you didn't know for sure—who, besides the two alternates, was going to get sick at the last minute.

Naturally Imogene wasn't the only Herdman who showed up in the lunchroom after school. They were all there, slouching around ready for action, draped over the tables, scraping gum from underneath the benches, chewing it—and this was *old* gum, shiny with germs and hard enough to tear your teeth out.

There was at least one kid from every grade on the Fire Safety Team and they all had one eye on the Herdmans, so Mr. Crabtree couldn't just *ignore* them, which is probably what he wanted to do.

"School's over, Ralph," Mr. Crabtree said, "Imogene, Ollie. Unless you people have some reason to be here, it's time to go home. We're just having a meeting."

"We came to sign up," Ralph said.

"Sign up for what? This is the Fire Safety Team."

"Right," Leroy said. "That. We want to sign up for that."

94

"It was on the announcements," Gladys put in, "about the meeting after school."

Mr. Crabtree opened his mouth and then he shut it again because there wasn't anything he could do about this. He had made it a major rule that anybody at the Woodrow Wilson School could sign up for anything they wanted to, no exceptions, and he had made another rule that everybody had to sign up for something whether they wanted to or not. So you had kids who signed up for two or three things, and you had kids who signed up for everything, and you had kids who wouldn't sign up at all till their teacher or their mother or Mr. Crabtree made them be something. What you didn't have was Herdmans signing up for anything.

Till now.

My mother said it was a good idea for the Herdmans to be on a Fire Safety Team. "Who needs to know more about fire safety than those kids?" she said. Some people said at least this way you could keep an eye on them during the assembly. My father said it was like inviting a lot of bank robbers to demonstrate how to rob the bank.

Three kids quit the Fire Safety Team right away before anything could happen to them, but their mothers said they ought to get the T-shirts anyway in view of the circumstances.

Mr. Crabtree knew what circumstances they were talking about—Herdmans—so he didn't even mention that. He just said he didn't have anything to do with the T-shirts. "That's up to the PTA," he said. "The PTA is providing T-shirts for the Fire Safety Team in honor of this special occasion."

The president of the PTA said they weren't providing T-shirts for kids who *quit* the Fire Safety Team. Mrs. Wendleken said they better not be providing T-shirts for the Herdmans, who had muscled their way *onto* the Fire Safety Team.

All anybody could talk about was T-shirts, but I agreed with Charlie, who said he wouldn't be on the Fire Safety Team if you paid him, not even for fifty T-shirts. "I watched them practice," he said, "and when Mr. Crabtree yells 'Drop and roll!' all the Herdmans drop *on* somebody, like in football."

They dropped on Albert Pelfrey and nearly squashed him flat, which wasn't all bad because as I said Albert is this really fat kid, but Albert quit the Fire Safety Team anyway. "I've got enough trouble just being fat," he said. "I don't want to be fat and dead both."

At the last minute two kids got sick (or said they did) and right away both the alternates quit, which didn't surprise anybody.

"You don't want to quit," Mr. Crabtree told them. "This is a big opportunity." He meant it was a big opportunity to take part in Fire Prevention Day and get a T-shirt and have their picture taken. But it was also a big opportunity to get pounded two feet into the ground by the Herdmans.

"I can only be an alternate," Roberta Scott said. "I can't actually be in it or anything."

"Roberta, that's what an alternate *is*," Mr. Crabtree said. "It's your responsibility to be in it and everything. You too, Lonnie."

Lonnie Hutchison was the other alternate, and he said he had to quit because of his asthma.

"Nice try, Lonnie," Mr. Crabtree said, "but you don't have asthma. I *know* who all has asthma. I know who has pinkeye and poison ivy and athlete's foot, also coughs and colds and nervous stomachs."

Mr. Crabtree didn't mention any other diseases, and when Lonnie's mother called the school to say that Lonnie was sick with a rash, Mr. Crabtree didn't believe it.

"Too convenient," he said. "It's probably finger paint or Magic Marker, something like that. Two or three weeks ago I saw Leroy Herdman walking around with red spots all over *his* face, looking for trouble. I just told him, 'Leroy, go wash your face,' and the next time I saw him all the spots were gone."

But it wasn't finger paint on Lonnie.

It was chicken pox, and before you could say "Speed and Safety Award assembly" there wasn't anybody left to go to it.

Mr. Crabtree wanted to postpone Fire Prevention Day but the fire chief said he couldn't do that. "It's Fire Prevention Day all over town," he said, "all over the state. You can't just have your own Fire Prevention Day whenever you want to. Tell you what, though. If you'll get together a small group of whatever kids you've got left—your Fire Safety Team would be good—and bring them down to the firehouse, we'll have the award presentation right here. We'll make it a big event."

It turned out to be a bigger event than anybody expected because the pizza-parlor ovens caught fire half an hour before the presentation. They put the fire out right away but Mr. Santoro made all his customers leave because of the smoke, and most of them just followed the fire engine back to the firehouse and stayed for the presentation. Some people thought the fire was *part* of the presentation, especially when Mr. Santoro showed up with all his leftover pizza and handed it out free.

Everybody said this was a great way to advertise fire prevention, and they congratulated the mayor and the fire chief for thinking it up, and the fire chief congratulated Mr. Santoro for donating the pizza.

The newspaper reporter got it all wrong too. "MOCK FIRE STAGED TO HIGHLIGHT FIRE PREVENTION DAY," he wrote. "RESTAURANT OWNER CONTRIBUTES PIZZA FOR LARGE CROWD ATTENDING AWARD CEREMONY. SCHOOL STUDENTS HONORED FOR SAFETY TECHNIQUES."

The "honored students" were what was left of the Fire Safety Team—Ralph, Imogene, Leroy, Claude, Ollie, and Gladys—and there was a picture of them standing in front of the fire truck, looking like a police lineup. You could imagine an officer saying, "Now, which one did it?" and the victim saying, "I can't be sure. They all look alike."

They did look alike, except for being different

sizes . . . plus, of course, they had on the famous matching T-shirts.

"If I didn't know better," Mother said, "I would think this was the Herdmans being honored instead of the school."

This turned out to be the general opinion, and so many people called the newspaper to complain that they printed another story—"WOODROW WILSON SCHOOL, DESPITE CHICKEN POX EPIDEMIC, WINS SPEED AND SAFETY AWARD," which my father said was better than nothing, but not much. "What does chicken pox have to do with it?" he wanted to know, but my mother said he was just tired of watching Charlie and me scratch.

Mrs. Wendleken made Alice sit in a bathtub full of baking-soda water so she wouldn't scratch, and made her wear these white cotton gloves so she wouldn't scratch, and when Alice came back to school, besides having puckery seersucker skin, she was still wearing the gloves.

"I don't think that's necessary, Alice," Miss Kemp said.

"I have to wear them while I'm thinking," Alice told her, "so I won't forget and scratch. If you scratch chicken pox, they get infected and leave scars."

"Not on Leroy," Imogene said. "Not on Ollie. Not on . . ."

"Wait a minute," Miss Kemp said. "Leroy? Ollie? I wasn't aware that any of your family was absent during our epidemic."

"Oh, we weren't absent," Imogene said.

Miss Kemp frowned. "But you had chicken pox?" she asked.

"You mean, did I have chicken pox?" Imogene said.

This was like talking long distance to my grandmother without her hearing aid, and—just like my grandmother—Miss Kemp didn't try to pin it down.

"If you have chicken pox, you can't come back without a note from the doctor," she said, and Imogene said, "Oh. Okay," and got up and left.

So no one ever knew for sure whether they did actually have chicken pox, or how many of them had chicken pox, or exactly when they had chicken pox, and no one ever knew for sure whether they came to school and breathed on everybody and ruined our big award assembly, or whether they were all sick and stayed home on the fire-drill day so we won the award in the first place.

9

The last day of school is pretty loose and they probably wouldn't even bother to have one except that that's when you clean out your desk. If you didn't have to clean out your desk, Mr. Crabtree could just get on the PA system any old day in June and say, "All right, this is it, last day of school. Go on home. Have a great summer. See you in September."

But then everyone would go off and leave their smelly old socks and moldy mittens and melted Halloween candy and leftover sandwiches. Once a kindergarten gerbil got loose and climbed in Boomer Malone's desk and died there.

Nobody knew what to do with the gerbil

because, like all the kindergarten animals, it had a name and a personality and we knew all about it from the notice on the bulletin board—"Our friendly gerbil is missing. His name is Bob. If you see Bob, please return him to the kindergarten room."

So this wasn't just any old dead gerbil—this was friendly Bob. It didn't seem right to drop him in the trash, so Boomer took him back to the kindergarten room. We all thought the kindergarten would stop whatever it was doing, hunt up a cigar box, write a poem for Bob, and have a funeral, but according to Boomer they couldn't care less.

"Not even the teacher," he reported. "She took one look and said, 'Oh, that's not Bob,' and dropped him in her trash basket."

If there was a moral to this, I guess it was: Don't show up with dead animals on the last day of school.

You couldn't show up with live ones either anymore. We used to have a pet parade every year on the last day of school, till the year Claude Herdman entered their cat.

The Herdmans' cat was missing one eye and part of an ear and most of its tail and all of whatever good nature it ever had, so you wouldn't expect it to win any prizes in a pet parade. If it was your cat, you would probably try to clean it up a little, but you probably wouldn't whitewash it and then spray it with super-super-hold hairspray, which is what the Herdmans did.

According to Claude, they thought it would win the Most Unusual Pet prize, but it was too mad from being whitewashed and hairsprayed to do anything but attack. So the pet parade turned into a stampede of dogs and cats and turtles and hamsters and guinea pigs. Some kids held on to their animals but most didn't, so there were cats up in the trees and on top of telephone poles, and dogs running off down the street, barking . . . and the Herdmans' cat in the middle of it all, tearing around the playground, hissing and spitting and shedding flakes of whitewash. It took all day to get the cats down and the dogs back, and there were two hamsters that never did turn up.

So that was the end of the pet parade, and it left a big empty spot in the day's activities, which the teachers had to fill up somehow. We had spelling bees and math marathons, or we stood up and said what we were going to do that summer, or what we would do if we were king of the world.

One year everybody brought their collections. There were baseball cards and Cracker Jack prizes and bubble-gum wrappers . . . and belly-button lint.

The belly-button lint came from Imogene Herdman, but she said she wouldn't recommend it as a hobby. "I don't even collect it anymore," she said. "This is left over from when I *used* to collect it." I guess that was the last straw—old belly-button lint—because we never did that again.

This year there was no big surprise about what we would do on the last day. It was up on the blackboard—Compliments for Classmates—and we had each drawn a name from a hat and had to think of more compliments for that one person.

"We've been thinking about this all year," Miss Kemp said. She probably knew that some kids had but most kids hadn't—but now everybody would think about it in a hurry. "And on the last day of school," she went on, "we're going to find out what we've learned about ourselves and each other."

I had finally thought of a word for Albert. Once you get past thinking *fat* you can see that Albert's special quality is optimism, because

Albert actually believes he will be thin someday, and says so. Another word could be *determination*, or even *courage*. There were lots of good words for Albert, so I really hoped I would draw his name.

I didn't. The name I drew was Imogene Herdman, and I had used up the one and only compliment I finally thought of for Imogene—*patriotic*.

"Patriotic?" my mother said. "What makes you think Imogene is especially patriotic?"

"When we do the Pledge of Allegiance," I said, "she always stands up."

"Everybody stands up," Charlie said. "If everybody sat down and *only* Imogene stood up, that would be patriotic."

"That would be brave," I said.

"Well, she would do that," Charlie said. "I mean, she would do whatever everybody else didn't do."

Would that make Imogene brave? I didn't really think so, but I had to have some more compliments, so I wrote it down—*patriotic, brave*.

Two days later I still had just *patriotic* and *brave* while other people had big long lists. I saw the bottom of Joanne Turner's list, sticking out of her notebook: "Cheerful, good sport, graceful, fair to everybody." I wondered who *that* was.

Maxine Cooper asked me how to spell *cooperative* and *enthusiastic*, so obviously she had a terrific list. Boomer must have drawn a boy's name, because all his compliments came right out of the Boy Scout Rules—*thrifty, clean, loyal*.

I kept my eye on Imogene as much as possible so if she did something good I wouldn't miss it, but it was so hard to tell, with her, what was good.

I thought it was good that she got Boyd Liggett's head out of the bike rack, but Mrs. Liggett didn't think so.

Mrs. Liggett said it was all the Herdmans' fault in the first place. "Ollie Herdman told Boyd to do it," she said, "and then that Gladys got him so scared and nervous that he couldn't get out, and then along came Imogene . . ."

I could understand how Boyd got his head *into* the bike rack—he's only in the first grade, plus he has a skinny head—but at first I didn't know why he couldn't get it *out*.

Then I saw why. It was his ears. Boyd's ears stuck right straight out from his head like handles, so his head and his ears were on one side of the bike rack and the rest of him was on the other side, and kids were hollering at him and telling him what to do. "Turn your head upside down!" somebody said, and somebody else told him to squint his eyes and squeeze his face together.

Boyd's sister Jolene tried to fold his ears and push them through but that didn't work, even one at a time. Then she wanted half of us to get in front of him and push and the other half to get in back and pull. "He got his head through there," she said. "There must be some way to get it back out."

I didn't think pushing and pulling was the way but Boyd looked ready to try anything.

Then Gladys Herdman really cheered him up. "Going to have to cut off your ears, Boyd," she said. "But maybe just one ear. Do you have a favorite one? That you like to hear out of?"

You could tell that he believed her. If you're in the first grade with your head stuck through the bike rack, this is the very thing you think will happen.

Several teachers heard Boyd yelling, "Don't cut my ears off!" and they went to tell Mr. Crabtree. Mr. Crabtree called the fire department, and while he was doing that the kindergarten teacher stuck her head out the window and called to

Boyd, "Don't you worry, they're coming to cut you loose."

But she didn't say who, or how, and Gladys told him they would probably leave a little bit of ear in case he ever had to wear glasses, so Boyd was a total wreck when Imogene came along.

She wanted to know how he got in there—in case she ever wanted to shove somebody else in the bike rack, probably—but Boyd was too hysterical to tell her, and nobody else knew for sure, so I guess she decided to get him loose first and find out later.

Imogene Scotch-taped his ears down and buttered his whole head with soft margarine from the lunchroom, and then she just pushed on his head—first one side and then the other—and it slid through.

Of course Boyd was a mess, with butter all over his eyes and ears and up his nose, so Jolene had to take him home. She made him walk way away from her and she told him, "As soon as you see Mother, you yell, 'I'm all right. I'm all right.'" She looked at him again. "You better tell her who you are, too."

Even so, Mrs. Liggett took one look and screamed and would have fainted, Jolene said, except she heard Boyd telling her that he was all right.

"What do you think of that?" Mother asked my father that night. "She buttered his head!"

"I think it was resourceful," my father said. "Messy, but resourceful."

"That's like a compliment, isn't it?" I asked my father. "It's good to be resourceful?"

"Certainly," he said. So I wrote that down, along with *patriotic* and *brave*.

I thought we would just hand in our compliment papers on the last day of school, but Alice thought Miss Kemp would read three or four out loud—"Some of the best ones," Alice said, meaning, of course, her own—and Boomer thought she would read the different compliments and we would have to guess the person. So when Miss Kemp said, "Now we're going to share these papers," it was no big surprise.

But then she said, "I think we'll start with Boomer. LaVerne Morgan drew your name, Boomer. I want you to sit down in front of LaVerne and listen to what she says about you."

LaVerne squealed and Boomer turned two or three different shades of red and all over the room kids began to check their papers in case they would have to read out loud some big lie or, worse, some really personal compliment.

LaVerne said that Boomer was smart and good at sports—but not stuck up about it—and friendly, and two or three other normal things. "And I liked when you took the gerbil back to the kindergarten that time," she said, "in case they wanted to bury it. That was nice."

It *was* nice, I thought, and not everybody would have done it, either. To begin with, not everybody would have *picked up* the gerbil by what was left of its tail, let alone carry it all the way down the hall and down the stairs to the kindergarten room.

"Good, Boomer," I said when he came back to his seat—glad to get there, I guess, because he was all sweaty with embarrassment from being told nice things about himself face to face and in front of everybody.

Next came Eloise Albright and then Louella and then Junior Jacobs and then Miss Kemp said, "Let's hear about you, Beth. Joanne Turner drew your name."

I remembered Joanne Turner's paper—"Cheerful, good sport, graceful, fair to everybody." I had wondered who that was.

It was me.

"I know we weren't supposed to say things about how you look," Joanne said, "but I put down graceful anyway because I always notice how you stand up very straight and walk like some kind of dancer. I don't know if you can keep it up, but if you can I think people will always admire the way you stand and walk."

It was really hard, walking back to my seat now that I was famous for it—but I knew if I did it now, with everybody watching, I *could* probably keep it up for the rest of my life and, if Joanne was right, be admired forever. This made me feel strange and loose and light, like when you press your hands hard against the sides of a door, and when you walk away your hands float up in the air all by themselves.

I was still feeling that way three people later when Miss Kemp said it was Imogene's turn.

"To do what?" Imogene said.

"To hear what Beth has to say about you. She drew your name."

Imogene gave me this dark, suspicious look. "No, I don't want to."

"You're going to hear *good* things, you know, Imogene," Miss Kemp said, but you could tell

Miss Kemp wasn't too sure about that, and Imogene probably never *heard* any good things about herself, so she wasn't too sure, either.

"That's okay," I said. "I mean, if Imogene doesn't want to, I don't care."

This didn't work. I guess Miss Kemp was curious like everybody else. "Imogene Herdman!" Louella had just whispered. "That's whose name you drew? How could you think of compliments for Imogene Herdman?"

"Well, you had to think of *one*," I said. "We had to think of one compliment for everybody."

Louella rolled her eyes. "I said she was healthy. I didn't know anything else to say."

Louella wasn't the only one who wanted to hear my Imogene words. The whole room got very quiet and I was glad, now, that at the last minute I had looked up *resourceful* in the dictionary.

"I put down that you're patriotic," I told Imogene, "and brave and resourceful . . . and cunning and shrewd and creative, and enterprising and sharp and inventive . . ."

"Wait!" she yelled. "Wait a minute! Start over!"

"Oh, honestly!" Alice put in. "You just copied

that out of the dictionary! They're all the same thing!"

"And," I went on, ignoring Alice, "I think it was good that you got Boyd's head out of the bike rack."

"Oh, honestly!" Alice said again, but Miss Kemp shut her up.

Of course she didn't say, "Shut up, Alice"— she just said that no one could really comment on what anybody else said because it was very personal and individual. "That's how Beth sees Imogene," she said.

Actually, it wasn't. Alice was right about the words. I did copy them out of the dictionary so I wouldn't be the only person with three dumb compliments, and I didn't exactly connect them with Imogene, except *sharp* because of her knees and elbows which she used like weapons to leave you black and blue.

But now, suddenly, they all turned out to fit. Imogene *was* cunning and shrewd. She *was* inventive. Nobody else thought of buttering Boyd's head or washing their cat at the Laundromat. She was creative, if you count drawing pictures on Howard . . . and enterprising, if you count charging money to look at him. She was also powerful enough to keep everybody away from the teachers' room forever, and human enough to give Howard her blanket.

Imogene *was* all the things I said she was, and more, and they were good things to be—depending on who it was doing the inventing or the creating or the enterprising. If Imogene could keep it up, I thought, till she got to be civilized, if that ever happened, she could be almost anything she wanted to be in life.

She could be Imogene Herdman, President . . . or, of course, Imogene Herdman, Jailbird. It would be up to her.

At the end of the day Miss Kemp said, "Which was harder—to give compliments or to receive them?" and everyone agreed that it was really uncomfortable to have somebody tell you, in public, about the best hidden parts of you. Alice, however, made this long, big-word speech about how it was harder for her to *give* compliments because she wanted to be very accurate and truthful, "and not make things up," she said, looking at me.

"I didn't make things up," I told her later, "except, maybe, brave. I don't know whether Imogene is brave."

"You made her sound like some wonderful

115

person," Alice said, "and if that's not making things up, what is?"

When the bell rang everybody whooped out to get started on summer, but Imogene grabbed me in the hall, shoved a Magic Marker in my face, and told me to write the words on her arm.

"On your arm?" I said.

"That's where I keep notes," she said, and I could believe it because I could still see the remains of several messages—something pizza . . . big rat . . . get Gladys . . .

Get Gladys something? I wondered. No, probably just get Gladys.

There was only room for one word on her skinny arm, so Imogene picked *resourceful*. "It's the best one," she said. "I looked it up and I like it. It's way better than graceful, no offense." She turned her arm around, admiring the word. "I like it a lot. I'm gonna get it tattooed."

I didn't ask who by—Gladys, probably.

Charlie was waiting for me on the corner, looking gloomy. He always looks gloomy on the last day of school, and it's always for the same reason.

"It happened again," he said. "Leroy Herdman didn't get kept back."

"Leroy Herdman will never be kept back," I

told him. "None of them will."

"He's going to be in my room forever!" he groaned. "What am I going to do?"

"Charlie," I said, "you're going to have to learn to be . . . resourceful."

"How?" he said. "What is it?"

"Ask Imogene," I said. "I think it's going to be her best thing."

BARBARA ROBINSON was born in Portsmouth, Ohio, but now makes her home in Berwyn, Pennsylvania. The recipient of a B.A. degree from Allegheny College, Ms. Robinson has written several books for children, including the critically acclaimed and enormously popular *The Best Christmas Pageant Ever* and *My Brother Louis Measures Worms*. *The Best Christmas Pageant Ever* has received numerous awards, and was among the ALA Notable Children's Books of 1971–75. It was produced as an ABC television film in 1983. Ms. Robinson has also published numerous short stories in well-known magazines.

She and her husband have two daughters, Carolyn and Marjorie.

My
Brother
Louis
Measures
Worms
And Other
Louis Stories

BARBARA ROBINSON

My
Brother
Louis
Measures
Worms

And Other
Louis Stories

A Charlotte Zolotow Book
An Imprint of HarperCollins*Publishers*

For my very special aunt, Jean Dodds

Contents

My
Brother
Louis
Measures
Worms
And Other
Louis Stories

Louis at the Wheel

I was ten years old when my little brother Louis began driving my mother's car, and by the time I was eleven he had put over four hundred miles on it. He figured out that if he had done it all in one direction, he would have landed in Kansas City, although I'm not sure he allowed for rivers and mountains and other natural obstacles.

I also wasn't sure that my mother was really as astonished as she said she was when all this mileage came to light. And, in fact, she finally acknowledged that she probably knew what Louis was doing, but she just didn't believe it.

"It was like one of those dreams you have," she

told my father, "that seem so real when you wake up. Let's say you dream that the President of the United States shows up for dinner. And you say, 'Oh, I'm sorry. All we have tonight is meat loaf.' And he says, 'That's just fine, Mrs. Lawson. Meat loaf is my favorite. Do you cook it with bacon across the top?' "

She hurried right on before my father could comment on the story so far. "Now, when you wake up, you know it was a dream. You know perfectly well that the President of the United States didn't come to dinner, and isn't going to come to dinner. But if he *were* to come, you know, beyond a shadow of a doubt, that he would say, 'Meat loaf is my favorite. Do you cook it with bacon across the top?' . . .

"That's the way it was with Louis and the car—as if I dreamed that he was driving the car, woke up and knew absolutely that he wasn't . . . but if it turned out later that he *was*, I wouldn't be surprised."

My father said that was the wildest kind of reasoning he had ever heard in his life; that dreaming the President came to dinner had absolutely nothing to do with why Louis, at his age, was driving up and down the street and all over the place. He also said that anyone who dreamed about meat loaf probably needed to get up and take some Alka-Seltzer.

"Well . . . you don't like meat loaf," my mother said.

This was a good example of how her mind worked, and to say my father found the process mysterious is an understatement. He never understood her brand of logic, but at least it never surprised him.

Nor did it surprise him to learn, when the whole thing was sorted out, that it was Mother who first told Louis to drive the car—though of course she didn't say, "Louis, go on out and drive the car. Pull the seat up as far as it will go and sit on one or two telephone books."

Mother was not that casual about cars and people driving them, probably because she didn't learn to drive till she was almost thirty-five years old. As a consequence, she never enjoyed driving and would go out of her way to avoid it unless she absolutely had to go someplace and there was absolutely no other way to get there.

She was, therefore, dismayed when my father bought her a car for Christmas. It wiped out her number-one excuse.

"Now you won't have to depend on buses," he said, "or other people, or using my car. I hope you like the color. Do you like the color?"

Mother said she loved the color, that it matched the living room. This was very much on her mind because what she really wanted for Christmas was a new sofa, which would also match the living room.

My father led her in and out of the car, showing off its many features, while Mother oohed and ahhed, stuck her head in the trunk and under the hood and nodded knowingly at the mysterious innards coiled up there.

It was a difficult performance, since all she asked of a car was that it would start, keep going and stop when it was supposed to—and that she would not have to drive it very much.

But there was worse to come. Having provided Mother with the means of mobility, my father wanted to hear all about how she was enjoying it.

"Well, where did you go today?" he asked every evening, and he was always disappointed if she hadn't been off and running. So she had to lie, which she didn't do very well; or tell the truth, which was not what he wanted to hear; or hedge, by saying she was sick, or worn out or cleaning the oven.

In view of all this stress, it was probably not surprising that she should absentmindedly tell Louis to pick me up from my flute lesson on a day of complicated comings and goings. My father was out of town; Mother was leaving at noon with her friend Ada Snedaker to go to a flower show forty miles away; I had missed my regular flute lesson and, hence, my regular ride.

As we ate breakfast that morning Mother tried to work all this out: "If *I* drive to the flower show I could leave early and get you at your lesson—but I can't fit all the plants in my car. Your father won't be home till after nine o'clock. The *car* will be here but what good is that? I suppose Louis could pick you up, he gets home from school at three thirty. . . ."

"All right," Louis said, but nobody heard him—and of course my mother didn't really intend that Louis, not yet eight years old, should drive her car all the way across town and get me at my flute lesson. She was simply thinking out loud, dissecting a problem: people who must be picked up; plants which must be transported; cars in which to do all this; and people to operate those cars.

"Or you could take a bus," she suddenly said. "That's what to do. You get the bus outside Miss Cramer's house, and then transfer to the Mabert Hill line."

Satisfied with this arrangement, she put the whole thing out of her mind and went off to the flower show, or so I assumed. I was therefore surprised, while waiting for the bus, to see Mother's car coming down the street very slowly and, as far as I could tell, entirely on its own.

The car stopped about a foot away from me and a disembodied voice said, "Let me have your geography book."

7

It was Louis.

"What are you doing?" I said. "Are you crazy? You can't drive a car!"

"Yes, I can," he said. "It isn't easy, but I can do it—but I need your geography book to sit on so I can see."

I was too horrified to think straight. Never a rambunctious child, I was a born follower of orders and obeyer of the law, and here was my own brother running amok—or so it seemed to me.

The most puzzling thing was that Louis was not a rambunctious child either, and I couldn't imagine what had gotten into him.

"I just thought I should try it" was all he would say as we drove home . . . down back streets and alleys where no one could possibly see us. No one could possibly see Louis anyway, even sitting on my geography book. I wanted him to sit on my flute case too, but he wouldn't do it.

"Then I couldn't reach the pedals," he said, which was true.

Thus it began; for, since we were neither killed nor arrested in the course of this trip, it seemed to me, in retrospect, less harum-scarum than I first thought. And in no time at all, I accepted the fact of Louis at the wheel, as people *do* accept the most unlikely or bizarre circumstances if they happen often enough and nobody pays any attention to them.

It turned out to be a great convenience. If I didn't want to ride my bicycle to a friend's house, Louis would take me; if we ran out of peanut butter or notebook paper or Cheerios, Louis would go get some. On tiresome rainy afternoons we could go downtown, or to the library, or to the YMCA.

To be sure, we could never go very far or stay very long. There was always the remote chance that Mother would want to go somewhere in the car, or the equally remote chance that she would notice the car was gone and wonder why.

Of course, Mother's apathy about the car was our great ace in the hole. When absolutely necessary she would go do whatever errands had to be done; but at all other times the car simply didn't enter her thinking. For one thing, she was perfectly happy *not* to go anywhere, having dozens of puttery projects at her fingertips at any given moment. Then too, most of her friends were tremendous get-up-and-goers, car keys always at the ready, and they counted on Mother to go along— to lunch, to various sales, to flower shows and needlework exhibitions. So she was always busy, quite contented, and able to ignore the car for days on end . . . though she didn't want my father to know that.

Our other ace in the hole was Louis himself. He was probably the only eight-year-old boy alive who would drive all over town in his mother's car and never tell anyone about it, never see how fast he could go, never take a friend for a ride.

His attitude was never "Hey, look at me!"—so no one ever did. We might have been children and a car from outer space, touring the countryside unseen, which was a little spooky.

There were spooky aspects as well for my mother—unexplained peanut butter and Cheerios—but she tended to dismiss such minor mysteries on the grounds that she must have bought the thing, whatever it was. Being unwilling to run to the store for this or that, she shopped like a bear about to hibernate.

She could not, however, anticipate every whim.

"Do you know what I'd like?" my father said one evening. "I'd like some old-fashioned gingersnaps. They used to sell them in bulk, by the pound. They were hard—almost broke your teeth off."

Mother frowned. "I could try to make some, but I wouldn't make them hard, to break people's teeth off."

"Well, that's what they were," my father said. "Hard, like rocks."

The very next night, while rummaging around for something to nibble on, he found a big brown sack labeled *Old-Fashioned Gingersnaps*, which he brought into the living room for all of us to share.

"Well, where did you find those?" Mother said.

"I found them in the bread drawer."

"No, I mean where did you buy them?"

"I didn't buy them." He grinned at her. "Come on, Grace, I know you bought them, and I appreciate it. Here you go. . . ." He handed the sack to Louis and me.

"Don't break your teeth off," Mother said automatically, but her mind was clearly elsewhere, her eyes puzzled, as she tried to figure out how this sack of cookies got into her bread drawer all by itself.

"I bought them at that little store where they sell the airplane models," Louis told me later. "I used my airplane-model money."

"That was nice, Louis," I said.

"Well . . ." He shrugged. "I figure, I never buy any gas."

Of course, there was no way that we *could* drive up and buy gas; but we didn't have to, because Mother always bought gas whether she needed it or not. Since we knew this, and since we never went very far anyway, we didn't even think about gas. We also didn't think about other people using the car, since no one consulted us about such matters.

Consequently we didn't know that my father had used Mother's car on a Monday, when his was

11

in the shop—and we didn't know that Mother's friend Helen Moulton borrowed the car two days later, when *hers* was in the shop.

So it was that on the following day, Louis, driving downtown, ran out of gas and, not knowing what else to do, simply left the car parked on Grandview Avenue. He carefully locked it up and walked home, a distance of some five miles.

Long before he arrived my father had come home, missed the car and, after a tangle of misunderstanding involving Mother, Mrs. Moulton's cleaning lady and Vinnie Tedesco at the service station (who seized the wrong horn of the dilemma and thought that *he* had mislaid *Mrs. Moulton's* car) called the police.

An officer came and took down all the information, much of it dealing with Mrs. Moulton, who was two hundred miles away in Cincinnati.

". . . and driving my car, probably," Mother said. "I *told* Helen to use the car. I didn't say when, or what for." Mother hadn't wanted to call the police at all, and was uncomfortable about the fuss being made.

"Well, Helen Moulton wouldn't drive your car to Cincinnati without telling you," my father said.

"When did *you* last drive the car?" the policeman asked.

Of course Mother didn't want to go into that

because she hadn't driven the car for two weeks, and she knew my father would be so exasperated with her, which he was.

They were both edgy and a little cross, but I was just scared to death because I couldn't imagine what had happened to Louis.

He arrived home eventually. After the police called to say they had found the car—undamaged, locked and out of gas. "Unusual for it to be locked," the officer said.

Louis, unaware of all this commotion, had automatically put the keys right back on the hook where they belonged and where they were discovered ten minutes later, to further complicate matters.

"How can the car be locked on Grandview Avenue, while the keys are here?" my father puzzled.

"Well—maybe Helen left them?" Mother suggested, but with little conviction.

"That would mean that Helen stole the car."

"Maybe you just didn't see them when you looked before?"

"That would mean that no one stole the car." He shook his head. "Well, I have to go get it before it rolls away all by itself. I wonder where on Grandview Avenue it is?"

"It's in front of the eye doctor's house," Louis said.

I had known, I think, that he was going to say this, or something equally damning. He was worn out from his long walk and only half awake and responding by instinct.

"Well, at least it's not the way downtown, but even so. . . ."My father stopped.

In the heavy silence that followed, Louis came to, realized what he had said and was, I suppose, too tired to wiggle his way out.

"I just ran out of gas," he said, which was true in every way.

We were grounded, of course, forever; and several other punishments were considered. But we were not easy children to punish, because of those very traits of character and temperament which had allowed us to drive around, unnoticed, for a year: our caution, our modest goals (in terms of destination), our quiet ways while motoring. Besides, my father seemed more inclined to blame himself, my mother and the public at large for failing ever to see what we were doing.

So, in the end, nothing much happened to us.

Mother, however, continued to fret. She seemed to think that Louis would now be driven to drive, as people are driven to drink, and saw the car as a dangerous temptation . . . or so she said.

I suppose my father saw no reason to maintain a car no one wanted to drive—except Louis, sitting on telephone books.

"Well, you'll be out one Christmas present," he told Mother. "So you have one coming. Make it a good one."

"Oh"—she eyed the sofa, which was old and rump-sprung and didn't match the living room—"I'll think of something."

The Mysterious Visit of
Genevieve Fitch

Maxine Slocum lived two houses down from us, and when Maxine's cat got pregnant, Mrs. Slocum called up all the mothers in the neighborhood to say that all children would be welcome at the lying-in unless their mothers objected. It was the beginning of an enlightened era and no mother wanted to seem unenlightened, so everybody accepted Mrs. Slocum's invitation.

My father said it was the craziest idea he had ever heard in his life. "There must be thirty-five kids in this neighborhood," he said. "What are they going to do, put up bleachers?"

"They have that big basement," Mother said.

"Suppose the cat decides to have her kittens in the hall closet, or under the bed? Poor damn cat. . . ." He looked at me and my little brother, Louis. "Take my advice, don't go. Be kind to a cat. How would you like to have a baby in front of thirty-five people?"

"French queens used to have to," Louis said, "to prove the succession."

When Louis said things like that, people always raised their eyebrows and whispered to Mother that he must be a genius. He wasn't, though; he was just one of those people who remembered odd, unrelated facts. Ask him to tell you what "the succession" meant, and he would have been up a tree.

I was only worried that the cat would have her kittens in the middle of the night or something, but Maxine promised that if that happened she would run out in the street and ring her father's antique cowbell.

"Don't worry, Mary Elizabeth," she told me. "You'll hear that."

In the meantime, we all kept the cat, whose name was Juanita, under close surveillance and privately hoped to get a kitten out of the whole thing.

According to my father, that was really Mrs. Slocum's dark purpose. "It isn't that she wants to provide this rich educational experience for everybody under sixteen," he said. "She just wants to get rid of the kittens."

In any case, the approaching accouchement of the cat had us all in a state of fevered anticipation; and so when Genevieve Fitch took up her sudden and mysterious residence at our house, I was too preoccupied to wonder why.

This suited my Mother right down to the ground. The less said about Genevieve Fitch the better, in her opinion; but she had to make some kind of explanation because nobody else in the family was quite sure who Genevieve Fitch was.

Genevieve wasn't exactly a perfect stranger, but her relationship was so remote—third or fourth cousin, two or three times removed—that I had never before laid eyes on her, nor had Louis, nor had my father. But Mother was one of a large family with whom she tried to keep in some kind of touch, and my father didn't begin to know who all of them were. When strange relatives showed up from time to time he always made them welcome, but he didn't always remember, later on, just who they were.

Of course, when Genevieve showed up, he didn't know the nature of her predicament (or even that she was *in* a predicament), because Mother didn't tell him the whole story. She simply said that Genevieve would be staying with us for a few days while the inside of her house got painted.

Though this seemed odd—every three or four years the inside of our house got painted and nobody moved out—it was the kind of oddity that children can understand and accept. I had one particular dress that I would never wear on Wednesdays. Louis would eat no sandwich that was not cut on the diagonal. Genevieve Fitch would not stay in a house that was being painted. Who knew why?

After a day or two of Genevieve, my father decided that he would like to know why. Had she been a sprightlier person he might have been more willing to take Mother's vague explanation at face value . . . but Genevieve was a pale, somewhat doughy young woman with all the personality of wallpaper paste, and I suppose he was honestly bewildered that my mother, who had lots of snap and hustle, would be willing to put up with so flat a presence for so silly a reason.

"Does Genevieve always move out when her house is being painted?" he asked.

"I don't know," Mother said.

"Probably everything is being painted this time— walls, woodwork, ceiling—just one big mess all over the place. Easier to move out and let them get it done. Is that it?"

"Yes," Mother said, much relieved. "That's it."

But of course that wasn't it, and as new, puzzling scraps of information came to light, the plot thickened. We learned, for instance, that it wasn't Genevieve's house at all, but her mother's house; and that her mother, Ethel Fitch, was still in it despite the big mess all over the place.

We also learned that my mother and Genevieve had not seen each other for almost six years; and that, in fact, for the first few days of her visit, Genevieve had mistakenly believed herself to be visiting Cousin Olive Underwood and *her* family.

My father immediately saw the possibilities in this. "Well, it's all a big mistake," he said. "She isn't even supposed to be here. And this Olive Underwood cousin is watching and waiting for her . . . probably worried to death. We'd better get her packed up and take her there right away."

"No, no," Mother said. "Certainly not. Genevieve just got mixed-up. And you can't blame her. Look at you, you can't keep all my relatives straight either."

"Maybe not, but if I planned to move in with one of them, I would at least pick one I knew by sight."

Shortly thereafter he happened to run into one of the few he *did* know by sight, Mother's brother Frank, and Frank knew all about Genevieve.

"Good thing she could stay with you," Frank said. "Had to get the poor girl away from the smell of that paint, you know. Believe me, I gave her mother a piece of my mind. Not that it does much good. Ethel never did have any sense . . . crazy woman."

From this conversation my father deduced that Genevieve was seriously allergic to paint (the one interesting thing he had yet learned about her); and that her mother, Crazy Ethel, either didn't know or didn't care about her daughter's allergy. While he didn't like the sound of it, at least it was some kind of explanation.

In later years, when recalling the whole affair, Mother always insisted that she did not intend a deliberate deception; that she simply wished to spare my father the burden of Genevieve's problem. And she always pointed out that if he had ever asked her, flat out, "Is Genevieve pregnant?" she would have said, "Yes." But he never asked.

"Why in hell would I ask?" he always said. "Why would such an idea occur to me?"

Why, indeed? Genevieve, being shapeless and lumpy all over, didn't *look* pregnant, and nothing she ever said while living with us would lead to that conclusion. As for putting paint and pregnancy together, like two and two, my father would have come up with five every time, and when this danger was eventually explained to him—"The smell of paint can make a woman miscarry"—he said that sounded like something Louis would tell us without knowing what he was talking about.

Nevertheless, Genevieve was pregnant, and respectably so, though temporarily abandoned by her husband, one Leroy Fraley. This was Mother's initial understanding of the situation and though, like my father, she didn't like the sound of it, she did feel sorry for Genevieve. She felt the press of family obligation, however far removed, and she agreed with Frank that Ethel Fitch didn't have good sense. (In fact, this was a substantial understatement. Ethel was definitely closet kin: not quite loony enough to be committed, not quite sane enough to run loose.) Most of all, Mother believed that Genevieve's stay would be brief, her departure orderly, and that, in the meantime, efforts would be made to locate the footloose Leroy Fraley.

All of this added up to "Genevieve's problem," from the burden of which my father was to be spared, much as he was spared all sorts of minor domestic dilemmas. Mother never called on him to manage things that she could manage herself or to sort out awkward situations that, left alone, would sort themselves out. Besides, she knew that he would find the tangle of Genevieve's affairs preposterous, and she was afraid that he would object to having the whole thing dropped in his lap . . . or, to be precise, in his spare bedroom. He recognized that there were unfortunate people all over the place who couldn't seem to regulate their lives, but he didn't expect to find any such people under his own roof.

Of course, he didn't count sickness as mismanagement. It wasn't Genevieve's fault she was allergic to paint, he felt, and in the absence of anything else to talk to Genevieve about, he talked to her about her "condition."

"I know you get a very serious reaction to this," he said, "but just how does it affect you? Do you break out in a rash? There's a young woman in my office who has your same trouble, and her face swells up. She can't see, can hardly eat. . . . It's a terrible thing. Has that ever happened to you?"

"No . . ." Genevieve said, looking pretty worried. "But my feet swell up if I'm not careful."

My father said that was most unusual, he had never heard of that. "I understand the worst of all is the respiratory effect. These people who suddenly can't breathe . . . their throats just close up—" and then, as Genevieve looked *really* worried, he went on, "I'll tell you what you ought to do—you ought to get a shot. You know, they have shots now for people like you. But you don't want to wait till you're in trouble. You want to get the shot well ahead of time. Then, too," he added, "they can make tests and find out just what causes this condition."

"Oh, I know what causes it," Genevieve said.

"Not necessarily. It could be any number of things. It could even be something you eat."

From this, and similar cockeyed conversations,

Genevieve apparently concluded that my father was just as crazy as her mother, so it's no wonder that she grew restive for Leroy Fraley to come and take her away.

She mentioned this once or twice to Mother—"I surely do hope that Leroy can come pretty soon"—but Mother never knew what to say in reply, it seemed like such a pitiable state of affairs. It never occurred to her that Genevieve might know where Leroy Fraley was, until, in desperation, Genevieve decided to join him.

She had overheard the tail end of a conversation between Louis and my father, in which Louis asked how many kittens Juanita the cat might have. My father said that under the circumstances—the great publicity, the Slocums' damp basement and a cast of thousands—it would be a miracle if she had even one, and a greater miracle if that one didn't have to be taken away from its mother and drowned.

"Why would it be drowned?" Louis said.

"Well, maybe not drowned, but put out of its misery. Sometimes it's kinder. If it isn't healthy and vigorous, it won't survive anyway, and it's just better to do away with it."

It was this last speech that Genevieve overheard, and so harsh a view, coupled with my father's seeming belief that pregnancy was caused by any number of things, including diet, and that it could be prevented by inoculation, apparently convinced her that she had gone from a frying pan into a fire and had better get away while she could.

"But, Genevieve, where will you go?" Mother said.

"I'm going to Leroy. He can't come here, so I'll go to him."

"What do you mean, he can't come here?" Mother wanted to know. "And how can you go to him, if you don't know where he is?"

"I know where he is," Genevieve said. "He's in Latticeburg, Kentucky. He's in jail."

Mother certainly hadn't counted on this, but it did fit in with her notion of a man who would desert his pregnant wife. She called Frank with the news, and Frank said he would find out about it right away. He also said that Genevieve must stay right where she was; the smell of paint in Ethel Fitch's house was still too strong for safety.

This was very discouraging information for my mother, who by this time felt herself hopelessly caught in an intrigue for which she had no taste in the first place, and little aptitude. But there wasn't anything she could do about it except wait— for the paint to settle or for Leroy Fraley to be sprung, whichever came first.

The next day Frank called, sputtering over the telephone, to say that he had found Leroy and that Leroy was in jail for stealing a car—specifically, the car of Ethel Fitch.

"He says he borrowed it," Frank said. "She says he stole it. I believe him, because he doesn't sound smart enough to steal a car, and we all know Ethel's crazy. Either she lent it to him and forgot she did, or she lent it to him and had him arrested anyway. I don't know why she would do that, and I don't much care. I'm going to get him out of jail if I can and get him back here. He *wants* to come back. He loves Genevieve."

Mother, reeling from this series of fresh alarms, seized on the one bright spot. "It's wonderful that he feels that way," she said. "I'm sure everything will work out, and he can be with Genevieve when the baby comes."

In view of the imperfect communication on all sides, it's not surprising that nobody knew exactly *when* the baby was supposed to come. My mother assumed that it was due in four or five months because that was what Frank assumed—on the testimony of Ethel Fitch, who had told him something about Genevieve being "all set by the middle of September." Genevieve must have known when the baby was due; but since she had never even mentioned a baby to Mother, Mother assumed that she was unhappy about it or ashamed about it, and she didn't want to hound Genevieve with painful questions.

Consequently, when Genevieve went into labor, nobody knew what was going on, including Genevieve, who was expecting a monumental stomach-ache and did not associate low back pain with the onset of birth. She suffered in silence all day, and by the time she finally decided that this must be something more than muscle strain, things were very far along.

My mother hardly knew what to think. She had heard of miscalculation, but never of miscalculation by five months.

"But Genevieve," she said, "isn't this baby coming much too soon?"

"Not for me," Genevieve said.

Then there was the problem of my father. Having hoped to keep him in the dark about the whole thing or, at the very least, to surprise him with the news sometime next year ("You remember Genevieve Fitch? Well, Genevieve has a lovely baby!") Mother now had to bring him up to date in a hurry.

"Will you bring the car around front while I call Dr. Hildebrand?" she called downstairs. "We're going to have to take Genevieve to the hospital."

"What for?" he shouted up. "What's the matter?" And then, still believing Genevieve to be the victim of allergy: "I'll bet it was those oysters we had for supper, wasn't it?"

"You don't understand," Mother said. "Genevieve isn't sick. She's having a baby . . . this very minute."

My father, however shaken and mystified by this announcement, apparently recognized the urgency of the situation. For one thing, he could hear Genevieve moaning from upstairs that she dare not try to move. "Never mind the car," he said to my mother. "I'll call an ambulance. You see what you can do for her. I'd better call Hildebrand too." A few minutes later he rushed up the stairs. "Is there anyone else I should call?" he asked.

"You might call Frank."

"I was hoping there would be a husband I could notify."

"He's in jail," Mother said. "I couldn't tell you. You would have had a fit. You know you would. Did you reach Dr. Hildebrand?"

"He's on his way. Also the ambulance. Didn't you think I would catch on when this particular moment arrived?"

"Yes," Mother said, "but this baby is five months early." She did not add that this was Frank's estimate.

It was hours before the whole thing got straightened out, and in the meantime Juanita the cat escaped from the Slocums' basement and disappeared, and all the neighborhood children (summoned by Maxine ringing the cowbell) ran up and down the street and in and out of everybody's yards looking for her.

Amid all the clamor Genevieve had an eight-and-a-half-pound boy upstairs in the bedroom. She did it all by herself because the ambulance arrived too late and Dr. Hildebrand was busy trying to improvise some kind of incubator for what he believed to be a dangerously premature birth for a seriously allergic mother. But then he got most of his information from my father, who was, in this case, the worse possible source.

Eventually all the loose ends got tied up. Leroy Amos Fraley, Jr., being of great size and marked vigor, was obviously not even five minutes early, and Genevieve's allergy was only a figment of my father's misinformation.

Ethel Fitch, on hearing the good news over the phone, said it was the end of all her hopes and dreams for Genevieve, which had involved a three-month course in beauty culture, to run from mid-June to mid-September (which took care of another loose end) and a subsequent career of styling hair in the front room of the Fitch house. Why else, Ethel wanted to know, did Mother think she had embarked on this painting-and-decorating project? She had done it, she said, all for Genevieve, who had repaid her by taking up with a convict.

My father, trying hard to catch up, said that, crazy or not, Ethel had a point. "After all, " he said, "this Leroy *is* in jail, isn't he?"

"Yes," Mother said, "but only because Ethel lent him her car and then said he stole it."

At this point the ambulance, having shut its door and gone away, returned . . . with Juanita and four kittens.

"Didn't like to put 'em out in the street," the driver said, "and we figured they must have come from somewhere around here."

"Bring them right in," my father said. "We seem to be in the business."

Juanita the cat hung around our house for two or three weeks, much to Maxine Slocum's disgust; Louis and I got to keep one kitten, which we named Leroy in honor of the day's events; and Genevieve and the baby stayed with us for four days until Leroy, who had been released from jail, arrived to take them away.

We all stood around on the front porch watching them go, and my father said now that it was all over he felt like a man who had wandered into someone else's home movie and then wandered out again without ever knowing what it was all about. Louis and I felt much the same way. While watching and waiting for Juanita to have kittens, we had missed the main event; had overlooked the forest for the trees, so to speak, and then missed the trees too.

But, happily for us, there remained one final confusion.

"What do you mean, Leroy is going to have kittens?" my father said the next spring. "How can a male cat have kittens?"

"Well, we were wrong about that," Mother told him. "And since all the children were so disappointed last year when Juanita ran away, I thought I might call just a very few mothers and see whether their children would like to come—"

"No," my father said. "No . . . no . . . no."

Louisa May and the Facts of Life

Mrs. Slocum's plan to expose us all to the facts of life came a little too late. Everybody in our neighborhood had already been exposed to them, although we didn't know it at the time, and didn't understand that sex had reared its ugly head right across the street in the unlikely person of Louisa May Fuller.

Louisa May and her sister Alma lived on the corner in a little gray cottage, and were described by my cousins from Elyria as "crazy old maids." But Louis and I had known the Fuller girls all our lives, and didn't think they were very strange.

"Not strange at all," my father often said, "compared to some of your mother's family."

Alma was the older of the two, and therefore the head of the family, so she made all the big decisions, like how to get ready for Judgment Day. Louisa May decided what to have for dinner and when to paint the house. Louisa May did the washing and the cooking; Alma did the needlepoint and cross-stitched pretty thoughts on all the dish towels. Louisa May scrubbed the kitchen floor and waxed the furniture; Alma picked up the living room and straightened the doilies.

They both were officers of the Women's Missionary Society—Louisa May rolled bandages, made layettes for African babies, collected and mended everybody's used clothing for the mission boxes and kept careful track of the organization's funds; Alma was in charge of devotions every other month, which accounted for most of the pretty thoughts on the dish towels. However, despite this lopsided division of labor (or maybe because of it), they got along very well, agreeing on almost everything except Alma's special concern: a great passion for searching out and recording the genealogy of the Fuller family, which was a matter of very little interest to everyone else, including Louisa May.

After much correspondence, Alma would establish a family tie with somebody in Ponca City,

Oklahoma, or East Orange, New Jersey; and she would throw up the window and sing out the news to Louisa May in the garden. "Mr. Fuller, in East Orange, is a third cousin twice removed!" she would call, hoping vainly for some enthusiastic response. But Louisa May just didn't care about all these far-flung connections and considered Alma's fascination with the subject a terrible waste of time, and a little silly into the bargain.

"It's not as if we came from anything grand," she used to tell my mother, "and even if we did, what would be the good of knowing it?"

Louisa May's hobby was babies. She adored babies. To be sure, noboby in the neighborhood was known to harbor an active dislike of babies, but Louisa May went to the opposite extreme, and seemed to view each individual baby as the beginning and end of all human wonder. Wherever a new baby appeared, there too was Louisa May, hard on the heels of the doctor.

My mother was fond of her, and she worried about her. "Louisa May," she would say, "you ought to get married. It's just a shame, the way you love babies, that you don't have a family. And you don't want to wait forever. You're thirty-eight years old and it's time you had your own babies. Now, you just find some nice man and marry him."

"Oh, Mrs. Lawson," Louisa May said, "I don't

want to get married and have to fool with some old man around the house."

"But he wouldn't be old!" Mother insisted. "You want a respectable young man who's a good provider."

"Well, I don't want any young man either," Louisa May always said. "I don't know. . . . Sometimes I ask myself, Would it be worth it to put up with a husband so I could have a baby? But I just can't seem to decide it would. Alma and I have our own ways of doing and things go along pretty smooth, and I wouldn't want to bring a stranger into the house."

Louisa May's predicament was not openly discussed at home because my mother was particular about discussions of babies and how to get them. But my father was equally particular about having all of us under his nose at the supper table, and at least two or three times a week he missed my little brother Louis.

"I suppose Louisa May Fuller has got him again," he would grumble. "Why in hell doesn't Louisa May get married and have her own children and quit borrowing Louis?"

Of course this was partly Louis's fault—he loved to have Louisa May borrow him because she let him eat raw cookie dough and ride around on her vacuum cleaner.

"Louisa May doesn't want to get married," Mother said. "She doesn't want to fool with a man around the house."

"Well, she could fool with one long enough to get some babies, and leave mine alone."

I didn't see my mother kick him under the table, but I saw him wince, and the subject was changed to some less interesting topic of the day—less interesting to me, at any rate. Louis wouldn't have cared, because he was only five years old, but I was almost eight and just barely smart enough to know that there were mysteries beyond my ken, and that one such mystery had to do with babies.

I concluded that there must be mysteries beyond my father's ken, too, in view of his remark; for if I didn't know anything else about the subject, I did know that the only way in the world to get a baby was to get married. All the available evidence supported that conclusion. In the first place, that was what I had been told; and in the second place, no unmarried ladies of my acquaintance had babies. Like most little girls, I shared Louisa May's enthusiasm and took it for granted that if there were some other way to get babies, everybody would have a few—my schoolteacher, Miss Lincoln; my Aunt Blanche; Miss Styles, who worked at the grocery store; Louisa May, of course . . . maybe even Alma.

I was therefore both amazed and delighted to

discover that I was wrong when Louisa May—though still unmarried—got a baby.

Not all at once—she took the usual length of time. But since Louisa May was so large and so comfortably padded, it was five months before her condition began to arouse speculation . . . and another month before Alma noticed anything amiss.

Then Alma brought my mother half of a coconut layer cake. "Too bad to have it go stale," she said, "and Louisa May and I can't eat it all up—or shouldn't, anyway. I've noticed of late that Louisa May is putting on weight, and I try to help her curb her appetite."

Louis and I loved the cake and ate most of it feeling sorry for Louisa May who apparently *couldn't* eat it.

"Just because she's fat?" Louis shook his head.

Naturally there was gossip, but it was sketchy and disorganized. There was nothing anyone could put a finger on, so to speak, until one day when Mother quite innocently called across the street, "How are you, Louisa May?"

Louisa May came right over, beaming. "Oh, Mrs. Lawson, I feel wonderful, and I'm just going to tell you why because I know you'll be happy for me. I thought a lot about what you said—about getting married and all, and especially about being thirty-eight and not waiting too long; and, Mrs. Lawson, I just got afraid to wait anymore."

"Oh, I'm so glad," Mother said, puzzled but relieved.

"I knew you would be. I don't know what Alma will say. She's not as crazy over babies as I am, and I just know she'll think I should have got married anyway, but"—and Louisa May shrugged—"this opportunity came along and I just thought, Well, why not?"

My mother was speechless. In her moral firmament there existed good women and bad women, and though she had never personally known any bad women, she had a clear image of how they looked and behaved. They would be gaudy, she felt, and rough and coarse, with brassy hair and low-cut dresses. Louisa May, on the other hand, was as plain, and as good, as homemade bread.

Furthermore, Mother had a vague, uneasy notion that she herself had somehow aided and abetted this state of affairs.

Alma turned out to have the same notion. At some point she took a good look at Louisa May and realized that her weight problem was neither permanent nor proper, and she came charging across the street to accuse Mother of encouraging immoral behavior.

"I didn't encourage her," Mother said. "I never said it was all right. I just wanted her to get married."

"Oh, how lovely that would be!" said Alma

hysterically. "But she didn't, and just see the fix she's in, and she's not even ashamed a little bit. I don't know what in the world to do!"

Mother felt sorry for Alma. "Maybe she could go away somewhere. . . ."

"She won't. She says they might take the baby away from her but that old Dr. Barney will let her keep it, and he will, he will! You know how soft he is, and what will I do?"

This didn't make much sense to Louis and me but we were glad Louisa May didn't have to go anywhere she didn't want to go.

"She won't say who the father is," Alma went on. "She says it's none of my business. She says—" Here Alma choked. "She says he was a nice man and for me not to worry about it."

Mother was so flabbergasted by the whole affair that she had no shock left to spare for this, nor even much curiosity, and my father seemed torn between outright astonishment and a kind of grudging approval on the grounds that he would no longer have to hunt around for Louis.

Louisa May did in fact fail to exhibit the least shred of shame or regret and she did not go away somewhere, but she did oblige the neighborhood by staying within doors as much as possible until her baby was born. It was a boy, which was what Louis had said it would be, but he did not claim any special credit for this.

Louisa May bought a very expensive imported perambulator, and what little time she was not feeding the baby, bathing him or rocking him, she wheeled him up and down the street with a rose stuck through the roof of the carriage, humming little tunes and literally commanding people to see how beautiful he was. She called him "darling" and invited other people to call him that too until she hit upon exactly the right name for him.

Nobody needed a second invitation to view the baby, so great was the curiosity as to his parentage. No baby was ever scrutinized more carefully for identifying features, nor with so little satisfaction—for when he got to look like anybody at all, it turned out to be Louisa May: a distinct disappointment to all.

That was later, though. For the time being he looked pretty much like most babies: plump, bald, rosy. He was an unusually happy baby, which prompted someone in the neighborhood to remark, "Love babies always are"—although on the face of it, Louisa May's baby hardly fell into that category. He was so happy, I suppose, because Louisa May didn't allow anything to make him unhappy, and his healthy good humor was almost an affront to decent, respectable women whose babies were fussy or fretful or colicky or pale or cross-eyed.

Won over by the baby and influenced by Louisa

May's own attitude (she simply ignored the whole question of the baby's beginnings, as if he had just appeared one day out of thin air), most people quit trying to sort out the moral issues of the case. Reverend Seagraves was asked by one or two of his flock to please call upon Louisa May, and did so, but with no clear purpose in mind and no visible result. Had Louisa May sought counsel, he would have counseled her; had she sought comfort, he would have comforted her; but as it was, all he could do was hold the baby while Louisa May cut him a quarter of a Gravenstein apple pie and read him recent correspondence from the missionary in Bechuanaland.

He ended up by offering to baptize the baby on the first Sunday of the month, although, as he said, he wasn't sure how the congregation would feel.

He need not have worried. Nobody expected or wanted the baby to suffer, and even the most puritanical of the parishioners seemed to take the view that here was a baby who *needed* to be baptized. For most people, though, there was a less lofty consideration. Since the baby didn't *look* like anybody, they pinned their hopes on having him *named* for somebody, and there was every indication that church attendance on that Sunday would set new, towering records.

My mother was shocked by this. "There are

people planning to go to church this Sunday," she said indignantly, "who haven't been inside the church since *they* were baptized!" At first she said she wouldn't go, and then she said my father wouldn't go, and then Louisa May asked both of them to stand up with her and be the baby's godparents, which delighted Louis and me.

My father said at least that way they would be sure of getting a seat, which made Mother so mad that she didn't speak to him for over an hour. It was no joking matter, she said.

It was not, to her. My mother's moral code was simple, uncompromising and, up to now, uncluttered by doubt. She believed that virtue is its own reward and that the evildoer will reap the whirlwind, but Louisa May had scrambled these precepts. Besides, Mother loved Louisa May and didn't want her to reap any whirlwind. Neither, though, could she ignore what was a clear and definite lapse of virtue.

She agreed to be the baby's godmother because she knew Louisa May wouldn't ask anyone else, and she felt it would be compounded cruelty to deny the baby honorary parents when he didn't even have a full complement of real ones.

I was thrilled about the whole thing because I thought it would give me an in with the baby, and he was so generally admired that his good favor amounted to a juvenile status symbol. Neither I nor any of my friends understood exactly how Louisa May came to have him, and though we wondered about it, we didn't wonder nearly as much as our parents thought we did. We just assumed, variously, that he had been brought by a stork, found under a pumpkin or left on Louisa May's doorstep by a band of gypsies, and we really didn't much care.

On the morning of the baptism we were about fifteen minutes ahead of time, but already the church was filling with people. "The baby has a lot of friends," I whispered to Louisa May, and she smiled.

Father, Louisa May with the baby on her lap, Alma and I all sat together in one pew, saving a place for my mother. She and Louis were coming with our neighbors the Pendletons because there wasn't room in our car, and as the organist started the opening hymn my father began to look around and mutter, "Wonder what's become of her?" I tried to see too, but there were too many people. It was my feeling that Mother was probably stuck back at the door, unable to push her way through, but then I saw Mrs. Pendleton, with her hat on crooked, steaming down the aisle.

She leaned across me and said, "Louis stuck a bean up his nose and we had to take him to a doctor. They're still there. You'll just have to go ahead without her." She started away and then turned back. "Louis is all *right*, you understand. It's just that—"

"He stuck a bean up his nose," my father said. "I see. Thank you."

The hymn over, Reverend Seagraves came down out of the pulpit to the baptismal font.

"Never stuck a bean up his nose before," I heard my father mutter as he stepped out of the pew and started to follow Louisa May up the aisle. I was sorry for Mother, who was going to miss what I considered her big moment, but very proud of my father, who was going to stand beside Louisa May and assume responsibility for her baby before God and man and our entire congregation and a considerable number of total strangers.

I guess the same thought occurred to him, because he stopped three rows up, and then, after a moment's pause, came back and got me. "You come too, Mary Elizabeth," he said "You can take your mother's place."

Poor baby, to be represented by such a group. Only Louisa May seemed to be in full possession of herself. Reverend Seagraves was trying to sustain the shock of the unexpected size of his congregation, and to overlook the appearance of a distinctly minor child as a baptismal sponsor. I assumed that Louisa May would hand me the baby, according to the usual procedure, but instead she handed him to my father, who looked very much surprised and immediately handed him to Reverend Seagraves, who also looked surprised, because he already had his hands full. But I suppose he didn't like to hand him on to anyone else—especially not back to my father, who had almost dropped him the first time around.

Louisa May, however, remained perfectly serene, and at the appropriate moment pronounced the baby's name as if it were as common, say, as Charlie.

It was not, and all those who had hoped for revelation in the naming of this baby had their hopes dashed. Louisa May named her baby Hannibal—a name never connected with anybody or anything in our community. It was her one indirect concession to public opinion, for surely, all things being equal, she would have preferred a name more natural to the ear. But she offered neither explanation nor justification for the name, except to say that Alma thought there might once have been another Hannibal Fuller way back in the genealogy. Alma hadn't thought any such thing, but she liked the idea of it so much that she came to believe it was true, and from then on spent most of her time trying to track him down.

My father hurried us away right after church, and Louisa May let me hold Hannibal on the way

home. He was soft and warm and sleepy and probably quite uncomfortable, smashed against my bony
chest.

"Will you tell him someday that I'm his godmother?" I asked.

"Well, more like godsister, maybe," Louisa May
said. "Oh, yes, I'll surely tell him."

"I'll take him to school when he's old enough,"
I said, "and Sunday school. I'll watch out for
him."

"I count on you," she said.

The excitement of the day, the weight of Hannibal upon me, the warmth of the sun through the
window of the car, all made me as drowsy as the
baby.

"Where did you get him from?" I asked.

Alma gasped. "Why, we went out one morning
to fetch the milk . . ." she began.

"Not quite," Louisa May said, and then to me,
"The where and the how is a mystery. As for the
why, just say I wanted him a whole lot, and was
old enough to take good care of him."

My mother was home from the doctor and waiting for us. "I took a taxicab," she said. "There was
no use going to the church so late. How did it
go?"

"Well . . ." Father sat down heavily on the
living-room sofa. "You can just about imag-

ine . . . everybody and his uncle there in the church. I walked right past the Ferguson brothers. Saw Amos Ball a couple of pews over. Ed Wiggins . . ."

"Oh, well," my mother said.

"Oh, well? Comes the big moment and who walks up the aisle with Louisa May and her baby? Me! By myself."

"Well, people must have known . . ."

"What? That Louis stuck a bean up his nose? I doubt it. Besides, there were people there who don't know me from Adam's off ox—perfect strangers." He took out his big white handkerchief and mopped his forehead. "Worst spot I ever was in. Then Louisa May gave me the baby and I didn't know what to do with him."

"Why didn't you give him to me?" I asked, and Mother stared at me.

"Where were you?" she asked.

"I was there too. I went up with Daddy. I'm Hannibal's godsister."

"Hannibal?"

"Hannibal," my father repeated, and shrugged. "Well, she couldn't very well name him Frank, or George, or Bill."

"She could have named him Fred," I said, "for you."

He mopped his head again. "I thought of that.

47

Oh, yes, that occurred to me while we were standing up there."

I was sent upstairs to change my Sunday dress and heard only a snatch of their conversation: ". . . have to tell her *something*, I think. Louisa May told her it was all a mystery . . ." When I returned my father had gone out to look at the garden and Mother was sitting by the window, reading a church bulletin. She was holding it upside down.

"Come and sit down," she said. "Your father told me you asked Louisa May where she got her baby . . ." Poor Mother, she made hard work of the facts of life. By and large her remarks only served to confirm what Louisa May had said—it all sounded most mysterious, but more practical than finding babies under pumpkins, which had always seemed careless to me.

"Then Louisa May is bad?" I said when she was finished.

"Well, more misguided. Louisa May will have a hard time bringing up her little boy with no husband to help." I could see the sense of that. Certainly, I thought, I would want a husband to do all the things my father did around the house, but I didn't think Louisa May felt that way about it.

"Louisa May never wanted to put up with a

48

husband around the house," I reminded my mother.

"Well," she said, after thinking for a moment, "that comes of not knowing. Marriage isn't just a matter of putting up with a husband around the house. It's a kind of sharing of everything . . . good and bad, hard and easy. It's having someone who cares, to care about. It's ever so many things, and when Louisa May says she doesn't want to be married I expect she means it. But it's like saying you don't want any candy when you've never had any."

Later that day Mother and I made a freezerful of peach ice cream and took it across the street, and we all took turns giving Hannibal his first taste of summer in a spoon. I watched Louisa May cuddle the baby, putting her cheek against the downy softness of his head, and I still thought it strange that my mother should feel sorry for Louisa May when Louisa May so plainly didn't feel the least bit sorry for herself. But if, as Mother had said, her contentment came of not knowing, I was glad she didn't know.

We started back across the street when it was beginning to get dark, and my father came to meet us. "I told you to call over," he said. "That freezer's too heavy for you."

"Oh, it's almost empty now," Mother said.

"Still too heavy." He took the freezer from her,

pretending to stagger under its weight until Mother slapped him lightly on the arm. "Now you stop that," she said, laughing. "Why, people will think you're drunk. Now, stop. I mean it. . . . Oh, you!"

I lagged behind to catch lightning bugs for Louis, but I could hear them laughing all the way into our house, and even after I had gone to bed.

Big Doings on the
Fourth of July

My mother—though a person of quiet ways and simple tastes, primarily interested in meat loaf recipes and January white sales—was prone to accidents of fate which landed her, time and again, in unusual, vaguely dangerous, or downright loony circumstances.

She was usually able to get herself out of whatever tangle she was in, but every now and then she had to call on my father, who said the same thing every time—"I'll bet this was your sister Mildred's idea"—which, very often, it was.

They were an odd pair, I always thought, to be associated at all, let alone as sisters, for they were as different as ducks and owls. They didn't even look alike—Mother was small and fair and conservative in matters of dress and makeup, while Aunt Mildred was a very tall and solid woman with dark hair and eyes—impossible to overlook, since her taste in clothes ran to gypsy colors and extravagant use of fringe and beads and trailing scarves.

Even Louis, who was only nine, thought that one or the other must have been adopted.

"Which one, Louis?" I asked him, but he said he didn't want to know because he liked them both.

"Now what does that mean?" my father said. "Does he think that in such a case you could only keep one—like puppies?" He shook his head. "Well, certainly Louis isn't adopted. He sounds just like your mother explaining why she went downtown on a bus to buy new curtains and came home in a taxicab with a vacuum cleaner."

"I couldn't very well haul that big awkward thing home on the bus," she had told him, as if that answered everything, which of course it didn't.

Pressed for further details, Mother said that she had, in fact, bought curtains at one store; subsequently found different, prettier, cheaper curtains at another store; returned the first curtains and bought a bedspread to match the second curtains. She then ran into Aunt Mildred ("Aha!" said my father) who was in hot pursuit of eiderdown pillows advertised on sale somewhere, though she couldn't remember where.

They joined forces, tried on some hats, stopped for lunch and then proceeded down Main Street, in and out of stores, looking for Aunt Mildred's sale pillows, which they never found.

Along the way, however, they were reminded of other homey needs and picked up what Mother called "a few things." The vacuum cleaner came from the Baptist Church thrift shop, where Aunt Mildred made a purchase similar in terms of unwieldiness: a concrete birdbath for her Oriental garden, which was, strictly speaking, neither Oriental nor a garden, but a collection of ugly outdoor statuary and a stunted crab apple tree.

They then called not one, but two taxicabs, so Aunt Mildred could use one of them to take old Mrs. Tipton home from the thrift shop and see her safely in her house. Aunt Mildred also took all the soft goods they had accumulated—curtains, bedspread, assorted dish towels and cotton underwear and needlepoint yarn—while Mother conveyed the birdbath and the vacuum cleaner, stopping on the way home to leave the birdbath in Aunt Mildred's garden.

"There, now," she said, at the end of this lengthy account. "Is that so terrible?"

"No," my father said, "but it's silly—you and Mildred running all over town in buses and taxicabs, loaded down with packages. Why didn't you take my car?"

"I don't like to drive," Mother said. "You know that."

"Why didn't Mildred drive?"

"Why, I don't know. It isn't as if we *planned* to go shopping. We just happened to meet."

Actually, Mother *did* know, but didn't like to say, that Aunt Mildred's car was in the repair shop again.

In matters of transportation, as in all other ways, they were exactly opposite. Mother hated driving cars, but when called upon to do so, she performed with caution and common sense. Aunt Mildred, on the other hand, loved to drive anywhere, anytime, with such zest and zip and freewheeling independence that she could be said to be unsafe at any speed.

It was for this reason (and others) that my father took a dim view of Aunt Mildred's plan to dress herself and Mother up in old-fashioned costumes and ride a tandem bicycle in the Fourth of July parade, for which, as chairman of the town committee, he was responsible.

Aunt Mildred said that Louis and I could dress up too, and ride our own bicycles beside or behind

54

them, and we would all be a charming addition to the parade.

"I can't ride a bicycle," Louis said. This was unusual in a small town where everybody rode bicycles—but then, Louis was unusual. My mother once said that she believed Louis was born forty years old, and he did indeed have an air of solemn deliberation better suited to an adult. This kept him out of a lot of trouble—by the time he'd considered all the pros and cons of sneaking into some movie we weren't allowed to see, the movie was half over—but it also cramped his style, I thought, in matters of simple enjoyment, like riding a bicycle.

He'd considered the pros and cons of this, tried it in a dogged, down-to-business way, fallen off harder and quicker and more often than seemed reasonable to him, reconsidered and said he'd rather walk.

"Can't ride a bicycle!" Aunt Mildred said. "Why, it's the easiest thing in the world. . . . You know how a newborn baby will swim if you throw it into the water? Well, it's the very same thing—it's instinct."

I didn't think it was the same thing at all and neither did Louis, and my father said it would be a cold day in August before he threw any newborn baby into the water, just on Mildred's say-so.

He also continued to grumble about the proposed bicycle act—probably because he saw too much similarity between Aunt Mildred on a tandem bicycle and Aunt Mildred in a car, both being vehicles and subject to collision—but there wasn't much he could do about it, because there were signs all over town urging people to *Join the Celebration! Sign up for the Big Parade!*—and they were *his* signs.

"Mildred's just trying to help," Mother said. "Isn't that what you said you wanted—more people in the parade?"

"Yes, but not Mildred! I want Charlie Baker at the bank, and Floyd Gemperline at the Select Dairy—*business* people, to show some spirit and spend some money and enter some floats, so we'll have something to judge besides the V.F.W. and the Ladies' Hospital Auxiliary."

"Then you should have said so," Mother told him.

"I doubt that Mildred even has a tandem bicycle—and what makes you think she knows how to ride one?"

"Oh, of course she does; she was a very athletic girl," Mother said; but in fact she wasn't at all sure of this, and was somewhat lukewarm about her own role in the whole thing. Unlike Aunt Mildred, Mother was uncomfortable about any kind of public display—choosing always to dish up the dessert rather than introduce the speaker—and didn't really want to put on a lot of old petticoats and a floppy hat and ride down Main Street in a parade.

Furthermore, she had, at different times and in an offhand way, invited various relatives to a picnic supper on the evening of the Fourth; and since Mother was one of a large family this had gotten out of hand. She had mentioned some of the arrangements to my father—"Carl and Ava are coming over after the parade"; "I told Linnea and Walt to stop by for some fried chicken"—but she had not spelled out for him the exact dimensions of the guest list, which, when she added it all up, came to forty-seven people.

She had even invited my father's only sister, Della, to come from Zanesville, a hundred and fifty miles away—but she didn't tell him that, either; because Della, though always invited to festive occasions, never came—too far to go, she always said, and too hard to get there.

My father both understood and approved of this attitude. He was fond of Della, he said, and she was fond of him; but their family affection didn't require them to see each other every fifteen minutes, like most of Mother's relatives.

All in all, the Fourth of July looked like a complicated day, and Mother wasn't sure she wanted to begin it on a bicycle.

Louis, however, had no doubts at all. At my

urging, he made one last determined effort to ride my bicycle the length of the driveway, landed five times in the forsythia bush and said, once again, that he would rather walk.

My father, pleased by the response to his signs— nine floats, two high school bands, a drum and bugle corps, and a team of horses from the local Grange Association—was too involved with the logistics of the parade to notice that Louis was a little black and blue, or that Mother was frying chicken and peeling potatos from morning till night. But he did notice when she showed up at the dinner table wearing a pair of voluminous ladies' bloomers.

"Mildred got them somewhere," Mother said, "and I just feel so foolish that I thought I'd wear them around and try to get used to them. She said they'd be more practical than long skirts."

My father was so surprised and impressed by this display of good sense in Aunt Mildred that he changed his tune, and said the the bicycle would probably be a nice touch.

"I'll put you in right behind the drum and bugle corps," he said, "so no one will miss you."

The tandem bicycle which Aunt Mildred produced on the morning of the Fourth did not in fact belong to her, just as my father had predicted. It belonged to old Mrs. Tipton, who had put it out in the trash and was dismayed to find it still there on the day Aunt Mildred took her home from the thrift shop.

"Oh, they didn't take it!" she had said. "Now what will I do with the old thing?"—and of course Aunt Mildred had known just what to do with it.

"I had it tuned up," she told us, "at the repair shop where I always take my car."

"But that's an auto body shop," Mother said, eyeing the bicycle with justifiable suspicion.

"That's what they said," Aunt Mildred agreed, "and they didn't really want to do it; but with all the business I give them they couldn't very well say no."

She was dressed, as were we all, in a motley assortment of attic discards: petticoats, automobile dusters, ladies' shirtwaists of a bygone day . . . and hats as big around as turkey platters, but nowhere near as solid. Mother's hat was especially limp, falling down around her ears and almost to her chin, while Aunt Mildred's hat looked like a wedding cake; roses and feather birds and yards of trailing tulle.

Louis had suffered himself to be decked out like Buster Brown, in knickers and a straw boater, just as if everything was going according to plan. He reasoned that there would be no time, at the last minute, for Aunt Mildred to commandeer a bicycle, put him on it and throw him into the water, and he was right.

"You ride right in close behind us, Mary Elizabeth," Aunt Mildred told me. "We don't want to be strung out all along the street if we can help it. It's just a shame about you, Louis. You wouldn't want to climb up here with your mother and me?"

Louis said no, but if we didn't go too fast he would try to keep up with us on foot.

"Oh, we won't go fast," Aunt Mildred said. "You don't go fast in a parade. Grace, are you going to get on?"

"Where?" Mother said, holding up the front of her hat and hitching at her bloomers.

"Doesn't matter—front or back."

"Whoever's in front has to steer," I said.

"Well, you'd better do that, Mildred." Mother straddled the bicycle. "I'll pedal."

"You both have to pedal," I said. Louis and I looked at each other, aware now of what we should probably have known all along—that neither one of them knew how to ride the thing, and, even more surprising, neither one of them seemed concerned about it.

When asked about this later, Mother said she based her confidence on pictures she had seen of people riding such a bicycle—smiling, unruffled, hardly exerting themselves at all—and she concluded that two people on a bicycle produced great stability, no matter who the two people were. Of course, she realized almost at once that she was wrong about this.

Parade or no parade, Mother and Aunt Mildred had to go fast because that was the only way they could stay upright . . . and I had to go fast to keep up with them, as they swooped back and forth across Main Street, narrowly avoiding things and people, pedaling furiously or not at all, and never in unison.

Aunt Mildred seemed to be steering, after a fashion, with all her customary abandon; and Mother—resigned, as she later said, to six months in a body cast—was simply hanging on for dear life, unable to see much because of her hat.

Of course the rear rank of the drum and bugle corps was aware of all this, and though they continued to bugle and drum, they also tried to step up the pace of the march—torn, I suppose, between a desire to maintain order and a desire to stay clear of this runaway bicycle and its hapless operators.

In the meantime, my father, assured that all the floats and bands and marching units had started on time and in position, had gone on to the reviewing stand, where he had been much complimented on the organization and variety of the parade so far.

"Just fine, Fred," the mayor had told him. "Any surprises coming up?"

At that moment the police chief stood up and pointed down the street. "Something going on down there," he said. "That band's all over the place."

"That band"—the drum and bugle corps—was indeed all over the place, and for good reason. Aunt Mildred, increasingly hampered by the collapse of her hat—roses and birds were dangling from all sides of it, and she was nearly strangled by loose tulle—had suddenly yelled, "Look out . . . we're coming through!"

As the musicians scattered, my mother saw ahead the team of horses from the Grange Association. It was almost the only thing she had seen so far, and it was certainly the most hopeful, for the horses were hauling a low flatbed trailer carpeted with hay, in which sat three or four teenagers.

"Mildred!" Mother yelled. "Now listen to me! . . . We're going to jump. Come on, those kids will catch us."

Many of the onlookers seemed to think that this was a legitimate comedy act and applauded, but my father stood frozen to the spot, for what he saw was Mother and Aunt Mildred—"No mistaking *them*," he later said—jumping from their bicycle onto a hay wagon, while the bicycle itself crashed into the reviewing stand and died there, like a worn-out horse.

I did not see their landing, only their leap, and I dropped my bicycle and ran ahead . . . while Louis, puffing and panting, out of breath and wobbly-legged, rose to the occasion as people often do in moments of crisis. He got on my bicycle and rode to the hay wagon, thus accomplishing out of fear what he couldn't accomplish any other way.

Nor were we the only astonished and terrified family members: We passed a woman being helped to a seat on the grass, while people assured her, "I'm sure they're all right. I'm sure they aren't hurt." This woman looked pale and shaken . . . and vaguely familiar.

It turned out to be Aunt Della, who had arrived, unbeknownst to anyone, just in time to watch the parade. She had spotted Mother—not very hard, in view of the circumstances—had seen her take off in what looked like a suicidal leap through space, and immediately concluded that, through a cruel twist of fate, her first visit would turn out to be funereal.

That was also my thought, and I was relieved to find both Mother and Aunt Mildred safe and sound, though choking and sneezing from clouds of hay dust.

Since the whole thing took place directly in front of the reviewing stand, there was some talk of giving first prize to this combination float and acrobatic stunt, but my father refused to make any such award, on the grounds that it would encourage the prize winners to further lunacy.

He was so torn between relief and exasperation that he had very little emotion to spare when he arrived home to find the house, the yard, the front porch and the back porch full of Mother's relatives eating fried chicken and potato salad, except to say that it looked like a convention. He did, however, take Mother aside to tell her that if he heard Aunt Mildred say one more time, "All's well that ends well," he would not be responsible for his actions.

"You could have been killed," he told her. "You know that, don't you?"

"But we weren't," Mother said. She wanted him to look on the bright side: the great success of his parade; Louis, now riding my bicycle up and down the driveway with all the confidence of one who has slain his personal Minotaur; Aunt Della, at last present and part of a family reunion ". . . and having a wonderful time, too," Mother added.

"Should have come long ago," Aunt Della said. "Just got set in my ways, that's all. Don't you get set in your ways, Fred. Have a little fun, have a little excitement."

"It's not always the same thing," he said; and then, "Why didn't you say you were coming? I'd have met you at the bus station."

"Didn't come on the bus," Aunt Della said. "I came in a taxicab."

"From Zanesville?" My father stared at her.

"Well, I didn't start out to come *here* in a taxicab. I started out, you see, to go spend the day with my friend Audrey Wilson. Normally I wouldn't go *there* in a taxicab either, but I was taking along three dining room chairs for Audrey's nephew to repair, and then there was the quilt we're making for the church bazaar . . ."

Even to Louis and me, this was beginning to sound like bedspreads, curtains and vacuum cleaners all over again, and I could see from my father's face that he thought so too.

". . . said I was his last fare, that he was going to Piketon to spend the day with his brother, and I said *I* had a brother living not twenty miles from Piketon . . ."

Aunt Mildred had drifted over by this time and was listening with interest.

". . . just thought, oh, why not? It's the Fourth of July, after all. But don't worry, Fred, I don't expect to drive down here in a taxicab very often."

"Surely not," Aunt Mildred chimed in. "Della, I just love to drive, and Grace and I . . ." She put her arm through Aunt Della's and led her over

65

to where Mother was dishing up potato salad, and they all fell into animated conversation, of which we heard only one snatch: "We'll just drive along, and see what we can find to do. . . ."

Louis wondered what happened to the dining room chairs and the quilt, and I wondered whether Audrey Wilson was still waiting for Aunt Della to show up at her door, but my father didn't ask about those details.

He just stood there, shaking his head and muttering to himself. "Three of them," I heard him say. "From now on, there'll be three of them."

The Wedding of Willard and What's-her-name

Of Mother's great swarm of relatives, my father had no special favorite and no special bête noire because, he said, they were all alike—and all perilously close to crazy.

They really weren't, of course, day in, day out. But he seldom saw any of them day in, day out, pursuing their ordinary rounds of activity. He saw them, instead, in great numbers, on holidays or on occasions of family celebration, all talking at once and recalling past events: "Remember when Louella blew up the beer?" ". . . when Ralph left the baby on the bus?" ". . . when Blanche brought the convict home for supper?" Details were never spelled out, and though my mother sometimes tried to fill them in for him, she usually made the whole thing sound even worse.

"Well, Ralph got off the bus in Chillicothe to go to the bathroom," she would explain, "and the bus went on without him."

"Went on to where?"

"To Columbus. He was going to Columbus."

"Ralph was going to Columbus?"

"Yes, but he got off in Chillicothe to go to . . ."

"Yes, I understand that. What about the baby?"

"The baby went on to Columbus on the bus."

"But didn't Ralph tell someone? Get them to stop the bus?"

"Why, he didn't know what to do, poor little thing. He was only—oh, I don't know—eight or nine years old."

"Eight or nine years old! What was he doing on a bus with a baby?"

At this point in the story—in any story—Mother's recollection would fizzle out. "I just don't remember," she would always say, "but there must have been a good reason for it."

It was a miracle, my father often said, that so many of them had lived to tell these tales; and he only hoped that my little brother Louis and I would learn something from all the mistakes in judgment.

We did, of course, learn some things—not to hobnob with convicts, not to leave babies on

68

buses—but, despite my father's hopes, we continued to stumble into exactly the same kinds of dilemmas and to solve them, or not solve them, in exactly the same ways.

When Louis won the magazine contest, it didn't look at first like a dilemma at all, but like a great triumph. Louis entered magazine contests all the time and had never won anything, so I was very excited. Louis, mysteriously, was less so.

"It's just the second prize," he said.

"But, Louis, second prize is always something good! It's honorable mention that gets the soap and the dog food. What did you win?"

"I won a wedding." He read from the letter: "'. . . flowers, reception, bridal wardrobe, limousine . . .' and some other things. Three thousand dollars worth of things. *First* prize was a honeymoon in Paris, France."

I couldn't believe that when Louis finally won a prize it would be a wedding. "Why did you enter this contest, anyway?"

"I didn't know what it was. I found the entry blank on a table at the dentist. The top was torn off, so I just filled it out and sent it in." He looked at the letter again. "The magazine's called *Bridal Daze.*"

"Daze is right," I said. "You'll have to write and tell them you're nine years old, so you can't use the prize—unless they'll keep it till you're old enough to get married, but I don't think they'll do that."

"I can't write to them," he said. "There's a place on all the entry blanks where it says 'I certify that I am twenty-one years old.' They'll arrest me."

"I don't think so," I said.

"They'll yell at me. Besides . . ." he looked stubborn. "I won the prize. I ought to get something."

"Louis, face it. This prize is for someone who wants to get married. Maybe you can trade it to someone who wants to get married."

Louis stared at me for a minute and then he nodded. "You're right," he said. "I'll give it to Willard."

That sounded perfect to me. Willard Armstrong was my mother's cousin, and our favorite relative. He gave us rides in his truck and took us to the movies, and he always sent us birthday cards signed *Very truly yours, Willard Armstrong.* Besides, he was grown up, he had a job and a girlfriend and—most of all—he wanted to get married.

Even my father liked Willard, though with reservations. He thought Willard lacked gumption and let people walk all over him. Mother said he didn't mean "people"—he meant Willard's girlfriend, Janine, who was also called Althea and sometimes Ginger, depending on what she said to call her.

"I like to try out all different names," she told

us once. "You can change your name, you know, if you don't like it."

"Don't you like your name?" Louis asked her.

"I like it better than I used to, but I'm not crazy about it." Janine whipped out a compact, rearranged one or two curls, and studied her face carefully. She did this a lot—hoping, we assumed, to suddenly hit upon exactly the right name to go with what she saw in the mirror. "I don't want to make a mistake though. I was all set to change it to Rosalie but I'm glad I didn't, because now I hate the name Rosalie. I may change it, or I may not, but I want to be sure."

When my father heard about this he said it was clear to him that Janine, or whatever her name was, must be a member of Mother's family, so it was no wonder that she kept turning down Willard's marriage proposals. "Doesn't want to marry her own third cousin," he said.

"That's the only thing," I told Louis. "Willard wants to get married, but Janine doesn't."

"Why not?" he said.

"I don't know why not."

"Maybe she doesn't want to get married till she knows for sure what her name is going to be—because, once Willard says 'I, Willard, take you, Janine . . .' that would be it, wouldn't it?"

My mother said no. "You marry a person," she said. "You don't marry a name. No, your father's right—Willard is too easygoing. Janine always has some silly reason why they shouldn't get married, and Willard just won't put his foot down. I don't know what will finally persuade her.'"

Louis and I thought we knew: three thousand dollars worth of flowers and food and limousines and bridal wardrobe, especially the bridal wardrobe.

Besides trying on all different names, Janine liked to try on all different clothes, and we never saw her in the same outfit twice. She said she had to look her best at all times because of her job at Kobacker's, where she sold ladies' dresses. "Besides," she said, "I get a discount, and it would be wasteful for me not to use it."

"I don't think they sell wedding dresses at Kobacker's," I told Louis, "and she probably doesn't have enough money to buy one somewhere else, because of using her discount. That may be one of the reasons she won't marry Willard."

Willard said he didn't think that was it. "I surely *hope* that's not it. No—Janine is just a very cautious person. Look how she is about her name. She's been trying out names ever since I've known her, which is six years. She doesn't want to make a big mistake—and I admire that." He sighed. "Of course, six years is a long time."

"I still think you ought to tell her about the

prize wedding," I said. "She might not want to waste it. You know how she is about her discount."

"Well . . ." Willard nodded. "There's that, all right."

Two days later Janine had set the wedding date, reserved a country club, located an eight-piece orchestra and gone off to Cincinnati to get fitted for a wedding dress.

We learned about all this from my mother, who was pleased for Willard but mystified by the arrangements. "I don't know what's the matter with her," she said. "Why, that country club's thirty miles away! What's wrong with the V.F.W. hall? And when your Aunt Rhoda called to say she'd make the wedding cake, the way she always does, Janine said she would take care of that because she wants a cake with a waterfall and continuous music. Rhoda said, 'Good luck.' I think she's crazy."

"Of course she's crazy," my father said. "Here's a grown woman who hasn't figured out what her name ought to be. Willard better think twice."

"Willard's had six years to think twice," Mother told him, "and all he can think is Janine."

It all seemed very romantic to me. "Just think, Louis," I said, "if you hadn't won your prize and given it to Willard, he'd still be waiting and thinking."

As it turned out, that had occurred to Willard

too, and it bothered him enough to discuss it with my mother.

"Of course, I know a nice wedding is important to a girl," he said, "especially a girl like Janine, who has to think about her appearance and all . . . and I don't really believe it was just the wedding that brought her around to say yes. You know, Janine doesn't make up her mind in a hurry."

"No," Mother said.

"I believe, though, that she'd about *decided* to make up her mind—and then, here came this wedding. And, naturally, she didn't want to see it go to waste. That's what she said. She said, 'Willard, we can't let this go to waste.' "

At this point, Mother realized that she must have missed something somewhere in the conversation, and that, in fact, it was not even the conversation she originally assumed it to be—a discussion about expenses, and the relative importance of certain details, such as musical wedding cakes—and wet ones, at that. She had planned to suggest that Willard put down, if not his foot, at least a toe or two, and rein Janine in a little bit. Now he seemed to be saying that Janine was doing the whole thing out of frugality.

". . . should think she'd be running out of ways to spend three thousand dollars . . ."

Mother didn't miss that. "Three thousand dollars! Willard, surely Janine doesn't have three

74

thousand dollars—*you* don't have three thousand dollars, do you?"

"I guess not!" Willard said. "Nowhere close."

"Then where's it coming from?"

"Why—from Louis," Willard said.

It had not occured to him that Louis's prize was a secret, nor had it occurred to Louis and me that it *should* be a secret.

Louis said that if anyone had asked, "Did you win a magazine contest?" he would have said yes; and if they had asked, "What did you win?" he would have said, A wedding . . . and if they had then asked, "What are you going to do with a wedding?" he would have said, Give it to Willard.

"But nobody ever asked," he told my father.

"But, Louis, why in God's name would we ask—out of the blue—if you'd won a magazine contest?" Once again, my father said, we were up the river without a canoe; and, as usual, the details were buried in fog. He turned on Willard. "Why didn't you say something about this?"

"I did," Willard said. "When Aunt Grace asked where the money was coming from, I said, 'From Louis.' "

"But Louis doesn't have three thousand dollars!"

"I know that!" It was interesting to hear Willard raise his voice, even a little bit, because he never had before. "It isn't Louis's money, it's Louis's prize."

"It is not Louis's prize! Louis is nine years old. This magazine isn't going to give Louis the prize, so he can't give it to you!"

Willard thought about that for a minute. "I believe you're right," he said.

"In the meantime," my father went on, "Janine has been out ordering dresses and flowers and cakes, to the tune of three thousand dollars. So she's either going to have to come up with the money or call off the dresses and the flowers and the cakes."

Willard shook his head. "Janine's not going to want to do that. Why, she doesn't even like it when people return things at the store because they've changed their minds. You know, Janine's slow to make up her mind, but when she does . . ."

"Now, Willard," Mother said. "Listen to me, because I'm all out of patience with Janine's cautious ways. You just tell her that she doesn't need to drag us all thirty miles to a country club to hear eight perfect strangers play fiddles . . . and she doesn't need to drape the church from stem to stern with orchids, which Mr. Herms the florist doesn't know where he's going to get them all, anyway. She doesn't need any limousine to ride two and a half blocks, either. She doesn't need any of those things . . . now, you just tell her so."

To everyone's surprise (including his own, I guess) that was just what Willard did.

He told Janine to cancel the reception and the orchestra and the orchids and the cake, and to find some dress closer to home.

He never did tell her what happened to Louis's prize.

"Don't know why I didn't," he told my mother. "That would have been the place to start. But it seemed like when I left here I was mostly worried, and by the time I got to Janine's I was mostly mad. And then, right off the bat, she told me we had to have a lot of white doves to fly around outside the church. *Had* to have them, she said. So I knew right then that this whole circus was a big mistake, and I just told her we weren't going to have any part of it."

He did give in about one thing, though. He told Janine that she could go ahead and get her wedding dress if she would give up forever all thoughts of changing her name, because he didn't want that hanging over him for the rest of his life—and Janine, astonished, perhaps, by the demonstration of strength and purpose, agreed to everything.

It all turned out so well that my father had a hard time getting Louis to see the error of his ways, and Mother was no help.

"If Louis hadn't won the wedding," she said, "they probably wouldn't be getting married."

"Exactly," my father said. "Is that a reason to get married?"

"No. That's why it's such a good thing that Louis didn't *really* win the wedding. Willard would always wonder if that was why Janine married him, and now he knows it isn't."

My father sighed. "Now, this is typical," he said. "Louis has done a foolish thing and caused everyone a lot of trouble, and you seem to be saying that we should congratulate him. But just because this turns out all right doesn't mean that he can go on doing foolish things. When Ralph left that baby on the bus, it turned out all right, but . . ."

"Well, it did and it didn't," Mother said. "We got him back, of course—but I don't know how much babies remember. Maybe somehow he always remembered that he got left on a bus and taken to Columbus, and it affected his personality. Maybe he's never had much get-up-and-go because that scared it out of him."

"Who?" my father said. "What are you talking about?"

"Why . . . Willard."

"Willard! Willard was the baby Ralph left on the bus?"

Of course this was big news to Louis and me, and we could hardly wait to go find out whether Willard did, in fact, remember the experience, because Louis always claimed *he* could remember being a baby and could remember that he didn't much like it.

My father was amazed. He made Mother tell him the whole story again, and when she was finished he said it seemed even worse now that he knew who the baby was.

He also said there was probably no way to keep Louis's wedding out of the family history—"Remember when Louis was nine years old and won the wedding?"—but he did hope there would be someone on hand to fill in the details.

Trn Rt at Chkn Frm

Until Mother's mysterious malaise, my father had always believed her to be somewhat disorganized in her thinking but perfectly sound of mind—and when, for a brief time, he had reason to doubt this, it affected his own common sense.

"I was too worried to think straight," he said—and in the absence of *his* common sense and straight thinking there was no one in charge of the store, so to speak, and misunderstandings multiplied.

At first Louis and I didn't even know Mother was supposed to be sick—but, of course, Mother didn't know it either.

"I just wish I had known," she said later. "I

would have gone to bed with a lot of magazines and all the Perry Mason mysteries and had some pleasure out of it."

My father said she didn't deserve to have any pleasure out of it, that she had put him through a terrible time of strain and worry.

"I didn't put you through anything," Mother said. "You put yourself through it, being so secretive. If you thought I'd gone crazy, why didn't you say so?"

That was, indeed, exactly what he thought; but it was not what he told Louis and me, out of respect for our tender years. He simply said that Mother wasn't feeling well: that she might seem nervous and edgy, and we should try hard not to upset her.

We knew what that meant, or thought we did, and immediately began to wonder whether the baby would be a boy or a girl, and—since we were always bone honest with each other—whether we would like it, whatever it was.

We thought it odd that no one gave us the straight dope on the matter, babies being commonplace around the neighborhood and their origins no longer any special mystery. But we didn't think it was any big secret . . . and so, unwittingly, we complicated the whole misunderstanding.

I said something about our new baby to Mother's sister Rhoda, who, having just been told that Mother was in a precarious mental state, immediately put two and two together and got six.

She decided that Mother, then thirty-nine years old, either was pregnant and didn't want to be, or wanted to be pregnant and wasn't—and, in whichever case, had retreated from reality.

Aunt Rhoda also thought it odd that my father had not given *her* all the facts, but put it down to a sense of delicacy, this being so personal a matter. She also decided that if my father, a wholly practical and forthright man, couldn't even bring himself to suggest the details of the situation, she shouldn't say anything to him about it and must simply bide her time, be available and await developments.

Mother, unaware of all this, thought it odd that Rhoda should suddenly start dropping in every other day for no good reason, but finally concluded that she was just lonely or bored or maybe feeling old before her time. So, while Aunt Rhoda was watching Mother for signs of pregnancy and/or mental collapse, Mother was watching Aunt Rhoda for signs of despondency about her fading youth.

"Come with me to Circleville to judge a flower show," Mother would say, thinking that was just what Rhoda needed.

"Isn't that a long way to go? I don't think all this travel is good for you; you look tired to me. Why not stay home and rest?" Aunt Rhoda would say, thinking that was just what Mother needed.

As a matter of fact, Mother thought it was a long way to go, too. She loved the flower shows and the sociability and the tea and cookies, but she didn't love getting there.

My father had again provided her with a car—for his own peace of mind, he said, lest in some emergency she find herself crashing through traffic with Aunt Mildred—but Mother still had little confidence in her driving skills, and no sense of direction at all, and continued to avoid any expedition which required her to drive very far or to figure out where she was going.

Still, when elected a judge by her garden club, Mother must have decided that the pleasure involved outweighed the perils. Once or twice a week, at the height of the flower show season, she would set out, clutching maps and instructions on how to get to the appointed place in Circleville or Athens or Wilmington, but even so, she was either lost or late most of the time until she stumbled on a way out of this continual dilemma.

While she was traveling down the highway one morning on her way to a distant flower show, a sudden gust of wind blew her vital information out the window, leaving her stranded; because, as she said, "If I get lost with a map in my hand, I would certainly get lost without one."

At that moment she noticed a station wagon

ahead of her on the road—loaded with green growing plants, driven by a lady in what looked like a pretty hat; and, having nothing to lose, she simply followed this car on the reasonable assumption that it was going to a flower show.

"And not only was it going to the show," she added triumphantly, "but that lady won first prize for her tuberous begonia. It wasn't a hat after all, it was a tuberous begonia."

Thereafter Mother spent less time studying her maps (which didn't seem to help much anyway) and more time studying the traffic around her, with surprising success. Time after time she was able to locate, identify and pursue some member of the local flower show crowd . . . and thus arrive at the right place, on time and unruffled. Sometimes the clues were obvious: many plants, ladies holding dried arrangements; sometimes more subtle: a horticultural society emblem in the window, a bumper sticker reading I Grow Gladiolas.

Of course, my father had no idea that this was going on. He knew that Mother liked flowers and was a judge of them, but he had no interest in such activities. If she enjoyed doing it, whatever it was, he was happy for her, and that was that . . . and Mother, knowing this, chose not to bore him with details.

He was very much surprised, therefore, while having lunch with a customer in a town some forty

84

miles from home, to look up and see Mother in conversation with the cashier of the restaurant— getting change for a dollar, as it happened, so she could use the phone in what was an emergency situation.

She had followed a car absolutely loaded with flowers and greenery all the way to its destination, which turned out to be a funeral home. She was not only distressed but somewhat indignant, because the driver of the car, a florist, had not used his delivery truck, in which case she would not have followed him in the first place.

My father excused himself to his customer and went to see what this was all about. Had anyone asked him that day about Mother's whereabouts he would probably have said, "Oh, Grace is at home—not much of a gadabout, you know," for so he believed.

"Well, this is a surprise," he said, and kissed her. "What are you doing in Fredonia?"

In Mother's reply lay the crux of the whole ensuing tangle . . . for what was she to say? That she had, by mistake, followed a car full of plants to a funeral home? That she was really supposed to be in Semperville, ten miles away? Most of all, that this was not a unique experience?

Various harmless fictions crossed her mind—she had come to visit a friend, to get the dining room chairs reglued, to buy something big and important on sale that very day in Fredonia—but Mother was no good at fictions, harmless or otherwise. An uneasy liar, she always fell apart two sentences into the lie.

However, it seemed to her that any answer involving the truth of this situation would surely lead to lengthy explanations, and might well produce some kind of public scene.

Hoping to avoid all this, she simply said, "I don't know," and immediately hurried back to greet the customer, to make polite small talk and to leave before my father could pin her down.

He said later that she seemed distracted, not herself, her eyes vague and troubled (all perfectly true, since she was then half an hour late for the flower show and had no idea how to get there). He was puzzled by her answer, but not alarmed . . . until the same thing happened several days later.

Mother had pursued what looked like a sure thing: an elderly Packard, gleaming clean and bearing three ladies in hats. They led her to a high school auditorium—a common flower show arena—and took from the back of their car three different flower arrangements, all of which turned out to be table decorations for a luncheon-lecture on Yugoslavian folk art.

Mother didn't know that, though; it looked to her like a flower show, and a very fancy and elegant one, which pleased her. She sat down at a table to make preliminary notes: *Good use of daisies in Number 7. Awkward larkspur in Number 10.* —and was served, and ate, a dainty appetizer of pineapple and cream cheese before she caught on.

Thus trapped—"I couldn't very well eat their food and then just get up and leave, could I?" she said—she stayed until the room was darkened for a slide presentation and then raced for a telephone to call, first, the flower show committee, and then Louis and me, to be sure we were all right.

As it happened, my father had stopped home between appointments, was already surprised to find Mother gone ("Not much of a gadabout"), and even more surprised to answer the telephone and learn that she was in Concord.

"What are you doing in Concord?" he asked.

Of course Mother was surprised too. She didn't expect my father to answer the phone and, caught unawares, had no ready reply. Once again, she had followed a strange car to an unknown destination, felt a little foolish and didn't want to go into it over the phone or, indeed, at all. No doubt she reasoned that what worked before would work again and said, "I don't know—but I'm coming straight home to fix the fish."

The idea here, a spur-of-the-moment notion, was to get his mind off one thing (her whereabouts) and onto something else (supper); and she thought the fish would do it, fish being his favorite meal.

It had no such effect. Had she gone to Concord to buy fish? he wondered. That made no sense, with a perfectly good fish market not ten minutes away. And even supposing there were better fish, or cheaper fish, or bigger fish in Concord, why hadn't she said so?

Louis and I were not only no help to him, but added fuel to the fire.

"When you left for school this morning," he asked us, "did your mother say she would be gone for the day?"

We said no.

"Well, was she dressed to go out?"

"I don't think so," Louis said. "She was in the kitchen, making meat loaf."

"For supper?"

He shrugged. "I guess so."

The meat loaf proved to be in the refrigerator with strips of bacon across the top of it, clearly ready for the oven—and in light of this, Mother's telephone conversation seemed not just strange and disjointed, but downright loony.

As my father later said, it was now clear to him that from time to time—indeed, *frequently*— something came over Mother; she would get in the car and drive somewhere (Fredonia, Concord) and then come to her senses and, exactly as she had told him, not know why she was wherever she was. The reference to fish struck him as an attempt on her part to hang onto reality: home, family, routine household matters.

It was at this point that he told Louis and me that Mother was not well, for he pictured a rocky time ahead and wanted to prepare us. He also planned to sit down quietly with Mother and try to talk about it—but then Mother came home with an enormous fish, complete with head and tail, opened the refrigerator and said, "Why, here's a meat loaf!"

She had forgotten about the meat loaf in all the confusion of the day, but her tone and choice of words suggested that she had never known anything about it in the first place. This convinced my father that she was in worse shape than he thought and needed more help than he could provide.

From here on, events marched off in all directions.

My father consulted Dr. Hildebrand, who said that Mother was the last person alive he would expect to go off her rocker; that if she had, it was out of his line; but that he would set up an appointment with her for a regular checkup and see what he could conclude.

He subsequently reported that Mother appeared

to him to be perfectly sane, though overconcerned about her sister Rhoda, and that to satisfy Mother, he had set up an appointment for Rhoda.

Following that consultation he told my father that if anyone had a problem it was Rhoda. "She's got pregnancy on the brain," he said. "Doesn't want to talk about diet and blood pressure. Wants to talk about babies; who has 'em, who wants 'em. I don't know"—he shook his head—"have to keep an eye on her."

Still, my father was not encouraged. Mother appeared to him to be perfectly sane, too, most of the time—but what about her amnesia jaunts to Fredonia and Concord? What about the meat loaf and the fish?

Meanwhile Louis and I were still waiting to be told about the baby, and Aunt Rhoda continued to come and go, waiting for Mother to break down and reveal whatever was troubling her and making her do the strange things my father said she did, and Mother went right on scrambling around the countryside from one flower show to another.

After the luncheon-lecture incident she was extremely cautious about following cars; but, as she later said, this system had worked for her more times than it hadn't. . . . When she next found herself heading into strange country with sketchy directions (*Trn rt at chkn frm; tke scd rt Briley?*

Borly?) she looked around for something likely . . . and found it, in a car whose rear window was literally abloom with pink and white blossoms.

She couldn't see the driver or the passengers, but neither had she seen anything along the road that might be a "chkn frm" and time was ticking by; so when this car turned off the highway she followed it.

The first thing that met her eye was a large billboard advertising Brown-Broast Broilers, which she took to be the Briley or Borly of her directions; and so she proceeded, confident and pleased with herself, until the flowery car stopped in front of the bank, and out stepped my father.

She had already pulled in behind him and there was no escape; but at least, as she said, this time the shoe was on the other foot. What was he doing in somebody else's car full of flowers? she demanded. And what was he doing here in Albion?

First of all, my father told her (gently, he later insisted), they weren't in Albion, but in Conneaut; he was here to make a business call; he was driving George Colgate's car because George asked him to; the flowers were all petunia plants to be delivered to George Colgate's mother-in-law, who lived in Conneaut.

"That is the craziest tale I ever heard!" Mother told him. She was, once again, upset with herself; exasperated with a driver who had led her astray; astonished that that driver should be my father; sick and tired of being late to flower shows; and fed up with the whole thing. "I'm supposed to be in Albion this very minute, judging a flower show. But because I followed you, I'm a long way from there."

"But why did you follow me?" my father asked.

"I thought you were going to the flower show."

"Why would I be going to a flower show, for God's sake?"

"Well, I didn't know it was *you*!"

And so it all came out—right there in front of the Citizens' Bank of Conneaut, before what my father called a cast of thousands.

"Let me try to understand this," he said. "Do you mean to tell me that for weeks you have been following just any old car, hoping it will lead you to where you want to go?"

"Not just any old car!" Mother said. "Do you think I'm crazy?"

Since that was exactly what he had thought, he said so, in the heat of the moment . . . and so all *that* came out—the consultation with Dr. Hildebrand; Rhoda's reason for being underfoot all the time; even the cautions to Louis and me— and it made Mother so furious that she got back in her car, slammed the door and drove away in a screech of tires.

By evening, though, they had both simmered down. They began to see the humor of the situation and produced appropriate peace offerings: My father brought a pot of the petunias home and set it in the middle of the table, like a flower show exhibit, and Mother presented him with a large baked haddock for dinner. They even became a little slaphappy, recalling to each other significant steps along the way: "You kept saying, I don't know why I'm here." "I just forgot about the meat loaf." Louis and I, encouraged by the convivial atmosphere, picked this time to say that we knew all about the baby, were very happy about it, and wanted to know when it was due.

My father, recalling his conversation with Dr. Hildebrand, instantly connected "baby" with Aunt Rhoda, assumed that Mother knew all about it and said, "I don't know. Grace, when is the baby due?"

Mother said, "Baby? What baby?" and my father said, "Why, Rhoda's baby"—which was, of course a big surprise to Louis and me.

Mother, though a little miffed that she was last in line to know this news, was overjoyed at the prospect of a new baby in the family. The very next day she dragged the crib and the buggy and the playpen out of the attic and hauled everything over to Aunt Rhoda, who, though fearful that Mother had finally slipped over the brink, nevertheless declared categorically that she, Rhoda, wasn't going to have any baby.

"Oh, yes, you are too," Mother said happily, hugging her. "And I should have guessed, because I was that very same way with Louis—nervous and a little blue, not quite myself, wondering whether I was too old . . ."

"What very same way?" Rhoda bristled. "I'm not nervous or blue and you're the one who's not quite herself!"

Mother said that was just a little misunderstanding, and she didn't want to talk about it, she'd rather talk about the baby.

"There *is* no baby!" Rhoda insisted.

"Then why did you say there was?" It suddenly occurred to Mother that she had been right all along about Rhoda, and she immediately adjusted her voice and manner to one of solicitous concern, saying things like "Don't get all excited" and "If you don't want to talk about it, we won't talk about it."

"Now, just stop that," Rhoda said. "I'm not crazy—you're the one who's supposed to be crazy!"

At this point a neighbor, attracted by the noise, stuck her head out a window, saw the pile of baby equipment and caught disjointed, but arresting, scraps of the conversation. And of course this news, such as it was—either my mother or Aunt Rhoda or both were either pregnant or crazy or both—spread through the neighborhood with the speed and spark of electricity and kept everyone alert and interested for a long time.

Mother refused to be embarrassed. She said it really didn't have anything to do with her . . . that she had simply been the calm center around which all the high winds blew. Aunt Rhoda was pretty mad, but eventually she cooled off too. My father said it was a good lesson for Louis and me.

"What did you learn from all this?" he asked.

I hadn't really learned anything except that Mother wasn't crazy, which had never occurred to me in the first place, but I knew that wasn't the right answer.

"Louis?" My father looked at him. "What do you have to say?"

Louis was ready. "Oh, what a tangled web we weave . . ." he said.

My father was absolutely delighted, but I was pretty sure that Louis didn't know what he was talking about, and I was right.

"What did I say?" he asked me later. "Dad loved it."

"It was exactly right," I told him. "It meant that if you tell lies, or don't tell the truth, or make things up, you'll get in a big mess. That was the lesson."

He frowned. "What about the other one?"

"There wasn't any other lesson, Louis."

"Sure, there was."

I could see that he meant it, that in all the confusion he had found some scrap of wisdom.

"If you're lost," he said, "find someone who isn't, and follow them."

The Adoption of Albert

There were so many children in our neighborhood that my mother was never surprised to find unfamiliar ones in the house, or in the backyard, or in my room, or in Louis's room.

"Well, who's this?" she would say, and she would then go on to connect that child with whatever house or family he belonged to.

But when Louis showed up with his new friend Albert, Mother had other things on her mind: the family reunion, which was two days away; the distant cousin who would be staying at our house; most of all, my Aunt Rhoda's famous Family Reunion cake, which, in Aunt Rhoda's absence, Mother felt obliged to provide.

Aunt Rhoda's absence, and the reason for it, were both first-time events: She had never before missed a family reunion, and neither she nor anyone else had ever before been called into court to testify about anything. Aunt Rhoda was to testify about an automobile accident she had witnessed— the only automobile accident in local memory, my father said, that did not involve Aunt Mildred.

All in all, it was a complicated time for Mother— cake, cousins, company—and when Louis appeared at the kitchen door and said, "This is Albert," she was too distracted to ask her usual questions.

Nor did she ask them at suppertime. By then she was up to her elbows in cake batter and left the three of us to eat alone with my father, who also didn't know Albert, but assumed that everyone else did.

I didn't know Albert either, but there was no reason why I should. He was Louis's friend, he was Louis's age, he even looked a lot like Louis—small and quiet and solemn—and it didn't occur to me to find out any more about him. I did ask, "Where do you live, Albert?"; and when he said, "Here," I just thought he meant here in the neighborhood instead of someplace else.

Mother thought the same thing. "Where does that little boy live?" she asked me the next morning, and I said, "Here," and she said, "I wonder which house?"

Albert had spent the night, and there was a note propped against the cereal box: *Albert and I have gone to dig worms.*

Louis had been collecting worms all summer and measuring them to see how long a worm got to be before it died. "I think that's what kills them," he said. "I think they die of length."

So far his longest worm was between four inches and four and a half inches. All his worms were between one size and another because they wouldn't hold still. "It's really hard," he said. "I have to stretch them out and measure them at the same time, and if I'm not careful they come apart."

"Oh, Louis," I said, "that's awful! What do you do then?"

He shrugged. "I bury the pieces. What else can I do?"

Of course, most kids wouldn't even do that, but Louis was neater than most kids.

It was late afternoon when he and Albert came back, and they had big news. They also had two coffee cans full of worm parts.

"I thought you buried them," I said.

"I didn't have to! Albert says . . . Albert

says . . ." I had never seen Louis so pleased and excited. "Tell her what you said."

"It doesn't kill them," Albert said. "The tail ends grow new heads, and the head ends grow new tails."

I looked in the coffee cans, but I couldn't tell the difference between head and tails. Louis said he couldn't tell the difference either. "But it doesn't matter," he said, "because the worms can. *They* know. We're going to keep them, and watch them grow, and measure them . . . and maybe name them."

"They're no trouble," Albert said. "They just eat dirt. We've got some." He held up another coffee can.

They took all three coffee cans up to Louis's room, and this worried me a lot because I knew I would have to sleep in Louis's room when everybody came for the family reunion.

My father said he was always astonished that there was anybody left to *come* to the family reunion. "Your whole family is already here," he told Mother, "living around the corner, or three streets away, or on the other side of town."

"Not everybody," Mother said. "There's Virginia and Evelyn and Clyde . . ." She reeled off the names—cousins, mostly, whom we knew only from Christmas cards, and from their annual appearance at the reunion.

100

Some, in fact, had already appeared and were upstairs unpacking their suitcases. Mother, who was busy catching up on their news and shuffling food around in the refrigerator and getting out all the dishes and silverware, either didn't realize that Albert was still with us or just didn't remember that she had ever seen him in the first place.

My father had gone off to borrow picnic tables for the next day, and since I didn't want to sit around and watch worms grow, I went next door to play with my friend Maxine Slocum and forgot all about Albert.

That night when I took my sleeping bag into Louis's room, he was already asleep in a mound of bedclothes . . . and there was another mound of bedclothes beside him.

"Louis." I shook him awake. "Who is that?"

"It's Albert," he said.

"Why doesn't he go home?"

Louis looked surprised. "He *is* home. He's going to live here now. Remember? He told you. . . . Don't worry, Mary Elizabeth," he added. "You'll like Albert."

"I already like Albert," I said, "but I don't think he can live here. I think he has to live with his parents."

"He doesn't want to," Louis said. "He even told

them so. He told them, 'I don't want to live with you anymore,' and they said, 'All right, Albert, you just go and live someplace else.' "

I had never heard of such a thing, except when my friend Wanda McCall baptized the hamsters with her mother's French perfume. The house smelled wonderful, but all the hamsters got sick and so did Mrs. McCall, and Mr. McCall gave Wanda two dollars and told her to get lost. But he didn't mean forever.

Neither had Albert's parents, I decided. They would probably call tomorrow and tell him to come home.

"Louis." I shook him again. "Where are the worms?"

"They aren't worms yet," he reminded me. "The cans are in the closet."

I didn't think either half of a worm could go very far, but I put my sleeping bag on the other side of the room anyway, just in case.

When I woke up the next morning Louis and Albert were gone, but they had made the bed and folded up their clothes and left a note that said, *We'll be back for the picnic. Please don't move the worms.* There was a P.S.: *Tell the lady cousin in the purple underwear that I'm sorry. I didn't know she was in there.* Then there was another P.S.: *It was really Albert, but pretend it was me and tell her I'm sorry. Or if you don't want to, just find out who she is and I'll tell her.*

That was nice of Louis, I thought, but I really didn't want to ask around about everyone's underwear.

"I guess not," Louis said later. "It's okay . . . Albert felt bad about it, that's all."

"Where is Albert?" I asked.

"Over there." Louis pointed to where Mother's brother Frank was taking pictures with his new Polaroid camera.

"You'll have to get closer together," we heard him say, "and put Clyde's boy in front of you, Blanche."

"Who is Clyde's boy?" Louis asked me.

"I think it's Albert," I said. "He's the only boy there."

I was right. "Looks just *like* Clyde," we heard Aunt Blanche say.

I thought Albert looked a little worried, but Louis said he was just worried about the worms. "We're going to move them someplace else," he said. "Albert thinks they might get out and crawl around—especially the head parts, Albert said, because they could see where they were going."

That made me shiver, so I hoped they would put them somewhere up high.

By then Aunt Rhoda had arrived, to everyone's

surprise. She never did get to testify, she said, because "the litigants" had to go to the police station to look at "mug shots" and "supply ID's." Aunt Rhoda had picked up a whole new vocabulary.

"Mug shots?" my father said. "ID's? Now, what does that mean? This was a traffic accident, not a holdup."

"I don't know," Mother told him. "Rhoda just said they had to study mug shots of children."

"There is no such thing as mug shots of children. Mug shots are of criminals. Rhoda's got it all wrong." He went to question Aunt Rhoda further and stumbled into the one event he always tried to avoid: the big family photograph, with everyone in it.

Uncle Frank had set up a different camera and lined everybody up, but he was missing some people: my parents, Aunt Mildred . . . "And Louis," he said. "And Clyde's boy. Clyde, where's your boy?"

Clyde looked surprised. "He's in the Army."

"I mean the little one."

"Looks just like you," Aunt Blanche put in.

"He doesn't look one bit like me," Clyde said. "He looks like his mother."

"No," Aunt Blanche said stubbornly. "He looks like you."

Clyde was stubborn too. "How do you know

what he looks like, Blanche? You haven't seen him in six years!"

"I saw him fifteen minutes ago!"

"Who?" my father said, arriving on the scene with Mother.

"They're talking about Albert," I said. "Louis's friend Albert."

"Albert!" Mother looked amazed. "Is that little boy here again?"

"He never left," I said.

So I was sent to get Albert, and find out where he lived, while Mother explained to everybody who he was (which was hard, because she didn't *know* who he was), and my father pressed Aunt Rhoda for more details about her experiences in court—fearful, he later said, that she had wandered into the wrong courtroom and the wrong trial, and was now mixed up with a bunch of criminals.

I found Louis crawling around the floor of his room. "We dropped some of a worm," he said, "but only one, and I'll find it. We took the rest of them out of the closet."

"Mother wants to know where Albert lives," I told him.

"You mean . . . besides here?" Louis was being stubborn too, just like Aunt Blanche and Clyde. "I don't know."

"Well, what's Albert's name?"

105

"You mean . . . besides Albert? I'll ask him."

"But, Louis—don't you know?"

"I only met him day before yesterday," Louis said. "He was sitting on the curb outside the model-airplane store, after his parents told him to go live someplace else. He didn't know anyplace else, so I told him he could live here. And after that, all we talked about was worms."

Albert didn't know where he lived either. "I can't remember," he said. "We haven't lived there long enough for me to remember. I think it's the name of a tree."

Albert was right. He lived on Catalpa Street, and his name was Henderson. But it was Aunt Rhoda, of all people, who supplied the information, while Louis and Albert were upstairs looking for the missing worm.

Aunt Rhoda recognized Albert in the Polaroid picture because, when she witnessed the automobile accident, she had also witnessed Albert in one of the cars with his parents—the very same people, she said, who were at this moment examining mug shots at the police station.

"Isn't it a small world!" Aunt Rhoda said . . . and everyone agreed, except my father.

He had assumed, all along, that Mother knew who Albert was and knew where Albert came from. "And I suppose," he said, "that Albert is staying with us now because his parents have to be in court—but didn't the Hendersons mention *why* they had to be in court?"

"I don't know the Hendersons," Mother said.

"Well, did Albert . . ."

"I don't know Albert either." Mother was getting testy under all this cross-examination. "Obviously, Louis said it would be all right for Albert to stay here—and it *is* all right," she said. "Those poor people have enough trouble. That's the least we can do for them."

In the meantime Louis and Albert came downstairs—"We found the worm," Louis assured me—went to get more fried chicken and potato salad, and ran into Aunt Rhoda, who said she was certainly surprised to see Albert again and to see him *here.*

"I live here," Albert said.

"Oh, no," Aunt Rhoda laughed. "You live on Catalpa Street."

"Not anymore," Albert said.

Of course Aunt Rhoda reported this to Mother, who was by then completely mystified about Albert, and pretty fed up with all the sketchy bits and pieces of news about him. She left Aunt Rhoda to cut the Family Reunion cake and make the coffee, and went off to find Louis. My father, having also concluded that Louis was the key to it all, had done the same thing.

Between them, they quickly figured out that

Louis did not know the Hendersons and that he barely knew Albert . . . and that Albert had left home and was prepared to live with us forever.

My father called the police station, where the Hendersons were indeed studying pictures of missing children and supplying information about their own missing child . . . and in no time they arrived at our house and were reunited with Albert.

This was exactly the kind of happy ending my mother loved best—even Albert seemed happy to be back with his family.

"Well, now he has a friend," Mrs. Henderson said, beaming at Louis. "That was the trouble. He didn't know anyone, didn't have anyone to play with or talk to. Thank goodness for you, Louis!"

The Hendersons obviously saw Louis as the hero of it all, which exasperated my father.

"I don't know why you're so grumpy," Mother said. "Just suppose Louis hadn't come along and found Albert outside the airplane store—then what?"

"Then Albert would have gone home where he belonged," my father said, "and none of this would have happened."

"Exactly!" Mother said. "And he would still be a lonely, unhappy little boy . . . way over there on Catalpa Street."

She invited the Hendersons to stay for cake and coffee, and to meet all the relatives. Aunt Rhoda said she couldn't meet them officially, or talk to them, because of being a witness, but she waved to them from the back porch, and Mrs. Henderson waved back and called to her, "Your cake recipe is wonderful!"

"Have some coffee," Mother said. "It's Rhoda's coffee, too."

Aunt Rhoda said later that it was pretty silly to call it *her* coffee just because she'd made it, and she also said that she didn't feel one bit responsible for what had happened.

"In my house," she said, "if a can says coffee, that's what's in it, and it wouldn't occur to me to look."

Mother said, in all fairness, it wouldn't occur to her to look either. . . . "Except, of course, I don't keep my coffee on that high shelf, so I might have looked."

My father, who had been the first one to sip the coffee—and, therefore, the *only* one to sip the coffee—said he wished *someone* had looked.

"Was it the can full of dirt?" I asked Louis, and he shook his head no.

"Oh, I'm sorry, Louis," I said, "but you and Albert can get some more worms."

"And it was only the tail ends, anyway," Albert said . . . although I hadn't really wanted to know that.

Marcella and Me

Until he was seven years old, Louis thought he would eventually catch up with me, and we would be the same age.

"Then what?" I asked. "Would we be the same age forever?"

"Wouldn't you like to?" Louis said. "We could be seventeen."

Like most of Louis's ideas, this one was wonderful but weird. "Sure I'd like to, Louis," I said, "but it won't work. I'm always going to be older than you are. I'll be seventeen before you are and then I'll have to go on and be eighteen, and you will, too. We can't do anything about it."

He was looking stubborn, so I said, "Believe me, Louis. It's like being *who* you are. We can't do anything about that either."

"I don't want to do anything about that," he said. "So far, I *like* that, don't you?"

Louis never changed his mind about being who he was, but I had to change my mind in a hurry when Aunt Rhoda joined the local Historical Society and began to trace the family's background.

Until then, no one even knew there *was* a local Historical Society, and my father said he would like to keep it that way. "You have enough family around right now," he told Mother, "without Rhoda digging up all the ones who *used* to be around."

Louis's eyes got wide. "She's going to dig them up?" he said. "Can you do that?"

"Not the actual people," Mother told him. "She's going to look up everyone's records: births and deaths and marriages, things like that. I think it's wonderful of Rhoda to do this. Now you and Mary Elizabeth will know who all your ancestors were, right back to the beginning."

Louis thought the beginning would be George Washington, but my father said not to count on it. He also said that Aunt Rhoda might get some surprises.

The first surprise turned out to be the biggest.

"Rhoda has found a whole new person in the family," Mother reported. "Someone we never knew

111

anything about." She had no further details, because, she said, Rhoda was very mysterious about the whole thing and wanted to tell us in person. But when Aunt Rhoda arrived that evening she refused to tell anybody anything until Louis and I left the room.

"But it's their family too," Mother said, and Aunt Rhoda raised her eyebrows and nodded her head up and down very fast.

We left the room, but as soon as Aunt Rhoda passed on her news my father made so much noise about it that we heard everything anyway, so we went back in.

"Our baby!?!" we heard him say, his voice rising. "What baby? We don't have any more babies, you know that. What's wrong with you, Rhoda?"

Aunt Rhoda said there wasn't anything wrong with her now, but she had nearly passed out from shock when she found this birth certificate. " 'Marcella Lawson,' " she read aloud. " 'Parents, Fred and Grace Lawson.' "

Louis poked me. "That's us," he said, "but who's Marcella? Do we have a sister? Where is she?"

"I don't know," I said. Where, indeed? Hidden away someplace? Given away to somebody?

"It must be some other Fred and Grace Lawson," Mother suggested, but Aunt Rhoda said that would be pretty unusual in such a small town; and, anyway, they weren't in the phone book.

"Maybe they moved away," my father said. He looked at the birth certificate. "This was eleven years ago . . . eleven years next month. They had this baby, and then they moved away."

"What day next month?" Mother looked at the birth certificate too. "Well, what do you know about that? We must have been in the hospital together, because that's Mary Elizabeth's birthday, and she'll be eleven."

Louis poked me again. "You're twins," he said.

"And what's more," Mother went on, "we have a second cousin named Marcella—Marcella Potter."

"But it couldn't be her," Aunt Rhoda said. "She lives way out in Denver, Colorado."

My father stared at both of them. "Of course it's not her! She doesn't have anything to do with this."

"I know she doesn't," Mother said, "but it *is* a coincidence, because she's the only Marcella in the family. She told me that once, in a letter, and she said why didn't I name a baby after her, and then there'd be another Marcella."

There was a long silence.

"Well, I didn't *do* it!" Mother said, but she didn't sound too sure, and there was another long silence, while everybody looked at the birth certificate, and at Mother, and at me.

"Apparently that's just what you did," my father

said finally. "You must have been half asleep from the anesthetic, and they came and said, 'What's this baby's name?' and you said, 'The baby's name is Marcella.' "

At first mother refused to believe that she had done such a thing, and then she refused to believe that it made any difference anyway. . . . "Everybody knows who Mary Elizabeth is."

My father said that wasn't the point. "Someday, somewhere, Mary Elizabeth is going to have to produce a birth certificate to prove that she is who she says she is, and *this* birth certificate"—he waved it in the air—"just proves that she isn't."

I must have looked worried, because Louis said, "Just tell them you don't have one. Say it got burned up in a fire."

That sounded good to me, but I was pretty sure it wouldn't satisfy the authorities, and in the meantime . . . who *was* I?

"I think you have to be Marcella," Louis said. "I think it's the law."

I thought so too. We were both scared of the law and anxious not to break it, and we were both impressed by the birth certificate, which looked too important to ignore.

I didn't get much chance to be Marcella, though, because Mother was right about one thing—everybody already knew who I was. What I needed was a lot of perfect strangers who would ask, "What is your name, little girl?" so I could say "Marcella Lawson" over and over again, till it sounded natural.

"You should ride the bus to Chillicothe and get lost," Louis said. "When you're lost, everyone wants to know who you are, and you have to say your name about a million times."

This was a good idea, but I didn't have any money to ride the bus to Chillicothe. Mother had promised us a nickel apiece for every Japanese beetle we picked off her rosebushes; but I couldn't bear to touch them and Louis couldn't bear to drop them into the can of kerosene, so between us we only captured four and only collected twenty cents. Chillicothe was out.

Whenever Louis thought about it, *he* would call me Marcella; but he didn't think about it very often, and when he did, I never remembered who he was talking to.

Neither did anyone else. My father never said, "Good for you, Louis. She'd better get used to Marcella, because that's going to be her name forever." My mother didn't call up all her friends and relations to tell them who I was now, and when the new Avon lady said, "Is this your daughter, Mrs. Lawson?" Mother said, "Yes, this is my daughter, Mary Elizabeth."

This was very puzzling to Louis and me, but, as we eventually learned, my father had taken the birth certificate back to the Town Clerk right away, explained the situation, had it corrected and put the whole thing out of his mind—while Mother had managed to convince herself that it was all somebody's else foolish mistake—the hospital, the town clerk, maybe even Aunt Rhoda—and put the whole thing out of her mind, too. Consequently, there was no one to help me remember who I was except Louis, who was willing but unreliable.

"Listen, Louis," I said finally, "this is too complicated. I'm just going to be Mary Elizabeth."

Louis frowned and began to shake his head, and I knew he was thinking about the birth certificate, with its big official seal and all the signatures that said WITNESS in fancy writing, so I said, "I know my *real* name is Marcella, and I have to be Marcella if I do anything that's legal. But I won't have to do anything legal till I'm all grown up . . . except say the pledge of allegiance, and you don't have to say your name for that." I knew that Louis *did* say his name: "I, Louis, pledge allegiance . . ."; but that was just his own idea.

Like Mother, I put the whole thing out of my mind, too; and when, a few days later, a package arrived for my father—"Have to sign for it," the delivery man said. "Insured freight, special delivery—sign right there"—I signed the only name I'd lived with for eleven years.

116

"Okay, that makes it legal," the man said. "It's your responsibility." He looked at my signature. " 'Mary Elizabeth Lawson'—right?" And he was gone before I could do anything.

"But what *could* I do?" I asked Louis. "I couldn't say, 'Wait a minute, that's not my real name.' He would have taken away the package . . . and, Louis, look at the package."

It was a big, long, heavy package, plastered all over with *SPECIAL DELIVERY* stickers, and *THIS END UP* stickers. It looked important and expensive—and most of all, legal.

My father was delighted. He had been waiting for it, he said, and he turned to my mother with a big smile on his face. "It's for you," he said. "It's just what you want."

Mother looked puzzled. "It can't be. It isn't big enough."

"It's the biggest size they make."

"The biggest refrigerator?"

My father stared. "It isn't a *refrigerator*! I didn't know you wanted a refrigerator."

Actually, Mother had not yet mentioned that she wanted a refrigerator, and she had been briefly (*very* briefly) surprised and pleased that he would have guessed this. She was also sorry to have spoiled his pleasure about the unexpected present, and she prepared herself to be crazy about it, whatever it was.

117

It was a big, round, ugly lamp on top of a long straight pole, and Mother said immediately, "Oh, you're right. I just love it. Where will we put it?"

"You don't even know what it is yet," my father said, "but you *will* love it. It goes outside. It's a Beetle Eater."

He set it in the yard beside Mother's rosebushes and plugged it in, while we all watched and waited.

Slowly the lamp began to revolve and to glow with a dark-orange light and to make a high, thin, screechy noise . . . and then, before our very eyes, Japanese beetles, by twos and threes, whirred away from the rosebushes and into the Beetle Eater and killed themselves.

It worked perfectly—the next morning there were four inches of dead beetles piled up inside the lamp—but Mother said she couldn't stand it.

"You can't stand the noise?" my father said. "The orange light bothers you? . . . What?"

"It's the beetles," Mother said. "All those dead beetles."

"But you drop them into kerosene!"

"It's not the same thing," Mother said. "If you're a beetle, you have to expect that."

This must have sounded as crazy to Mother as it did to the rest of us, because she went on, "I just mean, that's what happens to beetles. In a way, it's natural. But it's not natural to lure them into an orange lamp and burn them crispy."

She refused to change her mind, and my father said he wasn't going to spend thirty-four dollars and ninety-five cents for a Beetle Eater if we weren't going to let it eat beetles. "I'll send it back," he said. "I still have the receipt."

Louis and I looked at each other. I had signed the receipt, with my illegal name.

"You can't let him send it back," Louis said. "They'll come after you. Like Dad said, you'll have to prove who you are, and you can't."

"Louis," I said, "I'm only eleven years old. What can they do to me?"

"They can make you pay for the Beetle Eater."

"But we've already got the Beetle Eater."

"Not if Dad sends it back," he said.

"Of course I'm going to send it back," my father told me. "That's a lot of money. Thirty-four dollars and ninety-five cents is worth a fight." I must have looked alarmed, because he went on. "Well, they won't *want* to take it back. I can't very well say it didn't work, and I refuse to say that your mother feels sorry for the beetles. I'm just going to have to return it and say, here it is. And they won't like that. So"—he picked up his newspaper—"there'll be a fight about it."

This was the worst news yet. I pictured somebody pounding on a table and yelling, "Get hold of whoever signed for it!"; so I said the first thing that came to mind.

119

"Please don't send it back. Give it to me—for my birthday."

My father stared at me. "Why?"

I couldn't think of any reason why I would want a Beetle Eater: I didn't like beetles, dead or alive; I didn't like loud screechy noises; and I'd already said the orange light hurt my eyes. "I just want it. Please. You don't have to give me anything else."

I suppose my father, however bewildered by my request, saw in this an opportunity to avoid both a fight with the Beetle Eater company and a struggle with packing crates and wrapping paper—and Mother, despite her objections to *this* contraption, understood that people do, often, simply want an unlikely thing for no good reason except that they want it. She had once wanted, had bought and then stuck away in the attic a very large framed picture of dogs playing poker—and whenever she cleaned the attic she would say, of this picture, "I don't know why I wanted it so much. I just did."

Luckily, no one held me to my bargain, and I did get some other presents, including a package addressed, mysteriously, to *Grace Lawson and Daughter*.

"I don't know what it is," Mother said, "and I can't even read the postmark. But it does say daughter, and it's your birthday, so you open it."

It was a baby bonnet and a pair of pink booties

120

and the card said, *For my namesake.* It was signed *Cousin Marcella.*

When confronted with this evidence, Aunt Rhoda admitted that she had, in fact, mentioned Mother's mistake to Cousin Marcella Potter.

"I wrote to her for some information about the family background, and then I just said, *P.S. Did you know that Grace named a baby after you, by accident? I think* I said, by accident." She looked at the booties. "Obviously she got it all wrong."

I wondered whether I would have to write Cousin Marcella a thank-you letter, and what I would say in it. We weren't supposed to just say, *Thank you for the present.* We were supposed to say something *about* the present, and I didn't know what to say about the pink booties.

"Nothing," my father said. "You're off the hook. This woman thinks you're a new baby. And anyway," he added, "she sent the booties to her namesake, but she hasn't got one, because I had your birth certificate changed."

I was very relieved to hear this, because it felt peculiar to be somebody else, even secretly. As far as I was concerned, Marcella *was* somebody else (maybe somebody who could recite all fifty states, and do long division without a mistake and tap-dance) but even so, like Louis, I was satisfied to be me. I was sorry, though, that I had pleaded for the Beetle Eater instead of something equally ex-

121

pensive and more desirable, like my own telephone.

I assumed that the Beetle Eater would end up
in the attic, along with the bonnet and the booties
and the dog picture, but Louis and his friend Albert plugged it in one night after beetle season was
over; and in the still, clear night air, it caused a
sensation in the neighborhood. Two people called
the newspaper to report a strange orange light and
a weird unearthly sound in our backyard, and the
next day there was an article on the front page:
OUTER SPACE ALIEN?
VISITS LOCAL FAMILY.

For two or three days there was a steady stream
of cars driving past our house, and a parade of kids
perfectly willing to pay a dime to see the outer
space alien perform . . . and Louis and I made
$4.60 before the orange light burned out and the
noise died down and the first snow fell on the
Beetle Eater.

Vergil, the Laid-back Dog

Most of Mother's relatives had animals of one kind or another, and most of the animals, according to my father, were as strange as the people they belonged to.

"I don't know," he often said, "whether they actively seek out screwy dogs and cats, or whether the dogs and cats just turn screwy after a while." He included our cat Leroy in this overall opinion, although by then Leroy was gone. He/she had produced four kittens and immediately took off for greener pastures, abandoning both us and the kittens, which my father said was completely unnatural behavior, and proved his point.

Actually there were any number of perfectly ordinary pets in the family—faithful nondescript dogs, companionable cats—but, just as good news is less dramatic than bad news and therefore less publicized, these humdrum animals were never the ones my father heard about, and the ones he *did* hear about left him forever cool to the idea of having one of his own.

Mother knew this; but, as she later said, having a dog was one thing, and having a dog come to visit for a few days was something else. So when her cousin Lloyd Otway deposited his dog Vergil on our doorstep, Mother didn't think twice about offering to keep Vergil while Lloyd went off to Milwaukee, Wisconsin, to acquire a wife.

My father said he could understand that Lloyd might find the pickings slim and overfamiliar right here at home, "—but why take off for Milwaukee?"

"Because that's where Pauline lives," Mother said. "Pauline Swavel. That's where she went back to after she and Lloyd met and fell in love. Oh, Fred, you remember Pauline!"

Obviously he didn't; but in view of the romantic circumstances involving Lloyd and Pauline Swavel, I did; and I remembered, too, that my father had been out of town that day.

"That's right, he was," Mother said. "He was in Columbus. You were in Columbus that day, at your state convention. I know I told you about it, but you probably didn't hear me, or else you didn't listen."

"That *day?!?*" My father stared at her. "Lloyd and this Pauline met and fell in love in one day?"

"Yes," Mother said—and this was, indeed, the case: a one-day, whirlwind, love-at-first-sight affair, attended by the usual monkey puzzle of mistakes and coincidences.

Pauline Swavel, while driving through town on her way from West Virginia, was run into by Aunt Mildred, who had been distracted by the unexpected appearance in her car of Lloyd's dog Vergil.

"All of a sudden, there he was," she said. "Don't know where he came from. Just sat up in the backseat and yawned and stretched and groaned—scared me to death, and I hit the gas instead of the brake."

Vergil, equally alarmed, began to leap up and down in the car and to scramble from back to front, howling and barking. This behavior was so unnatural in Vergil—who had, at various times, slept through a fire, a burglary, and an explosion at the fertilizer plant—that Aunt Mildred lost all control, careened through a traffic light and bounced off a milk truck and into Pauline, who had pulled over to study her road map.

Pauline had taken a wrong turn somewhere north of Parkersburg and was not only completely lost but, now, involved in a traffic accident as well—

with a car that seemed to her, at first glance, to be driven by a dog.

At this point Lloyd appeared. He had been delivering lawn fertilizer to Aunt Mildred, missed Vergil, and knew immediately what had happened, since it was Vergil's habit to climb into whatever car was handy and open and go to sleep.

Lloyd set out at once to find and follow Aunt Mildred—never an easy task, but a little easier this time because of all the commotion at the scene of the accident.

He arrived; retrieved Vergil; assessed the damage, which was minor; ignored Aunt Mildred (or so she said); and, on the spot, fell in love with Pauline. That Pauline should, at the very same moment, fall in love with Lloyd seemed insane to Aunt Mildred and my mother; unlikely to Louis— "Unless it was a movie," he said—and gloriously romantic to me.

"But, Lloyd," Mother said when he arrived at our house later that day, arm in arm with Pauline, to tell us the news, "isn't this awfully sudden?"

"Like a lightning bolt," Lloyd said.

"And, Pauline," Mother went on, "of course we think the world and all of Lloyd . . . but you don't even know him!"

"I feel I do," Pauline said, "after just these few hours. I've never felt so comfortable with a person, nor found anyone so easy to talk to. I figure that

126

whatever I don't know about Lloyd, or what he doesn't know about me, will give us conversation for years. Do you believe in fate, Mrs. Lawson?"

"No, I don't," Mother said, "not when it's mixed up with Mildred and a bird dog."

"Neither do I," Pauline said, "or never did till now. But just think about it. . . . Why did I get lost and end up here? Why did Lloyd's dog get into someone else's car? Why did your sister run into me instead of someone else?"

Now, explaining it all to my father, Mother agreed that these were not mysterious events: Vergil was famous for getting into anybody's car, Aunt Mildred was famous for colliding with anybody's car, and . . . "I know all about getting lost," Mother said, "but even I know there are only two main roads north from Parkersburg, and if you miss the other one you'll end up here. But after all, they're both grown-up people—Lloyd's thirty-three years old, it's time he got married—and it wasn't as if they were going to get married that very minute. Besides, I thought it would all fizzle out. Of course, it didn't"—she smiled happily—"and now Lloyd's gone off to Milwaukee to marry Pauline."

My father eyed Vergil. "I think if I were Lloyd," he said, "I'd take that dog along with me for good luck, since he was in on the beginning of this romance."

"Well, so was Mildred," Mother said, "but she

can't just go off to Milwaukee either—and you don't fool me a bit. You just don't want Vergil underfoot."

Unfortunately, because of his large and rangy size, Vergil was automatically underfoot, and he usually chose to sprawl, full-length, in awkward places: at the top of the stairs or at the bottom of the stairs, under the dining-room table, under my father's car and, from time to time, on very warm days, in the bathtub.

The first time this happened Louis tried to make Vergil more comfortable by turning on the water; but Vergil scrambled out of the bathtub (moving faster than we had ever seen him move before) and tore all around the upstairs, barking and howling and shaking himself and spraying water everywhere.

"I think he was asleep," Louis said, "and it surprised him."

I thought so too, because Vergil was asleep most of the time . . . but when Louis tried it again, Vergil was awake and the same thing happened.

"He doesn't like the water," Mother said. "He just likes to feel the cool porcelain tub."

"So do I," my father said, "but I don't want to take turns with a big hairy dog. Isn't Lloyd back yet? He must be married by now."

"Yes," Mother said, "but they're on their hon-

128

eymoon. Surely you don't begrudge them a honeymoon?"

"That depends on where they went," my father said. "They could have a very nice honeymoon between Milwaukee and here—two or three days in Chicago, maybe."

"Yes," Mother said, "they could. Listen, is that the telephone?"

"Well, hurry up and answer it. Maybe it's Lloyd."

It wasn't Lloyd. Actually, it wasn't even the telephone—Mother just made that up because she didn't want to explain that Lloyd and Pauline had gone in the opposite direction—to San Francisco—and were going to stop along the way wherever Pauline had relatives who wanted to welcome Lloyd into the family. We found out later that all these relatives lived in places like Middle Mine, Wyoming, and Clash, Nebraska, and were probably overjoyed to see anybody at all.

Of course, after two or three weeks, Mother had to admit that they weren't in Chicago and, as far as she knew, never had been. "They probably aren't even to San Francisco yet," she said. "You know how southerners are—sometimes newlywed couples visit around for months."

"But Pauline isn't a southerner, she's from Milwaukee!"

"I was just giving you an example," Mother said.

"It wouldn't have to be southerners. Amish people do the same thing."

"Is Pauline Amish?"

"She didn't say."

My father thought that over briefly and then shook his head. "You don't have any idea where they are, do you."

"No . . . but I do know that Lloyd is lucky, to marry into such a close and loving family."

"Lloyd is lucky," my father said, "because he was able to unload this dog on us while he tours the entire western half of the country. Oh, well," he sighed. "I'm going to take a bath—he isn't in the bathtub, is he?"

"No," Mother said, "but be careful when you come downstairs. He's asleep on the top step."

Three or four minutes later Louis and I heard the unmistakable *thump, thump, bang, thump, bang* of something or somebody falling downstairs, and went to see who or what it was.

My father heard the noise too, assumed that Mother had tripped over Vergil and came stumbling out of the bathroom with his pants half off, calling for us to get help. Mother, in the back bedroom, heard both the thumps and the cries for help, came running from that end of house and fell over my father, who was trapped by his pants.

Meanwhile, Vergil lay at the foot of the stairs in his customary position: full-length and flat on his back—and ominously still. We thought he might be dead, and Louis got down on the floor to listen to his heart . . . which led Mother to conclude that it was Louis who had fallen *over* Vergil and then down the stairs along *with* Vergil.

"What else would I think?" she said. "Everybody on the floor in a heap." She felt responsible, though, and made my father pull on his pants and take Vergil to the animal hospital, where, as it turned out, he was well known.

"He isn't moving," Mother said. "He fell down the stairs."

"Does it all the time," the doctor told us. "This is the laziest dog in the world. He'd *rather* fall down stairs than stand up. Fell off a shed roof once. Fell out of Lloyd's truck that was loaded with fertilizer bags."

"But he isn't moving," Mother said.

"That's because he's asleep."

My father said this was the last straw—that he hadn't wanted a dog at all, and he especially didn't want a dog who was too lazy to stand up—but Mother was relieved.

"I'd hate to have Lloyd come back," she said, "and have to tell him that his dog died of injuries."

"At this rate," my father said, "his dog will die of old age before he shows up."

Vergil didn't die, but Lloyd and Pauline never did show up, either. Their car broke down in a place called Faltrey, Arkansas . . . *and we couldn't find anyone to fix it,* Lloyd wrote. *They had a garage, had a gas station, had parts and equipment, had no mechanic. The mechanic couldn't stand Arkansas, they said, and he got on his motorcycle and left. So I fixed our car and two or three other people's cars . . . and to make a long story short, they just wouldn't let us leave. And now you couldn't pay us to leave, because we love it here in Faltrey, especially Pauline. But don't worry, because we'll be back to get Vergil, the first chance we get.*

" 'Yours truly, Lloyd,' " Mother finished reading. "Well, what do you know about that!"

"I know it's a long way to Arkansas," my father said, looking at Vergil.

After that we got a few postcards from Lloyd and a few letters from Pauline, who sent us a picture of the garage and a picture of their house and, eventually, a picture of their baby. All the cards and letters said they would be back for Vergil . . . *as soon as Lloyd's work lets up a little* or *as soon as we get the tomatoes in the garden* or *as soon as the baby's old enough to travel.*

My mother believed all these assurances (or said she did), and she would never admit that Vergil was anything but a temporary house guest. If anyone mentioned "your dog," she would always say, "Oh, this is Lloyd's dog. We're just keeping him for Lloyd."

In a way, my father wouldn't admit it either, because he never referred to Vergil as "our dog" or "my dog" or anything except "that dog"; but when Lloyd and Pauline finally did come back they had a sizeable family—Lloyd, Jr., was in the second grade, and the twin girls were two and a half years old—and their car was full of infant seats and baby beds and toys. My mother said the last thing they needed was Vergil. "Where would you put him?" she said.

Lloyd agreed. "I guess I just forgot how big he is. We'd better bring the truck next time."

Mother didn't mention this to my father, and in fact, Lloyd and Pauline had been gone for three days before he realized that Vergil didn't go with them, although Vergil was in plain sight, asleep, the whole time.

"You're just used to him," Mother said, "and you would miss him a lot."

"How could I possibly miss him if I haven't even noticed him for three days?"

"There!" she said. "How could any dog be less trouble!"

She was right, of course. Vergil didn't bark, or bite people, or dig up gardens, or upset trash cans, and by then we were all used to stepping over him or around him. By then, too, he was too old to climb into the bathtub; but sometimes, on very hot days, my father would lift him in—to get him out of the way, he said—and then get mad because Vergil wouldn't climb back out.

Despite Vergil's lack of interest in us, Louis and I were very fond of him. We thought of him as our dog, played with him during those brief and very occasional moments when he was awake, and whenever we had to write a paper for school about *My Best Friend*, or *My Favorite Pet*, we wrote about Vergil.

We never got very good grades on these papers because there was so little to tell, but we did share the glory when Vergil won a blue ribbon in the YMCA Pet Show. He won it for "Unusual Obedience to Command"—we commanded him to "play dead," and no dog did it better or for so long.

Misplaced Persons

Mother was not the only member of her family to be intimidated by automobiles, just as Aunt Mildred was not the only one to have exactly opposite feelings. In fact, they all seemed to be either one way or the other, with the exception of my little brother Louis, who enjoyed driving a car (till he was found out and stopped), but did so without risk to anyone's life or limbs.

The extreme cases were Aunt Mildred, with whom Louis and I were forbidden to ride—and, at the other end of the scale, Aunt Blanche. My father said that with Aunt Mildred we were apt to be killed outright, but with Aunt Blanche we would probably die of old age while waiting to turn left at an intersection.

When, on one occasion, circumstances required him to be her passenger, he said that he saw parts of town previously unknown to him as she drove blocks and blocks out of her way to avoid crossing traffic.

"I would tell her, 'You can turn here, Blanche,' " he said, "but she would never do it. We would go on three or four streets, turn right, turn right, turn right again. We were trying to get to the bank, and you could *see* the bank, but it might as well have been on the other side of a river. . . . Never again!"

Aunt Blanche's travels were further complicated by her poor sense of direction (a failing she shared with my mother), and by her insistence on beginning any trip, long or short, at the post office. Since she didn't live very far from the post office, it wasn't unusual for her to drive past it often, in the natural course of events . . . but even if she was headed for the other end of town in the opposite direction she still drove first to the post office and then took off from there.

This seemed odd but harmless, and no one paid much attention, though there were various opinions about the reason for it. Aunt Rhoda thought Aunt Blanche didn't want the mailman to know all her business, and to prevent this, just picked up her own mail. This was a sore point with Aunt Rhoda, since *her* mailman was notorious for reading postcards and return addresses and, on at least one occasion, for observing that Aunt Rhoda certainly did a lot of business with the Spencer Corset Company.

My mother thought Aunt Blanche had a romantic interest in Clifford Sprague, who worked at the post office and, like Blanche, had been widowed young. Uncle Frank thought there was something vaguely crooked about it—not on Aunt Blanche's part, but on the part of someone else—someone using an anonymous post office box, maybe, and trying to peddle nonexistent real estate or gold mine stock to foolish widows.

Typically, no one ever asked for an explanation—probably because no one would ever allow himself to be driven by Aunt Blanche. My mother was usually willing to ride with her, but since Mother thought she *knew* the reason behind the post office stop, and wanted to encourage the romance of Aunt Blanche and Clifford Sprague, she said nothing for fear of upsetting the applecart.

Of course Louis would have asked, and would have accepted any of the above reasons, or any other reason, or, as it finally turned out, the *real* reason, without batting an eye, since his own reasons for doing things rarely had much to do with the logic of a situation.

But we almost never got inside Aunt Blanche's car. "We'd never see you again," my father always told us. "Is that what you want?"

To Louis and me this was both mysterious and intriguing, and we kept hoping for some combination of broken-down cars and urgent errands that would require us to be driven by Aunt Blanche. There wasn't much chance of this though—the only car which was consistently broken down or smashed or pushed in was Aunt Mildred's, and the only errands Mother considered urgent were those involving medical emergencies . . . in which case she would obviously not call on Blanche, lest Blanche haul the victim (bleeding or choking or giving birth) first to the post office and then all over town.

"I think I'm the only one who's really comfortable riding with Blanche," Mother often said, and this was true. Neither of them was ever in a hurry to get anywhere, or dismayed to end up at an unexpected destination. "We always have a good time," Mother said . . . and even after the misadventures connected with her Uncle John's funeral, she insisted that it had been a pretty ride to get there, despite the complications.

This Uncle John was a relative unknown to Louis and me: The first we heard of him was through a telegram, delivered to Mother over the telephone.

"Uncle John Lane has died," she told us, "in Springfield, and the funeral is the day after to-morrow. He was my father's brother," she went on, "and I knew he was at a nursing home in Springfield, but no one's ever heard from him, or anything about him, so that's all I know."

How could this be, I wondered, in so nosy a family? This was my father's first question too when he heard the news.

"I just don't know," Mother said. "Nobody knows. Frank thinks maybe he had a fight with my father years ago. Rhoda said maybe he got wounded in World War I and just never came home. Mildred never heard of him.

"Of course we're all going to the funeral." She hurried right on, handing out reasons for this as if she were dealing cards. ". . . last of his generation . . . must be nearly a hundred years old . . . some of us *have* to show up . . . Mildred says we owe it to the past and to the future. . . ."

Perhaps Mother considered this lofty thought the last word in reasons, but my father did not. "Mildred!" he said. "Mildred just wants to go to Springfield."

"Well . . . what's wrong with that? She's never been there. I've never been there. The children have never been there."

"You're not going to drag them all that way!"

"Why, of course," Mother said. "They're the future."

Louis said later that this worried him a lot—he was afraid it meant that someone was going to point us out at the funeral, make us stand up, maybe even recite something about life. Still, he wanted to go. We both did—"all that way" sounded to us like foreign travel.

The arrangements turned out to be difficult. Of those who wished to go, only two were willing to drive.

"Let me guess," my father said. "The tortoise and the hare."

"I suppose you mean Blanche and Mildred," Mother said . . . but she did not deny that they were, in fact, the very ones, and my father said he might just as well drive himself, that otherwise he would sit home and worry.

He ended up both driving and worrying, though, because at the last minute an extra cousin appeared, and in the ensuing scramble for seats (especially seats in our car) Mother was seen to climb in with Aunt Blanche, who immediately took off (presumably for the post office), while Mother stuck her head out a window and called, "We'll see you along the way!"

There had been some talk of forming a caravan, in which the three cars would stay together, but my father said he would have no part of it, and discouraged everyone else from such a plan. "If Mildred is the number-one car," he said, "you'll lose Blanche at the first traffic light, and if Blanche is number one, you'll never get there."

Nevertheless, he became increasingly uneasy as time passed and we saw no sign of Mother and Aunt Blanche along the road. "Don't know where they are," he muttered from time to time, ". . . all going in the same direction on the same highway."

The late-arriving cousin, Howard Grashel, picked up this mood and kept saying, "Seems like the earth swallowed them up—seem to you like the earth swallowed them up?" till my father finally said, "For heaven's sake, Howard, shut up. You'll scare the kids."

But Louis and I didn't think there was anything to be scared about, believing, as we did, that grown-ups (even the grown-ups related to Mother) could take care of themselves. Had Mother been riding with Aunt Mildred we might have been scared, for Aunt Mildred passed us—honking and waving and then disappearing in the distance—"Like a bat out of hell," Howard said.

My father seemed to feel better after that. It reminded him, he said, that it was better to be late to a funeral than to require one.

"What happens when you're late to a funeral?" Louis asked me, for he was still fearful of public recognition. "Do you just walk in, in the middle of it? Do they stop while you walk in and sit down?"

"We're not going to be late, Louis," my father said. "It's your mother who's going to be late, unless they stop somewhere and take a taxicab."

To everyone's surprise, this was what they did.

At the very last minute, as we stood outside the funeral home, looking up and down the street for any sign of Aunt Blanche's Ford sedan, a blue-and-yellow taxicab pulled up at the curb and out of it stepped Mother and Aunt Blanche.

"Let's go right in," Mother said, hurrying up the steps, "I'll explain everything later."

"At least explain the taxicab," my father said.

"We were so late—it seemed like the best thing to do—Oh! . . ." She smiled. "Look at all these people. Isn't that nice?"

There were a lot of people, all very old, and all, naturally, strangers to us except for Aunt Mildred and her passengers.

"I hope Mildred thought to tell the minister who we are," Mother whispered.

It was immediately clear that Aunt Mildred had done so, because the minister based his entire remarks on the fact that so many had come so far to pay final tribute. He talked about life and death, and generations, and the old and the young (here Louis scrunched way down in his seat) . . . "Mildred and Rhoda," the minister said, "Frank and Grace and their families . . ."

When it was over Mother went to thank the minister, but my father said it ought to be the other way around, that he should thank us. "Makes you wonder what he was going to talk about before we showed up," he said.

To our surprise Mother came back right away, looking distracted, and hurried Louis and me out ahead of her. "We're not going to the cemetery," she said. "I told him we had to get right back. He understood. Where is everybody? Let's get out of here."

"They're outside," my father said. "What's the matter with you?"

"Oh!"—Mother rolled her eyes—"I didn't know what in the world to say! Fred, that's not Uncle John in there!"

"What do you mean?" My father stared at her. "Who is it?"

"*I* don't know!"

"Well, didn't you ask the minister?"

"Why, I couldn't say anything to the minister! I couldn't ask him, 'Who is this?' He just preached his whole sermon about us being the family!"

There was a lot of discussion and disagreement: Was this the right funeral home? Had Mother misunderstood the telegram? "How do you know it isn't him?" Aunt Rhoda demanded. "You never saw him. None of us ever did."

"I saw pictures," Mother said. "He was a little,

143

short, bald man, and this is a big tall man with lots of hair and a beard."

While everyone argued about what, if anything, to do, my father went back in to talk to the minister, who was surprised and puzzled, but found a silver lining to it all. He said that Mr. Johnson (whose funeral we had just attended) had no family at all, that his mourners were simply fellow residents at a nursing home, and that since we were all children of God and therefore kin, our presence was in no way inappropriate.

Aunt Mildred and Aunt Rhoda seemed willing to let it go at that. For one thing, Aunt Blanche was beginning to worry about her car, which was parked at a restaurant called Randolph's Ribs. "They were all very nice," she said, "trying to give us directions, and then calling us a cab and all . . . but they're not going to want my car sitting there all day long."

Mother said she'd never heard of such a thing, and now that we were here, we were going to locate Uncle John Lane, dead or alive, if it took a week.

Fortunately it only took my father about twenty minutes to figure out, and to confirm, that there had been some mix-up at the nursing home, inhabited by both Uncle John Lane and Mr. Johnson.

"They don't know much at that place," he said,

"but they do seem to know that *one* of them is deceased, and the other one isn't." He also said that he intended to call someone to account for this outrageous mistake, but Mother wouldn't let him.

"That sounds as if we're mad because he isn't dead," she said; "and anyway, these things happen all the time."

"That is simply not true," my father said—but of course he was in the company of people to whom such things *did* happen all the time, and they bombarded him with examples: "Remember Pauline . . . took the wrong baby home from the hospital?" "Remember Lloyd's dog Vergil that got listed in the telephone book, and after that got all the mail and the phone calls?" "Remember Audrey? . . . Calvin? . . . Maxine?"

Aunt Mildred summed it up. "Happens all the time, Fred."

"Not to me," my father said . . . but he had no wish to sue the nursing home, or to take Uncle John Lane out of it—for it proved to be a bright and homey place—so he settled for firm assurances that such a thing would never happen again.

Uncle John Lane turned out to be just what Mother said he was—a little, short, bald man: very old, very cheerful and very deaf, who said he was glad to see us and invited Louis to help him do his jigsaw puzzle. "It's a picture of some dogs," he said, "or the Rocky Mountains—hard to tell."

After a flurry of explanations and introductions, Mother and Aunt Rhoda tried to decipher the mystery of Uncle John, but they didn't have much luck. They had to yell, and neither one really wanted to yell about family matters for everyone to hear—and besides, Uncle John said yes to everything.

"I hope it wasn't a misunderstanding about money," Mother said, and Uncle John nodded. "That's right." "Political argument?" "That's right." "Heard you just never came home after the war. . . ." "That's right."

Louis, still doggedly assembling the puzzle, mentioned what was to him the most interesting feature of the day. "We went to your funeral," he said; and Uncle John nodded and said, "That's right."

"He just doesn't remember," Mother said finally, "and what difference does it make, anyway?" She raised her voice. "We're just all so glad we've found you. My goodness, the oldest member of our family! . . . And from now on, we're going to stay in close touch."

But as we were leaving we heard Uncle John ask a nurse, "Who in the hell were all those people?"; so my father said he didn't think Mother should count on much correspondence back and forth.

We all had dinner at Randolph's Ribs—"Seems only fair," everyone said—and headed home, after some reshuffling of people.

"I still think I ought to ride with Blanche," Mother said. "I'm not sure Howard knows the way."

"I don't know what difference that makes," my father said. "*You* were supposed to know the way, and look what happened." He wanted to hear all about what had happened, he said, and Mother could start from the time she stuck her head out the window and said, "We'll see you along the way."

"Well," she began, "it was a really pretty ride. . . ."

Louis and I listened for a while to a bewildering account of side trips to get gas and lunch and fresh country eggs, of misinterpreted road signs, of inaccurate directions from people at bus stops and grocery stores, of detours—"There were no detours on the highway," my father said; but it seemed that Aunt Blanche and Mother were not on the highway often, or for very long. It had been an eventful day, though, and Louis and I fell asleep somewhere south of Xenia and didn't wake up again till we were home.

My father was right about Uncle John Lane. He never answered any of Mother's letters, but the director of the nursing home did send monthly reports about his health and well-being. She also sent us a small package containing Mr. Johnson's personal belongings; photographs, Confederate money, five Zane Grey westerns, a collection of travel postcards, and other odds and ends.

My father said this had to be the last straw in confusion, but Mother thought it was nice and eventually came to refer to Mr. Johnson as a distant relative, and—even more eventually—just seemed to forget that he wasn't one.

Perhaps, in her mind, he took the place of Aunt Blanche's secret post office flame, Clifford Sprague, who got married (to someone else) and moved to Indianapolis, much to Mother's consternation. She wanted to know what went wrong between him and Aunt Blanche but didn't like to ask, until my father pointed out that Aunt Blanche was obviously not heartbroken and, in fact, seemed unmoved about the whole thing.

"Clifford Sprague?" Aunt Blanche said, when she was questioned. "I didn't even know him. Whatever made you think I did?"

When Mother reported this conversation she said everybody was wrong—that Blanche didn't care who read her postcards, and wasn't about to buy more real estate, when it was all she could do to get the grass cut and the hedge trimmed on the real estate she already had.

"There's a perfectly simple explanation for why

she always goes to the post office," Mother said. "That's how she learned to drive. She just followed the mailman around his route—first one mailman, and then another one. They always started at the same place and came back to the same place, and they never went very fast. It was perfect for Blanche, and it just got to be a habit."

"Now let me understand this," my father said. "Blanche would get in a car, and . . ." But then he stopped. He had finally realized, I guess, that he would never understand this, any more than he ever understood Mother's driving habits, Louis's contest entries . . . Aunt Mildred or Genevieve Fitch or Vergil the dog—any more than he would understand similar events and revelations yet to come.

Instead, he said, "It's the craziest thing I've ever heard . . . so far."